praise for *th*

"Let me state this very clearly: *I f......................* or those of us who care about the burgeoning New Zombie literature, and the powerful cultural metaphors it contains, *The Loving Dead* is a pivotal work."
— John Skipp, author of *The Bridge* and *The Long Last Call*

"Zombies are all over the place right now, but trust me, you've *never* read a zombie novel like this! Amelia Beamer's *The Loving Dead* is about zombies, all right, but it's zombies with Xanax, Zeppelins, Trader Joe's, iPhone apps, sex, humor, adventure, NPR, IKEA, and Indiana Jones! It's a rollercoaster ride of a read and a true original!"
— Connie Willis, author of *Blackout*

"Amelia Beamer's *The Loving Dead* is strange, sick, sexy, and scary. It's also wickedly funny and a damn good read."
— Jonathan Maberry, author of *Patient Zero*

"*The Loving Dead* is that rare zombie story that manages to remember the human aspect that makes the living dead so terrifying. It's modern, witty, and funny as hell without crossing the line into parody, and it makes the question of 'how will you survive the zombie apocalypse?' seem all the more important. Plus, how many zombie stories manage to feature Trader Joe's, iPhone applications, a Zeppelin, Alcatraz, and make it all make *sense*? Truly an awesomely wild ride."
— Mira Grant, author of *Feed*

"If you like raunchy comedy with whips, brains, and zombies, this is the book for you."
— Mario Acevedo, author of *Werewolf Smackdown*

"*The Loving Dead* is a Grand Guignol extravaganza, appallingly vivid and unrelentingly suspenseful. Though definitely not a book for little kids, mature readers won't be able to put it down until they get to the last page."
— Tim Powers, author of *Declare* and *On Stranger Tides*

the loving deAd

the loving deAd

ameliabeamer

NIGHT SHADE BOOKS
SAN FRANCISCO

First Edition

ISBN 978-1-59780-194-2

Printed in Canada

Night Shade Books
Please visit us on the web at
http://www.nightshadebooks.com

For Charles N. Brown,
whether or not he would have appreciated it.

I owe my gratitude for advice and support to Mars Jokela, Gary K. Wolfe, Tim Pratt, Liza Groen Trombi, AAron Buchanan, Francesca Myman, Jeremy Lassen, Cecelia Holland, Nalo Hopkinson, Joe Monti, Alan Beatts, Michelle Boussie, Zachary Smith, Joel Brandt, David Findlay, a number of Beamers and Jokelas, and the Second Draft writers group.

"Everyone was gray and speaking in monosyllabic tones. There was no class, no race... We've been beaten up. I mean, it's so much easier to forgive a zombie."
—Alaina Hoffman, in the *Chicago Tribune*, May 4, 2009

chapter one

The sun had set by the time Kate left the belly dance class. Jamie, the instructor, had stayed late showing Kate a move called "the sprinkler," where you swing your hips in a smooth figure eight, then four sharp ticks back to center. It looked like a lawn sprinkler when Jamie did it. Kate, watching herself in the mirror, thought that her attempts looked more like a dog with a hose. But after a few minutes, after all of the other girls had left, she got it.

They walked out together from the converted warehouse. This part of Berkeley was mostly artist studios.

"See ya next week," Jamie called. She turned, away from the streetlight.

"See ya," Kate called. "Thanks again." Despite her best intentions, she didn't attend every week. She walked towards her car, pleasantly tired. The party Michael was throwing would be in full swing soon, but she would have a few minutes of quiet between now and then.

"Hey," a woman's voice called. It sounded like Jamie. Kate looked back. Some guy had pushed Jamie up against a van. His face was dangerously close to Jamie's. She was pushing him away. "Fuck you," she shouted. She kicked at him. "Hey, anyone, help?"

Kate felt a rush of panic. She dropped her finger cymbals, which made a clatter on the sidewalk like a tiny, demented marching band. She ran towards Jamie, her shoulder bag bouncing against her thigh, wishing she had a weapon. There was the little Swiss Army knife on her keychain. As if that would scare anyone.

Kate found her voice. "Hey! Jamie?"

Jamie turned to look at Kate. So did the guy. It was enough of a distraction for Jamie to wiggle away from him. Kate, at full speed, ran into the guy anyway. He fell. The back of his head made a wet crack on the curb. Kate stumbled, finding her balance against the van.

"You OK?" She turned to Jamie. They both moved away from the guy.

"Shit, honey." Jamie spat to the side, then wiped her mouth on her bare arm. She let out a long breath. "Fucking drunk, thinking with his dick and leading with his chin," she said. "Yeah, I'm all right." She didn't sound all right. She spat again.

"What happened?" Kate asked, brushing hair behind her ears. "I heard you call out. He attack you?"

"Something like that," Jamie said. "You just don't expect that, not in Berkeley. Panhandling, maybe, but not this. He just came up on me before I knew what was happening. I was looking in my purse, for my keys, you know? And before I even hardly see him he's pushing me up against my van and trying to stick his tongue down my throat."

Both women looked down at the sidewalk. The guy's eyes were closed. He was in a bad way: obviously homeless, judging by the layers of clothing he wore against the still-warm summer night. Never mind the smell. His hair looked dirty in the yellow light from the street lamp, and his face was smudged. A liquid seeped from near his groin. It bubbled on the sidewalk. Malt liquor.

"Man." Kate nudged the guy's leg with her foot. He didn't move. "Um," she said. He could be bleeding to death from a head injury. "Hey," she called softly. "You all right, man? Anybody in there?" Kate knelt. If he died, it'd be her fault.

"Don't touch him, honey. You'll wake him up. Fucking drunk," Jamie said. "Thinking he could rumble me for a few bucks so he can go get a Chore Boy and a rock."

Kate didn't question Jamie's interpretation. It had looked to Kate like the guy had been trying to rape Jamie. "Um," Kate said. "Don't you think we should call the cops or something? Report that he attacked you? Get him help?" She didn't like police any more than the next twentysomething, but it felt wrong to just leave the guy. He didn't seem to be bleeding, though she couldn't tell in the low light, and she didn't want to touch him. She thought of spending all night trying to explain to the so-called peace officers what had happened, again and again, under migraine-inducing fluorescent lights. Who would she call to bail her out if they put her in jail? Michael would be drunk already.

Jamie gave Kate a look. She'd thought the same things, about cops and trouble.

The guy stirred, letting out a low moan. So he wasn't dead. That was a relief. Kate backed away from him. She glanced around. The street *was* dead. No one had seen what they'd done.

"You're right," Kate said. "Let's just go. My housemate's throwing this party tonight," she found herself saying. "There'll be people, and food, and we'll be safe." The idea of being indoors, surrounded by doors that locked and people she mostly knew and trusted, sounded very appealing.

Jamie shook her head. "I need a cigarette," she said. She pulled a pack from her purse, and lit one. She smoked Kools, which Kate found odd. Belly dancers were supposed to smoke American Spirits, or roll their own. Jamie lit it, then fished a set of keys from her purse. The metal gleamed in the low light.

"I don't want you going off alone. Not after this. Just come for a little while, check it out," Kate said. She didn't normally invite people over to Michael's parties, but she didn't normally attack dudes on the street, either. "Come on, let's go."

"All right," Jamie said. "Should I follow you, or…?" She used two fingers from the hand that was holding the cigarette to smooth a strand of her long hair.

"Sure," Kate said. She looked around again. It was unnatural, how quiet the street was. "I just want to go before someone else happens along. My house is up in the hills, and it's easy to get lost, so yeah, you should follow me. I'm just down the block, I'll go get my car."

"And leave me alone here?" Jamie glanced around the street. The end of her cigarette glowed.

"Well, how about you drive me to my car—" Kate said. She saw movement. The guy was sitting up, bracing himself against the curb. His mouth was bleeding. He blinked, touched the pocket that now held the shards of his beer bottle. He moaned in dismay.

"Come on. I'm getting spooked," Kate said. "He's going to be able to describe us. Pick us out of a lineup," she whispered. She was ready to run; ready to shove Jamie into a car if that was what it would take. She took Jamie's hand, pulling her to the other side of the van, so the guy couldn't see them.

Jamie unlocked her door, moving fast. "You get in on my side." Her tone had changed: she sounded scared. She was starting to get it.

Kate obeyed. She barely knew Jamie, had been going to Jamie's class off and on for a year or so. They hadn't spoken outside of that context before tonight.

The guy struggled to his feet. Kate saw him through the window. She covered her mouth with her hand. Jamie started the engine. The guy touched his jaw, then put his hand to the side window. The van lurched forward. The guy followed, but they soon lost him. His handprint remained.

chapter two

Hardly had Michael brought in Audrey and Cameron and showed them to the drinks than there was another knock on the door.

"Let someone else get it," Audrey said. "Check this out; I want you to admire my getup." She wore a black vinyl dress that showed off her legs. "And the nails," she said, offering her hand as if to be kissed. She had applied long black acrylics. "I already knocked off one of them on the way here," she said. In her other hand she held a small single-tail whip. The cutest girl at Trader Joe's and a redhead to boot: Michael still had a bit of a crush on her.

"If I had a hat, I would tip it," Michael said. "And your partner here, also a very fine job of costuming."

"We didn't really come together," Cameron said. "I mean, we came *here* together, but we're not together."

"We've *come* together before, baby," Audrey said, interrupting.

"Which is by way of saying," Cameron continued, "that if there's any particularly nice girls that I don't know who are coming to this party, you should point them out." Cameron wore a white T-shirt with a pair of handcuffs around one wrist, which he promptly applied to the cap of a beer bottle.

"Dude, it's a twist-off," Michael said.

"So can you tell who I am?" Cameron asked. He held the open beer as if it were a microphone. "Beyoncé had one of the best videos of *all time!*"

Audrey turned to Michael, holding a plastic cup she'd filled with wine. "Would you please introduce Kanye here to some other girl? He's going to think that we're back together."

Cameron shrugged. "George Bush hates black people?"

Michael wasn't sure if Audrey was joking. It was always hard to tell with her. "Chick on the couch there was in my AP English class senior year." He pointed. "Natalie. Top hat, holding the golden gun? She did a dramatic reading from Hunter S. Thompson's *Fear and Loathing in Las Vegas*, the speech about the hippie zeitgeist that would roll over the nation with the unassailable force of nature. You'd like her. I'd introduce you but I'm afraid of her myself. Excuse me. I hear the door. Again." Derek and Amy were standing in the foyer; Derek must have let Amy in, and now that she was there, Derek would see no reason to open the door ever again.

Michael opened the door. It was already nine o'clock and Kate wasn't back from her dance thing. He'd thought of texting her but had decided against it. Henry stood there, holding an IV pole. "Hey man, come on in." Michael shook Henry's hand. "Nice digs."

"Thanks." A few drops of Henry's costume dribbled onto his chin, and he wiped at it with the back of his hand. He was wearing a hospital gown. His IV pole held a clear bag filled with red fluid, with a tube leading to his mouth. "It's Merlot. I've been wanting to do this ever since they stopped making the metallic space bags and started making them clear. You know, box wine? Transfusion bags, I call them. I stole all of the medical gear from work, in between cleaning up people's vomit."

"You sure you won't come back to TJ's?" Michael asked.

"What, and leave show business? Naw, dude, I'm going to go to nursing school. Nurses work four ten-hour shifts every week, or three twelves, and I can arrange them so that I get a week or more off at a time."

"You'd have time for a second job! What about the generous employee discount?"

Another knock sounded on the door. "Drinks over there,"

Michael said. "Go ingratiate yourself with all of the people you left behind." He opened the front door and studied the young man holding the pizza boxes. The costume was impeccable, down to the baseball cap emblazoned with the Cybelle's logo. But the guy didn't look familiar. He must have heard about the party from someone. "Friend of the bride or the groom?" Michael asked. Then he remembered. "Shit, the pizza's here."

"Um, it'll be sixty-three forty-five. You said you had a coupon?"

"Just a second." He went and found the coupons, and tore off the applicable ones. He felt dumb. How many beers had he had already? Only three or so. He counted out cash, and paid the driver, giving him five bucks extra.

"Soup's up." Michael put the pizzas on the ancient electric range, making sure that he didn't accidentally press any of the buttons that turned on the burners. He set plates on the table.

There was a fumbling at the door. Michael went to check that it was unlocked. He turned the lock, then the knob. Finally he managed to pull the door open. Kate was standing there, holding the doorknob, her keys in the lock. She looked worried.

"Hey, roomie. You OK? Your timing's perfect: pizza just got here," Michael said. "Oh, hi," he said, seeing the woman Kate had brought. "C'mon in. I'm Michael."

Kate pushed her way in and shut the door behind them. She took something from the woman and hung it up on the key rack by the door. Keys.

"What are you supposed to be?" Michael asked.

"I told you I was coming as a belly dancer," Kate said. "This is what they wear to practice in. Also this is Jamie. She's a belly dancer, too."

"That's cool. So, you sure you're all right?"

"No shit. You won't believe what just happened," Kate said. "Seriously. Well, maybe you'd believe me. We're leaving class, and—oh, man. I just remembered that I left my finger cymbals on the sidewalk. Anyway, this guy straight up attacks Jamie. And then," she glanced at her friend, who had found her way to a couch and sat down.

"It's a good thing you were there, no shit," the woman said. She picked up a magazine from the low table. She was gorgeous, no two ways about it. Michael made a mental note to hang out with more belly dancers. Kate could introduce him. He could take up playing drums or something. Start dreading his hair.

"You're kidding," Michael said. "No, you're not kidding." He turned to the woman. "Are you OK? Would you like some pizza? Or a drink? Or should I call the cops or something?"

Jamie nodded and then shook her head no, then smiled. "I'll check it out. Thanks." She went towards the kitchen.

"So what did you *do*?" Michael asked.

"I shoved him down, and he conked his head on the side-walk."

"Shit. No kidding." This wasn't the Kate he knew.

"I thought he might have been dead, but he was breathing," she said, lowering her voice. "He scared the daylights out of me. I thought I might have killed him. There was beer everywhere; it must have broken when he fell. I wanted to call the cops, but I didn't. We just left."

"Sounds like he was just a drunk. He'll walk it off," Michael said. He wasn't sure whether it was true, but he didn't want to make Kate feel bad. "You OK, though? Want a Xanax?" he asked quietly.

Kate ran a hand through her hair, which smelled of cigarette smoke. "Yeah. I think so. At least until the cops show up and arrest me for leaving the scene of a crime, anyway." She lowered her voice. "And yes, on the Xanax. Also, my car's still on the street in Berkeley. Maybe you can take me there in the morning to get it? We ended up driving back here together. To tell the truth, I didn't want her to go off alone. Not that I don't trust her, I just didn't want her driving any distance by herself. She lives in the city, I think in the Sunset, by the ocean." They both looked at Jamie, deep in conversation with Natalie.

Michael put his arm around Kate's shoulders. She didn't shrug him off. He suspected that Kate didn't trust Jamie. That they barely knew one another. Jamie was a witness to whatever it was that happened, whether or not it was a crime. "I could make an anonymous tip, you know. If you were concerned about this guy. Have the cops go check on him. It wouldn't come back to you."

"And what would you say? No, don't worry about it. It's nothing. He's fine. I'm just overreacting."

"I believe you," Michael said. He didn't, not entirely, but he didn't want to make an issue of it. His arm was still around her. He had an urge to lean in, kiss her ear. Instead he took a tiny pill from his pocket and handed it to her. She smiled her thanks. He knew that she knew that there wasn't enough Xanax for everyone, and he appreciated her being quiet about it.

"You got one more?" she asked, her mouth near his ear again. He could feel the tickle of her words on his skin. "You know. For Jamie."

"My last one. For you, baby." He liked her. She had to know that. She must enjoy it, knowing that she had his attention. He could play this game as long as she could. He handed another of the tiny pills to her.

They went into the kitchen. Kate poured herself a glass of wine, surreptitiously put a pill in her mouth, and drank.

"So I was studying, like every afternoon, at Cato's," Sam was saying. He was holding court, leaning against the kitchen counter and gesturing with a slice of pizza. He was dressed as a hooker from the early 1980s, with teal leggings and black tube top. His long hair was curled into a Farrah Fawcett, and he wore fake eyelashes. "I look up, and there's this lady zombie looking at me through the window. Less than a foot away, through the big glass windows, you know? And I scream and spill my beer, because she caught me by surprise, and I see that the whole street is full of zombies. Walking slowly, with their arms out. Limping and staggering. Groaning and rolling their eyes."

"Dude, you study in a bar?" Michael asked. "You're going to paramedic school; don't you have to be smart for that?" He helped himself to a slice of pepperoni and mushroom, not bothering with a plate.

Sam didn't stop. "Zombies!" he was saying. "Walking down Piedmont Avenue! And everyone in Cato's is laughing. That lady zombie gives me a big grin, and she's got most of her teeth blacked out, and then, only then, do I see that it's makeup. There isn't even any on her neck, although her face was gray. Like a B movie. She blows me a kiss and then walks away." Sam heaved a theatrical sigh. "I chased after her, trying to get her number, but I lost her in the crowd."

"You hadn't heard about the Zombie Walk?" Audrey asked. "I missed that one because I was in L.A., but I'm totally going to do it. A bunch of people meet up and walk around, and then go on a pub crawl. You're not supposed to chase after people. But you can also arrange to be waiting on the route, and get turned into a zombie in public. It's all very consensual." Her tits jiggled as she laughed. "Did none of you know about it?"

Heads around the room shook, a few nodded.

"Let me know when it is, if you do it," Sam said. "That zombie stole my heart."

"You wouldn't judge a woman on appearance alone," Audrey teased. She and Sam had dated, years before, and they still got along pretty well.

"Carriage and vocals count for a lot," Cameron said.

"You got it," Sam agreed. He helped himself to another beer from the vegetable crisper in the refrigerator, and levered it open with his lighter.

Michael pulled a bottle of Jack from the cupboard above the range. "Who's doing a shot with me. Kate? What's your friend's name?"

"Jamie. Hey, Jamie, do a shot with me?" Kate called.

"I will. Give it here," Audrey said. "*I'm* not driving anywhere tonight." She smiled at Cameron.

"Somebody say shots?" Freddie came into the kitchen. Dressed as Heath Ledger as the Joker, he had already eaten most of his lipstick. He accepted a drink. "Here's to the best parties of all time!" Plastic cups converged in a toast. They did some damage to the bottle, and then Freddie got a group together for Rock Band in the living room. Audrey brought out a pipe, which circulated, leaving a sweet smell. People sat outside on the deck, smoking cigarettes and laughing. The house was full of happy, drunk people, some of whom could even sing. Kate and her friend seemed like they were having fun. Michael relaxed. Time passed. People started to say goodbye and leave, but that was OK. It must be getting late. He thought about picking up some of the dead soldiers. But he was comfortable.

Someone screamed. Inside the house. A girl. Michael stood, spilling his drink. His head swam. There was truth to that old rule about how you can drink twice as much sitting down, but then when you stood up you were twice as drunk. He stumbled into the hallway towards the bedrooms.

chapter three

Jamie pulled Kate away from the group while they stood in the kitchen, after a round of shots. "Give me the tour?" she said, putting her arm in Kate's. Kate's heart sped up. The booze and food and company were calming, but Jamie made her a bit nervous.

"Hey, this is for you," she handed Jamie the pill. "Xanax. You know. It'll help you relax. My friend Michael's got a scrip for it."

Jamie took it. "What's the dose?"

Kate tried to remember. "The little one. Whatever that is. That's all he could get."

"Point two five milligrams. That's still very nice. Thank you, my dear."

Kate grabbed an open wine bottle with her free hand. She led Jamie into the hallway. They passed a few people whom she knew from work or previous parties, and she nodded and said hi without getting entangled in conversations or introductions.

"You saw the kitchen and living room," she said. "Bathroom on the right. Master bedroom next door on the right, with another bathroom inside, that's Michael's. The guy who opened the door? He rents the house. My bedroom's on the left here, and Lena's is in back here. She's out tonight, probably with her boyfriend. She's not a big fan of these parties." Kate looked at Jamie, trying to gauge how Jamie felt about them. "I'm not much for them

12

either, sometimes, although the costumes are good. Michael's got a hard-on for costume parties."

"That hooker was pretty hot, for a dude," Jamie said.

They went into Kate's room, which was messy enough to be embarrassing. She flicked on the desk lamp rather than turning on the overhead, then slipped her arm out of Jamie's and pushed the clothes and books from the bed. "If you're tired I can make up the bed with clean sheets for you. If you wanted to stay over. Would you like to go to bed? I mean, to sleep?" She blushed, and was grateful for the low light.

"Not yet," Jamie said. She closed the door. "Sit down."

Kate sat on the bed. Jamie perched behind Kate and started rubbing Kate's shoulders. Kate was surprised. She tried to relax into it. She took a sip of wine and held out the bottle to Jamie.

"Don't want to mix the grape and the grain." Her fingers worked Kate's muscles and tendons, at just the right pressure.

"You're really good at this," Kate said. It had been a long time since anyone had given her a halfway decent shoulder rub, and this was better than halfway.

"I'm also a massage therapist, though I don't do it much these days; the lupus fucks with my hands. I also don't normally give it away for free, but you're being good to me tonight."

"Thanks," Kate said. "I didn't know you had lupus."

"It's mild, and it's not contagious, don't worry. Just means I have to watch my energy level and sometimes I have to take steroids. It's an autoimmune thing, in my joints."

"Oh, that sucks," Kate said.

"I suppose so," Jamie said, sounding unconcerned. Xanax did that; it was supposed to be for anxiety.

After a while, Kate said, "You know, I think our generation is possibly a little too concerned about zombies. You ask anyone, they've got a zombie contingency plan. The bat under the bed, or whatever, that's not for thieves."

"And yours? You have one?"

Kate pointed at the bamboo sword in the corner. "I know it's not much, but it makes me feel better. The whole zombie thing is a joke, and everyone knows it. That's how I met Michael, actually. Before he convinced me to work at Trader Joe's, back when I'd just moved here. We used to stick fight every week with this group in People's Park. Shinais, like the bamboo slat sword there, plus padded knives and swords and nunchucks made of PVC and duct tape."

Jamie laughed. "That's rad."

"It's exercise, at any rate. We'd always play this game called Yojimbo, after this old Kurosawa movie. It's like reverse tag. One person is It, and everyone chases them. Whoever landed the killing blow is the next It, and then anyone who got killed by the previous It gets to come back. The point is to kill everyone, and sometimes you can do it, if you're really lucky."

Jamie leaned forward and brought one of Kate's sleeves to her nose.

Kate froze. She probably smelled of sweat. The way Jamie exhaled, the hum in her throat, made it clear that she was enjoying herself. So maybe Kate didn't smell. Or whatever she smelled of, Jamie liked it. There was an inherent contract; smell led to taste. Kate felt a warm tingling in her belly. She knew where this might go. She was trying to decide if she wanted it. Jamie seemed to. She seemed to expect that Kate wanted it.

Jamie kissed Kate's shoulder. Once, as if tapping a microphone to check that it was on. "So do you have any brothers or sisters?" Jamie asked. She ran her fingers through Kate's hair.

"A brother, three years younger. Still lives with my parents. If you wanted to go home, I can get Michael to drive me to my car in the morning. I just didn't want you going off by yourself. I was worried."

"That's sweet. But I'm too drunk to drive now," Jamie said. "Just relax. Don't worry about it. So tell me, where are you from?" The smile in Jamie's voice told Kate that Jamie knew she was just teasing by making small talk. Prolonging what she was trying to make inevitable. Her fingers dug into Kate's shoulders.

Kate found it hard to talk. "Wisconsin. Near Madison. The Berkeley of the Midwest, except for Ann Arbor claims that. Calls Berkeley the Ann Arbor of the West." She stopped. Jamie was kissing her shoulder. Jamie bit, just hard enough. Kate shivered. She decided that she wanted this. It was the easiest way. And maybe it was the right thing to do, after what they'd been through already tonight.

"Turn around."

Kate did.

"You've never been with a woman, have you?" Jamie smiled like she found this amusing.

Kate nodded, forcing herself to meet Jamie's gaze. During the belly dance class, all of the girls would watch Jamie as she demonstrated the moves. Jamie would raise her shirt, tying it off to reveal a long, muscled torso. Sometimes Kate found herself watching the Ouroboros tattoo that coiled around Jamie's hips, the snake's mouth open to eat its tail above her navel. If Jamie didn't have that tattoo, Kate might have been able to pay more attention to the moves. Not that she was normally attracted to women, or that she would ever have acted on it. Maybe she had a *little* crush, she admitted.

"That's OK." Jamie touched Kate's cheek. "It's hard to meet women, you know? I think that's why some girls come to the belly dance class. It's why I started dancing in the first place, to meet women. Gay guys, they got it easy. Everybody knows they're gay: they're the only guys who style their hair, and when they check each other out, you know what they're thinking. But women check each other out no matter what. I'm walking down the street, and I see a chick, and I don't know if she thinks I'm cute, or if she's just trying to figure out where I bought my shoes." Jamie leaned forward, turning Kate to face her. Their mouths met. What happened then was complicated and friendly and different from anything Kate could remember.

"My boyfriend doesn't kiss like that," Kate said when Jamie pulled away. Boyfriend wasn't really the term for what Walter was, but the situation was too complicated to explain.

"Guys don't know. At least, not any guy I dated, when I was a kid. Sucking face, we called it, and that was basically what it was. People who think youth is the high point of life should be condemned to the lousy sex we all had back then, while the rest of us get it together and figure out what we like. Women don't hit their sexual peak until their thirties, anyway. You've got time." Jamie toyed with Kate's hair while she talked. She smelled so good. Kate wanted very badly to please her.

Kate understood that Jamie wanted to be kissed. Kate moved slowly towards Jamie, enjoying the tension. Jamie tasted of lipstick. Kate learned how Jamie liked to be kissed: starting gently, and building up. Jamie rubbed her thumbnail over Kate's nipple, through her shirt. Kate took an involuntary breath.

"Does your door lock?" Jamie asked. Her voice was low and husky.

Kate put her hands over Jamie's. "Yes," she said. She stood to lock the door. The room tilted just a little as she found her balance; she didn't think she was drunk enough that she'd regret this later. Muffled laughter came from down the hall; everyone was busy. They wouldn't be interrupted.

"You're beautiful when you smile," Jamie said.

Kate stood next to the bed. She was always nervous the first time with someone new. Things changed after you let yourself get naked. There would always be that between you, the vulnerability that comes from letting down your guard.

Jamie smiled, and held out a hand. Kate let Jamie pull her onto the bed. They lay together. As Jamie kissed her neck, Kate concentrated on remembering everything, so she could play it back later and understand it. She found Jamie's earlobe with her mouth, and nibbled the length of it. She put her tongue inside, tasting skin and wax, and was rewarded with a gasp. Jamie took Kate's hands in her own, kissing Kate's fingertips.

"First, this," Jamie said. She removed Kate's shirt and bra. She took Kate's nipples in her fingers. She pinched them gently, moving them around in slow circles. She bit Kate's shoulder. The sensations induced by Jamie's mouth, her hands, her proximity, were intense.

Jamie took Kate's pants down. She licked her fingers. Slipped one finger inside Kate, then two, and then three. She kept her fingers moving, in and out with a knowledgeable come-hither pressure on Kate's G-spot. She whispered gentle words. With her thumb on Kate's clitoris, Jamie kissed the insides of Kate's thighs, then her belly, working her way up to take Kate's painfully hard nipples into her mouth. Kate gasped. The world was collapsing to this; there was nothing else but this, and there was no shame in it. She had her hands in Jamie's hair.

"Don't stop," Kate said. Over and over, until she couldn't speak. It was a beautifully long orgasm. As it ebbed, Kate couldn't help but laugh. Lying on her back, she felt the tension leave her. She kept her eyes closed. She squeezed Jamie's fingers, still inside her, and Jamie took that as a signal to withdraw.

Jamie licked her fingers, then smiled. "You're not so straight after all," she said softly. She lay down next to Kate and put an arm around her. Their faces were close. "That's okay. Every girl can eat a little pussy and still be straight. Women's sexuality is more fluid, anyway."

"Thank you," Kate managed.

Jamie put a finger over Kate's lips. "That's not what you say." She stood and removed her shirt and bra, revealing a tattoo of a pomegranate on the inside of her left breast, and the Ouroboros tattoo around her waist. Her pubic hair was light brown, trimmed short, and her labia emerged beneath it like lips; her clitoris like a tongue.

Kate was transfixed. Jamie was so *hot*. Why hadn't she really seen it before?

Jamie took her bag from the floor, and removed something from it. She held out a length of rope. Two lengths of rope, it turned out. "I can't come without being tied up," she said. "So you get to do it. You don't have to hit me or anything. Not on the first date."

She winked. "Seriously though. Don't hit me."

"Thank you for trusting me," Kate said. The rope felt awfully heavy. This wasn't how she'd expected to spend the evening. But she wanted to do this. Wanted to do it right. Jamie demonstrated how to tie what she called a rolling hitch. Around and through, around and through, and then the circle went around Jamie's wrist. She pulled to tighten it, and tied the other end of the rope to the bedpost. Jamie tied a second rolling hitch, and told Kate to tie the other end to the bedpost.

Kate looped the rope around and started to tie it.

"Tighter," Jamie said. "Please, honey."

Kate pulled the rope tighter, until Jamie's arms were splayed and the skin was taut over her ribs. It was funny, and awkward, and sexy. Kate kissed the inside of Jamie's wrist, working her way up Jamie's arm as she finished securing the rope to the bed frame.

"I've never done this before," Kate said. "And I can't imagine why not," she added.

Jamie laughed, then grew serious. "Please. Come here," she said.

Kate kissed the spot between Jamie's neck and shoulder, then bit gently, and was rewarded with Jamie's intake of breath.

"Yes," Jamie said.

"Yes," Kate said. She put her tongue in Jamie's ear. Jamie's arms tensed, pulling against her bonds. Kate thought about where else she could put her tongue. She kissed the pomegranate tattoo on Jamie's breast, tracing it with her tongue. She circled Jamie's breasts with her mouth, enjoying the feeling. Finally she allowed her tongue to graze one nipple, and was rewarded with a gasp. She'd never had a woman's nipple in her mouth. It felt so large and sensitive.

"Harder," Jamie said.

Kate obeyed, wanting to please. She straddled Jamie's body, tonguing her nipples until Jamie's hips thrust upwards. Only then did she allow herself to kiss Jamie's stomach, marveling at the Ouroboros tattoo. She kissed the snake's head, flicked her tongue inside Jamie's navel, then moved down. Jamie spread her legs, and Kate started at one knee, moving to the other.

"Like that, yes," Jamie said. Her voice was deep and husky. "Oh."

Kate concentrated, kissing from knee to knee. She wanted Jamie to come, wanted to hear and feel her orgasm. Jamie's thighs were wet with saliva.

"Yes," Jamie said.

Kate moved Jamie's panties to one side, and flicked her tongue into Jamie's warm center. The taste was strong but not unpalatable. She did it again, hoping for a gasp or a moan. She put one knuckle of her index finger inside, resting her cheek against Jamie's thigh, waiting for a reaction. She brushed Jamie's clitoris first with her nose and then her tongue. Jamie was still.

"Jamie?" Kate said. "Am I going too fast?"

Jamie's breathing had slowed down. "Um, something's happening," she said. "It's not you, baby. Something. Wrong." She let out a low moan. Kate lifted her head.

"Jamie?"

Jamie was looking up at the ceiling. She let out another moan, deep and strange. "*Something's happening*," Jamie said. She grimaced. She tried to sit, but was stopped by the ropes. Jamie looked from one tied hand to the other, as if surprised.

"Jamie?" Kate said. She backed away until she fell off the bed. She stood up, stumbling over the clothes and books on the floor. "Jamie?"

Jamie moaned again, and pulled on the ropes.

Kate backed into the light switch. She turned, and fumbled it on.

Jamie's eyes were milky white, as if cataracts had suddenly developed. Her mouth was open, her teeth bared. Her skin had turned ashen gray. Jamie licked her lips with a tongue the color of well-done burger.

Kate screamed.

chapter four

Michael ran to Kate's room. The door was locked. He was sure the scream had come from inside. "Kate, are you all right? What's going on?"

There was a low moan. "I can explain," a weak voice called.

The remains of the party had made their way to the hallway by the time Kate emerged. She shut the door behind her. Her top was on inside out, and she was still pulling up her terrycloth pants. "I can explain," she said. Then she burst into tears. "Something happened!"

Another moan from inside the room only added mystery. "Where's your friend?" Michael asked. "She OK?" He reached for the door handle.

Kate blocked the door. "Don't. You don't know."

Michael could smell the sex. This was hot. But Kate was clearly upset. Something was going on, more than just embarrassment. He turned around and waved his hands, shooing at his friends. "Nothing to see here, ladies and germs. As you were." The guys let out a collective "Aww." They stayed where they were. Audrey and Natalie headed back towards the kitchen, sensing Kate's embarrassment, or maybe just ready for another drink.

"Kate, you all right?" Cameron asked.

"Clear out, please. Give us some space," Michael said. "Your friend drunk in there? Do we need to bring her something to vomit in, maybe?"

A low moan came from inside the room.

"She's not well," Kate said.

"Let me check it out." Cameron wore the classic stoner expression, eyes half-open and an amused, closed-lipped smile. He pushed past Michael. Kate blocked the door. She had stopped crying, and now just looked frightened. Michael wished he were a little more sober, so he could say something smart to calm her down. He patted her arm. "Kate, doll, what's going on? You can tell me."

"She's tied up," Kate said in a small voice. "She made this terrible moan. I think she's sick."

"Let's check it out," Michael said. "You can trust me. I'm not going to make fun of you."

Kate moved aside, just enough to let him pass.

Sure enough, Kate's friend was roped to the bed. Naked. She wore white contacts, and her skin was a fine gray. Her gaze moved among the men, and she licked her lips.

Michael was stunned. He knew Kate had a sense of humor, but this was beyond expectations. She'd turned her friend into a perfect sexy zombie. He turned to her. "You had me all worked up! You two must have been doing makeup all this time. And I never thought you were such an actor."

"I'm not," Kate said. She wasn't grinning like she should have been. "I don't know what happened."

"My compliments," Cameron said. "She looks awesome."

"Wow, Kate," Sam said. "You know, what would be even better is if you'd put some blood on her. Or some black goo, or something. I guess you don't want to mess up your sheets, though."

"Kate, you can cop to the joke," Michael said. "It was masterful. Smile already."

Kate blushed. "It's not a joke. I swear. She *wanted* me to tie her up. Before she turned into this. We'd been talking about zombies, and then…"

Michael examined the girl in the bed. She pulled on her ropes, moving towards him. There was a blank look in her eyes. He took a step back. She was an amazing actor.

"Where'd you get the contacts?" Sam asked. "They're perfect."

"I'd better get the girls so they can see this," Henry said. He didn't leave the room.

"Guys, you have to help me figure out what to do," Kate said. There was panic in her voice. "Michael, please."

He leaned forward, inspecting the rope. Maybe she wanted him to play along. Take the joke a little further. "The knots are pretty good."

Jamie moved towards him, licking her lips. Even her tongue was dark.

"I didn't think you knew how to tie knots like this, Kate," Michael said. He tried to pitch his voice so that only she could hear it. "You know how I like rope, and knots. Is that what you were doing?"

"What?" she said. "I don't. She did it. We were," Kate let out a breath. "Well, shit. You *know* what we were doing."

"Hey, check this out," Cameron said. He locked Jamie's ankles together using his handcuffs. He climbed onto the bed and straddled her, sitting on her hips. She was straining against the rope to sit up. Her white-eyeball gaze was locked on Cameron. She winked, and pursed her lips.

"She wants me," Cameron said. "Michael, I knew you'd come through and introduce me to someone who could really appreciate me."

"Don't!" Kate said. "This isn't a fucking joke!" She grabbed Cameron's arm, but he shrugged free.

"I'm in love," Cameron said.

"Love," Jamie said. She could make her voice sound amazingly deep.

"Get off, Cameron," Kate said.

"I'm fin' to get off, that's for sure," Cameron said, slipping into his Kanye voice. He ran his hands up Jamie's stomach, cupping her breasts. "You cool with that?" he asked Jamie.

She moaned. Her nipples were a deep red, maybe painted with lipstick. She wore enough black makeup to make her eyes appear to sink in her face.

"We'd better take pictures," Sam said. "Cameron, get off of her before you mess up her makeup." He reached over and undid the handcuffs, freeing Jamie's ankles.

"Off!" Kate said. "Dude! Seriously."

"Her nipples are so hard," Cameron said. "Holla, girl, can I get a holla back?"

The woman tied to the bed did not holler back. She struggled to get closer to Cameron.

"So, Kate, how much is Michael paying you and your friend to do this?" Henry said. "Because I'm going to have a party. Everyone can come as different kinds of zombies. Belly dancer zombies, zombies in hardhats and shit. You know how in the movies, the zombies are always, like, a naked chick, and a bloody bride, and a businessman, and a fat dude wearing a bathrobe and a stained wife-beater, and a kid in a baseball uniform. Like, to show that zombieism strikes equally across all demographics, when really it would probably be a group of people who were all in the same place at the same time. A common interest group. Like if Trader Joe's were overrun and we're all Hawaiian-shirted zombies…"

"Dude," Cameron interrupted. "You want to give us some privacy, or you want to see me whip it out?" He turned around to grin at the guys, and then moved his face towards the zombie's. "I don't want to mess up your makeup. I just want a quick—"

"Cameron! No!" Kate screamed. She grabbed his arm and pulled. The zombie was biting him.

Cameron howled and fell back onto the floor, holding his hand to his mouth. Blood seeped between his fingers.

"Na funny," Cameron said. "I don't haf healf insuran'. You are hepin' me wif da bill fo dis."

"Cam, are you okay?" Kate asked. She knelt.

Cameron took his hand away from his mouth. Part of his lower lip was missing.

In the silence, Kate said, "I told you guys. This isn't a fucking joke."

The zombie in the bed was *chewing*. Michael took a step back, and then another. The rest of it he could believe as a joke, a joke that got steadily sicker, but not this. Cameron would have had to have been in on it, and he wasn't this good of an actor. Michael closed his eyes and opened them. Reality hadn't changed.

"Why didn't you *tell* us this was a real zombie?" Henry asked.

"I *tried*!" Kate said.

Sam bolted from the room, and shut himself in the bathroom. The door didn't block the sound of his retching.

Kate picked up the open bottle of wine from her desk, and took a sip. "We'd better clean you up, Cam," she said tonelessly. "If there's any hard alcohol left, will someone get it?"

The bedroom door opened. Audrey and Natalie came in, each carrying tumblers of a mostly clear liquid. The ice had been used up hours ago.

"Oh, my God. Cammy, what happened to you?" Audrey went to him, raised her hand to his face, but didn't touch him.

"We have to smash her head," Henry said. "That's the only way."

"No," Kate said. "Jamie wasn't hurting anyone until we got close. That's her name, Jamie. If Cameron had treated her with respect, none of this would have happened."

"What's going on?" Audrey asked. "Cammy, what did you *do*? Kate, um, why is your friend tied to your bed? And what's with the makeup?"

Jamie licked the blood from her lips and chin.

Cameron pointed at Jamie. He looked scared.

"I need to get some gauze." Kate left the room. "You explain," she said to Michael as she passed.

"I don't know if we should hang out in here," Michael said. Jamie was moaning.

"*We* shouldn't," Henry said. "But Cameron's infected now."

"We don' know dat fo' sho'," Cameron said.

"We should get you to a hospital," Michael said. "Who's sober enough to drive?"

Henry shrugged. Natalie and Audrey both shook their heads, looking worried.

"Damn," Michael said. Cameron didn't want to go to the hospital, anyway. Michael was reminded of their friend Rich telling him about how he'd had a bone spur in his foot, and had smashed it against the pavement in order to fix it. Rich hadn't had health insurance, either.

Kate came back into the room. She held a fresh bottle of Jack. Michael was glad that someone was thinking straight. It must be the Xanax. She pressed gauze over Cameron's mouth. He fainted.

"We need to wash this out," Kate said. "We have to get him into the shower, and Sam's in the bathroom. Michael, we have to use yours. Henry, hold this." She handed him the bottle. Kate put her hands under Cameron's armpits and started dragging him across the carpet. Cameron moaned softly. He was bleeding everywhere; the carpet would be ruined. A small, distant part of Michael observed that this would wipe out the security deposit.

Jamie let out a low moan as the group left the room. Henry shut the door behind them.

"Shouldn't we, like, tie him up or something?" Henry said. "Isn't he going to turn into a zombie now?"

"What the hell's going on?" Natalie asked. She was pale.

"Your boy here done got himself bitten, and we're trying to clean him up," Michael said. He suspected, nauseatingly, that Henry was right; they should tie Cameron up. He picked up Cameron's ankles and helped Kate move him. They maneuvered his head and shoulders into the shower. Kate took the bottle from Henry and uncapped it. "Alcohol's an antiseptic," she explained. She poured the booze over the side of Cameron's face. "I'm sorry, Cameron," she said softly.

Cameron cried out, coughing and spitting. His eyes opened. "Ah, fuck, fuck," he gurgled.

"You OK?" Michael asked. "Dude?"

"Ow," Cameron said. He reached up to wipe his face. His eyes were watering. "Dat fucking hurts."

"I'm sorry, Cam, I had to. Here, try sitting up. Michael, a towel?" A mixture of blood and booze was dripping down Cameron's shirt, coloring the white fabric.

Michael gave her a hand towel from the rack. Cameron sat, leaning against the tile wall of the bathroom. Kate applied the towel to his lip. He flinched.

"You're going to be OK," she said. "Faces and heads bleed a lot. And there's a lot of germs in the human mouth. I just wanted to make sure it was disinfected. I know it stings."

"Fuck," Cameron said.

"Here, use this." Audrey leaned over them, holding out a bag of frozen peas. "Stop the bleeding, at least."

Kate took it, wrapping it in the towel and applying it to Cameron's face. She seemed so calm; like she knew what she was doing. She was glowing with sweat, a smear of blood on her cheek. It was disturbing, how attractive she was.

"I don' feel so good," Cameron said. He sounded spacey, and he still wasn't pronouncing consonants very well. The frozen peas on his face probably weren't helping.

"Do you want to go to the hospital?" Michael asked. "I can call for an ambulance. Just give me the word. There's a fire station a few blocks away. They'll be here fast."

"Naw, dude. Gimme a minute."

"We shouldn't have let you climb on top of her," Michael said softly. "It wasn't cool."

"See, the bleeding's slowing down," Kate said. "Let's just call you an ambulance, and get you taken care of. I'll go with you. It's going to be fine."

"No way," Cameron said. He took a breath, let it out slowly. "Ah," he said. His voice was deep. He looked at Kate, his eyes wet.

"Momma," he whispered. "Somefing's happening."

Kate recoiled. She didn't scream. She dropped the frozen peas, but managed to hold onto the towel. She gripped both ends of it, pushing the middle into Cameron's mouth.

"Shit, shit, shit. No," Kate said. "Cameron. Say something. Stay with me."

"Uhh," he said into the towel.

Cameron's eyes had gone white. He pushed his head towards Kate. She held the towel in his mouth. He reached both hands towards her face.

"Michael, help," Kate said. "Rope. *Something.*"

Michael moved as fast as he could. He grabbed a length of rope from a drawer just outside the bathroom. "Natalie," he called. "Help me get his hands."

Natalie shook her head, backing away.

"Michael, hurry. Please." The matter-of-factness in Kate's voice nearly undid him. Cameron was touching her cheek. Michael was panicking. He tied one of Cameron's hands to the shower door.

"Fuck," Michael said.

"Ulh," Kate said. Cameron had a grip on her throat with his free hand. He was trying to pull her closer. She held tight to the towel covering his mouth, trying to keep him at a distance.

"Can we get some fucking *help* here? I need to get his other hand." Michael shouted. He looked to his friends. They stood in the doorway, wearing identical expressions of bewilderment and fear.

Audrey seemed to snap out of her trance. "Hey, Cameron, come here," she said. She moved into the bathroom, waving her hand. "Cameron, babe, look at me."

Kate's face started turning red.

Audrey switched her whip, hitting herself in the ear. "Fuck," she said. She lashed the whip, making it snap.

Cameron looked at her. "Fuck," he said, through the towel. He let go of Kate and reached towards Audrey. Blood ran down his chin.

Kate fell back onto the floor, coughing and breathing hard. Cameron spat out the towel and smiled at Audrey. Michael hoped like hell that Audrey was going to keep distracting Cameron. He heard the whip snap.

"Look at me, Cam," Audrey cooed. She stayed outside of his reach. He strained towards her.

Michael tied a length of rope to the shower door and made a clove hitch. Now he just had to get Cameron's hand inside it. He took a breath, then lunged. Grabbed Cameron's hand. Secured it next to the hand he'd already tied.

Michael backed away, pulling Kate and Audrey with him. Cameron's skin was turning gray. His teeth clicked together.

Cameron had been right: something was happening.

Kate coughed and spat. "Gag," she said.

"Seriously," Michael said. "You OK? He looked like he really had you." They stood, catching their breath.

"I meant," Kate said, "gag him. I know you've got something we can use."

Michael understood. "Not really. My gear is mostly blindfolds, feathers, and shit I got from the pet store. All the good stuff is expensive." There were online catalogs full of it. Leather and metal. Gags and hoods and cuffs and rope. That's what you really needed when the zombies came.

Cameron's tongue protruded from his mouth, licking at the air.

"Plus I'm not touching him again," Michael said. He didn't realize he'd spoken until he heard it.

Michael shut the bathroom door, leaving the light on for Cameron. It seemed like the least he could do. It was a pity that the bathroom door didn't lock from the outside. "Fuck," he said. "I need to sit down." He could see haloes of light around people and objects. He moved to the living room, and his friends followed.

"What happened in there?" Audrey said.

"You ever seen *Night of the Living Dead*?" Michael asked.

"Um."

"But you know what zombies are, right?"

"You're not saying what I think you're saying," she said. "Because we're all high. This *has* to be a joke." She giggled, as if to prove it.

They walked past Kate's closed bedroom door. No one said anything.

"What do we do now?" Natalie asked.

"I'm going to sit," Audrey said. There was the sound of couches sighing.

Michael went into the kitchen. Kate followed him. They washed the blood from their hands with dish soap. The sink was full of plates.

"Dude, how do you work your TV?" Natalie called. "We gotta check the news."

"Universal remote on the coffee table," he said. He looked to Kate. She seemed small, after all of this. "Your cheek," he said softly, pointing to his own face.

Kate wiped at the wrong side.

"No, I mean this side." He raised his voice over the sound of the TV. "Like a mirror." He hadn't intended to touch her, but there was his hand, grazing her cheek. Her wet skin under his. His hand stayed there, longer than he had any right to. She didn't push him away. They'd shared something in that bathroom. Now everything would change. The world was broken, and they were going to have to try and put it back together. He leaned over to kiss her. She stepped towards him, opening her arms and turning her face away. He put his arms around her, startled by how thin she was. He could feel the outline of her spine and ribs. Her shirt was still inside out. He wanted to pick her up and carry her away. He settled for kissing her neck.

She pushed him away. "What was that about?" She dried her hands on her jeans. The blood was still on her cheek, smeared now.

He shrugged, unable to explain. She'd held him close. He picked up a dishtowel and offered it to her. "Your cheek."

She wetted it under the tap, and brushed at her face. She looked as tired as he felt. "You didn't gag him," she said.

"The ropes will hold."

"You should have gagged him."

"Why? What do you know that you're not telling me?"

She shook her head, moving away.

He was ashamed that he'd raised his voice. "Sorry, Kate, I'm just... I don't know what to do. Let's go check out the news." He went into the living room, as much to get away from her as to get to the TV.

The space was large, as living rooms went, with three couches in a U shape facing the TV. Two of the walls were entirely windows, which he normally loved about the house. The view of the blossoms on the plum tree outside had been what had convinced him when he had been looking for a place to rent, though it cost more than he'd intended. Now the expanse of windows seemed like a dangerous oversight. There was no way to board them up, even if he had any wood. The plum-tree side of the house didn't matter, because you needed a ladder to access those windows from the outside, but the other wall had a deck built right outside. He locked the sliding glass door and turned on the outside lights, half-expecting to see a crowd of the living dead standing there. The deck was empty, save for the picnic table. He thought about bringing it inside, using it to barricade the windows. That would probably be overreacting. The zombies were inside the house, anyway.

He sat down and took the remote from Henry, who'd been watching a music video with a few guys in sunglasses and a dance floor full of quivering booty. Michael looked at his friends for their reaction. They looked dazed. Sam was gone.

"Did Sam leave?" he asked.

Audrey looked around. "I guess so. Didn't say goodbye. He could have offered me a ride."

"Well, I guess we've got enough, then," Michael said. He dug into his pocket, feeling bad about how he'd told Kate that he didn't have any more pills. "Xanax, anyone?"

His friends held out their hands, and he distributed the pills. "This is the body of Christ," he said. He took the last one for himself, swallowing it dry.

"What do we do?" Henry asked, chewing his pill. "Are they safe?"

"They're tied up," Kate said. She swallowed her pill with a swig of wine. "They're safe enough. Now I'm worried about what might be wandering the streets out there." She sat down next to Michael, her thigh brushing his in a distracting way.

Michael remembered the remote in his hand. "If you guys know anything about zombies, you know that this won't be an isolated case. We should check the news." CNN had a story about a poodle show. NBC had some heads talking politics. He flipped through channels. Commercials, *Top Chef*, a rerun of a lousy episode of *Saturday Night Live*, and a black-and-white documentary about Hollywood at the end of World War II on PBS. Nothing about zombies.

"Jesus," Michael said. He closed his eyes. The room spun. There were too many things that didn't make sense. He looked at Kate. She bit her lip. He moved his thigh towards hers. She didn't move away. His head was starting to hurt, and he couldn't bring himself to believe that they'd hallucinated everything. Touch was the only thing that made any sense.

"*Night of the Loving Dead*," Kate said.

"What?" He was sure that's what she'd said. No way was there a zombie movie with that title. He'd have heard of it. He imagined a romantic comedy. Two girls are in bed, and one turns into a zombie, then a guy tries to fuck her and he turns into a zombie. Everything would end well, somehow. Either that or it was porn, and everything always ended well in porn. Maybe they could Netflix it.

"The Romero one?" Kate elbowed Michael. "*Night of the Living Dead*?"

Now he was sure he'd heard her correctly. He was disappointed.

That one ended badly; zombie movies always did. If anyone survived, they did it by losing the very things that made them human. He got up and put on the DVD.

Michael sat next to Kate, leaning his knee against hers.

"Is this really what we're doing?" he said softly into her hair.

"What are we *supposed* to do?" Kate whispered back.

"We're all going to die, like this. The zombies are going to get us." He inhaled. She smelled of smoke, and sweat, and fear. And shampoo.

"Oh, God," Kate said. She put her head on his shoulder. "We deserve it, don't we." It wasn't a question.

"No. That's not what zombie stories are about." He put his arm around her. He waited for the movie to get underway. He fingered her hair. She'd never let him do that before.

"What the hell are we doing?" Audrey asked. She'd spent the last few minutes holding her head in her hands. She sat up straight now. "Why aren't we helping him?"

"It'll show up on the news soon," Michael said. "We can't be holding onto Patients Zero and One here. It's only a matter of time. If we go to the hospital it'll be like the *Day of the Dead* scene when everyone is turning into zombies. Or, worse, the CDC, or FDA, or whoever, will quarantine the lot of us. Imprison us and run tests. Who knows if this is transmitted by contact, or by blood, as well as by bite?"

"Or even through the air," Kate said. "And that movie was terrible. Plus the Food and Drug Administration won't have anything to do with zombies."

"We have to do *something*," Audrey said.

"Right. Absolutely," Michael said. "What do you propose?"

"Well, I'm calling an ambulance," Audrey said.

"That's five hundred dollars right there," Henry said.

"Then we can take him ourselves, both of them," Audrey said, but there was doubt in her voice now.

The group was quiet. On the screen, the young woman ran through the cemetery.

"OK," Michael said. "All those in favor of trying to wrestle our friends into a car and avoid getting bitten while we take them to the hospital, also dealing with whatever other zombies are out there wandering around, please raise your hands."

No one did.

"We could call the cops," Audrey said.

"I tell you what," Henry said. "If it were just a little thing, like his bits were burning, he can go to a doctor and pay a couple hundred to get himself sorted out, but for something like this, he wouldn't get out of the hospital for less than a million dollars. That's *if* they don't just cut him up for sport. I mean, research."

"Oh," Audrey said. "What do *you* want to do, then?"

"Fuck if I know," Henry said. "At least now, they're still in one piece."

"Michael?" Audrey turned to him.

"Sober up until we can think straight? I don't know. I really don't know. I'm sorry. Excuse me while I lock the doors and windows." Michael stood. He wished someone had a better idea. The way things were, it seemed like the zombies would be safe, for a while. Secure. He wouldn't fall asleep, not with them there. In a few hours, he'd be able to make a better decision.

Kate interrupted his thoughts. "Hey, does anyone else think that scene in *Living Dead*, where the white girl slaps the black guy, and he clean knocks her out and then lays her on the couch and undoes the buttons on her jacket—does anyone else think that scene is hot?"

"Racist," Audrey said.

"Liberal," Henry said, in the same tone.

Michael was stunned. It was the sexiest thing anyone had said in a long while. Deliberately provocative. And a total non sequitur. It took his mind off of their zombie problem for a blessed moment.

"It was 1968," Kate said. "You know, the same year as the first interracial kiss in *Star Trek*. Don't you get it? They were *trying* to push buttons. But, no, what I meant is the tension between them.

It's almost romantic. She's going nuts, and he's trying to hold them both together and keep the zombies at bay—"

"Shh," Natalie said. There was a zombie on the screen.

"I'm going to shower." Kate stood as Michael sat. He watched her walk, wanting to follow her. She obviously had more to say. Michael found it engaging, more so than the movie, which most of them had seen. It sounded a little like the third-wave feminism stuff she'd been talking about from one of her community college classes. He wouldn't have known what third-wave feminist theory was without her; at first he thought she'd said third-*rate* feminism, which just sounded mean. Still, he couldn't very well follow her into the shower. He imagined it for a while as the movie played. After they'd soaped one another, he'd lay her on her back in the tub, warm water falling over both of them. He focused on little things; things he'd done with girls in showers, and things he'd like to do. Her hand tight in his hair. The way the shower washed away a woman's taste, so that you had to put your tongue inside to find it. Her hips lifting. The way she'd be unsteady on her feet, after. Leaning on him and smiling that precious satisfied smile which always went away after a minute, as if she was embarrassed. He'd go down on Kate until both of them were pruney and the hot water ran out, if she'd let him. Trace the alphabet, over and over. Whatever she liked. His fantasies always centered on a girl's orgasm. He'd heard of women who could imagine their way to orgasm, literally no-handed. He wondered what they fantasized about: whether they thought about someone touching them, or if, like him, they thought about giving someone else pleasure.

A moan came from deeper inside the house. Henry took the remote from the table and turned up the volume. Michael was facing the movie but he wasn't paying attention. Images registered like patterns in clouds, and then disappeared. He found himself thinking of how much smarter than him Kate was. It shamed him. They both read books, and watched movies, and listened to music, and had conversations about culture and how well it was doing whatever it was that it was supposed to do. But Kate was probably brighter, and definitely more studious than he was. She actually talked about going to college full-time, whereas he hadn't managed to take a single class since high school. Maybe he just needed a study buddy. If they took classes together, that would get him on track.

Kate came back, her hair wrapped in a towel, wearing Sponge-Bob-printed pajama pants and a white T-shirt. She smelled edible. Lemony. She sat next to Michael, and he had a hard time not leaning over and putting some part of her in his mouth. He'd teased himself rigid, thinking about her. She dropped the towel on the floor. Normally that would bother him. He supposed that if there were zombies in the house, one wet towel on the carpet didn't matter.

"All's quiet," she said. "For whatever that's worth." She rested her head on his shoulder. There was such trust in that gesture. He decided that would be enough for him. They could take things slowly. She relaxed against him. A moment later, he worked a hand under her shirt. Up, over her belly, the skin soft. She wasn't wearing a bra. She tensed, and he slowed down. Ran his fingertips over her collarbone, down the center of her chest. Back up. He circled around her breasts. By the time he had a nipple in his fingers, it was hard. He put his tongue in her ear, enjoying her struggle to stay quiet, not caring if anyone was awake to see them. She pulled away from him, sitting up, then leaned back, unfolding a blanket over herself. She slipped a hand inside her pajama pants. He kissed her neck, surprised and pleased and a little jealous. He put an arm around her, so that he had access to both of her nipples under the blanket. She shuddered, and then her breathing became calm. He knew enough to let go. He put his nose in her hair, his hands wrapping around her waist.

If anyone had been watching, they had the decency to pretend to be asleep. The room was quiet, save for the movie and the regular breathing. Kate disentangled herself and went into the kitchen. She didn't turn on the light. The faucet ran for a while, like she was washing her hands. He'd never been with a woman who did for herself. It was sexy, how unabashedly in control she was of her own desire. He wanted to take her to bed, but he didn't want to frighten her off. Never mind the zombie in his bathroom.

She came back with two glasses of water. She held one out, and he took it. He found that he was thirsty. She was silent. He couldn't tell what she was thinking, if her expression indicated lust, or shame, or worry. Some combination. Something else entirely. He patted the couch next to him, wanting her to be near him. He ached for her to touch him. She hesitated, then sat. Two empty glasses were set onto the coffee table. She put her arm around him and leaned into him.

"Sorry," she whispered. "That was really inappropriate of me. First you catch me *in flagrante lesbiano*, or maybe it should be *lesbiana*. And now," she put her fingers in his hair, tightened them. "You'll think I'm such a—" she didn't finish.

He touched her cheek. "I started it. We both need to remember that we're alive. And you're not a—" He pulled her face towards his. She dodged his mouth, biting his ear gently. Her hair was wet against his cheek. He could feel her chest moving with her breathing, and all of the words she wasn't saying.

Impulsively, he took her hand and brought it to his crotch. He flexed, wanting her to know the effect she had on him. It was painful, how much he wanted her. She fingered his bulge, then lowered her head to his lap, inhaling. He gripped the couch so as not to grab at her, willing himself to hold still. She pulled away, her hand closing on his arm with surprising force.

"I can't do this," she said. She let go. "We should check the news." It was as if she'd turned on a light.

He realized that the movie was over. The introduction music had been looping. Kate found the remote and flicked through the channels. Nothing. Weather and sports. She sat at a distance from him now. Michael waited for his erection to go away. It didn't. He could feel the beginnings of a hangover. He closed his eyes. At least his head wasn't spinning any more. He stood, sick of it, sick of the tension between him and Kate. He went to the hall bathroom and closed the door. The mirror was opaque from the shower steam. The temperature in the room was slightly warmer than the living room. It made what he did easier. He came into a handful of toilet paper, then flushed it. He washed his hands, watching as if someone else was doing it.

Kate had put on *Shaun of the Dead*. She was lying on the couch, asleep. He worked up the nerve to join her, taking the side closer to the floor so that he'd be the one to fall off if she pushed him. She stirred as he slipped under the blanket. She wrapped a sleep-heavy arm around him.

He held her hand to his chest, not sure what he was supposed to be feeling. There was the emptiness that he got after masturbating, and the warm and real closeness of her. The way she'd arched her back when he had her nipples in his fingers. He listened to the movie for a few minutes. It made him think about zombies. He didn't know how to feel about them, either.

"You know, I think we're going to die," he said.

She tightened her fingers in his shirt, but didn't say anything.

chapter five

Kate's head ached. She was in a red room. No. She opened her eyes. The living room was bright with sunlight. She closed her eyes. The television was on, playing the DVD introduction to *Shaun of the Dead*. Michael's parties often ended this way, with people passed out on the available horizontal space, although Kate usually found her way back to her own bed. Now, though, she was on the couch, pressed up against someone warm and comfortable. She turned to look. It was Michael, which was perhaps not surprising, but in the time they'd been housemates, neither of them had made any overtures, and she liked it that way. She had a bad feeling that something had happened.

Audrey and Natalie were cuddled up on the opposite couch, Henry on the third. Kate stretched, catlike. She drifted through the fragments of her dreams: in one, all of her teeth had come loose, and then she was late for school. Classic anxiety dreams. She held onto the evaporating images. Then she remembered what had happened last night. Kate was immediately awake. She listened to the house. All was quiet.

She needed to leave. Needed to get away. Once, in middle school, she'd mistakenly gone to the first lunch period, instead of the second, skipping class. She'd sat with friends she didn't normally see at lunch, which was nice if strange. When she realized her mistake, she left the school. She used her milk money to call the school from a payphone, after calling Information to get the number. She pretended to be her mother, saying that she'd come to get Kate because of a family emergency, and she was sorry she hadn't checked in with the office. She spent the rest of the day walking through town, thinking that she was going to get into trouble for skipping. Obsessing over it. She'd gone home at the normal time, fearing there would be cop cars outside the house, and teary parents inside, or at least angry parents. None of that happened. But she felt the same instinct to flee. Something was wrong; she'd fucked up, and she needed to go.

As carefully as she could, Kate extricated herself from under Michael's arm, and sat on the edge of the couch. He woke.

"Shh," Kate whispered. "I've got to run."

He rubbed his eyes. "You're going to leave me?" His voice cracked with sleep. He looked about as hung over as she felt.

"I needs to get paid, you know." She smiled, trying to make it a joke. Michael never paid attention to her work schedule, and if he believed she'd be at work, that would save having to tell him what she was really doing. She may as well keep her date with Walter. The Zeppelin was scheduled to fly at noon, and it was already after ten, but maybe she could talk him out of it. If Michael knew about Walter, probably he'd think Kate was forward-thinking and empowered, but she had decided several houses (and several sets of housemates) ago that it was better not to talk much about her love life.

"You're kidding. You're really going to go? I thought you got today off." Michael put his hand over Kate's, and the touch was surprisingly electric. "What are we going to do about—" He stopped.

They considered one another. "Wake them all up and send them home. Or not. I don't fucking know. Why are we even still alive?" Her mouth tasted of warmed-over ass, and her mind was going in little circles trying to piece together the previous evening. She didn't dare say anything aloud. If they talked about it; if they both remembered the same events, that might make them true.

"You remember *Evil Dead*?" Kate whispered. "I know they're demons, not zombies, but I always thought that the most horrific ending would have been if the guy, after brutally murdering and dismembering his friends, realized the next morning that he'd imagined it all. I thought it was going to end like that when he touched the mirror and it gave way. You could see him coming apart." She could hear herself rationalizing, as if that situation was anything like theirs. Except their friends really had turned into *something*, and they'd left them tied up all night. Kate wanted to say something about how they needed to take responsibility for what had happened. "Um, so my car is parked on the street in Berkeley and I don't want to get a ticket," she finished.

"Don't leave me," Michael said.

"Will you still drive me to my car?"

Michael sighed. He was never great in the mornings. "All right. Just let me piss."

"I've got to get dressed." Kate went to her room. She took a deep breath, and knocked.

There was no answer. She thought about how well the knots may or may not have held in the intervening hours. If Jamie weren't a zombie, she'd be pissed off about being tied up all night. Kate would never be able to go to belly dance class again, that was certain. Maybe she'd go to jail for assault and battery, or whatever it was when you tied someone up and then didn't untie them. Unless maybe they could laugh it all off. "Jamie?" she whispered. "Are you all right?" Kate opened the door a crack, just enough to look in. There might have been a person in the bed, underneath the bedclothes.

Kate remembered that she had some clothes in the dryer. She must have gotten her pajamas there last night. She selected a decently revealing top, her Hawaiian-print TJ's shirt, and jeans. She calmed down in the bathroom, washing her hands and face in the sink. She popped some store-brand ibuprofen, drinking water from the tap as it spilled over her palm. In the mirror she looked a little worse for wear. She ought to put on some lipstick.

They got into Michael's car, a late-nineties Buick. He'd been proud of finding it for $900, though he'd bitched about having to get a new radiator and new brakes almost immediately. Michael wore a hoody against the morning chill. Kate realized she probably should have brought a jacket, but the car was already started. He wouldn't drive her to her car if he wasn't OK with her leaving, she thought. She put her bag on the floor. She'd cleaned it out recently, discarding the unnecessary socks and gym clothes and receipts. Now it held nothing but a book and yesterday's water bottle. "Sorry to leave you with this," she said as he drove. "I need to go in for a few hours. You know. Plus I don't want to leave my car on the street."

He gave her a sidelong look.

"It'll be ticketed. It's Berkeley. I'll be back as soon as I can. If we can keep everyone separated, we should be safe." She touched his knee, under the steering wheel.

"How long will you be out?"

"Um, not very long," Kate said. "Maybe a few hours. I'd call in, but I at least have to go and do the ordering. If TJ's runs out of wine, I'll be the one to blame. But I'll get it done, then take off early. Go home sick, or whatever. Plus, with any luck, you'll be back before anyone else even wakes up. They'll listen to you." She felt sick, lying to him.

"Sure," Michael said. "Probably it was a blood sugar problem. They just need a good breakfast. How do you know that the whole world isn't full of them?" He didn't have to say the Z word.

"Left here," Kate said. "And right after the light." A moment passed in silence. "Just up here, see my car?" He stopped his car, put it in park.

"Be careful," he said.

"You, too." She kissed Michael's cheek. Normally she wasn't this affectionate with him, but it seemed like he could use it. And after last night, she owed him something.

He reached for the back of her head, trying to bring her mouth to his. She pulled away, holding his hand against her cheek. He smelled like the guys she'd gone to high school with in Wisconsin, some combination of cheap deodorant, soap, and Northern ancestry. Against her will, she'd always had some chemistry with him. That must have been why she'd let him fumble up against her. She'd needed it, last night; they both had needed something to remind them they were still alive. After she came, though, it had been weird.

It wasn't that she hadn't wanted to touch him. But a quick tussle under the blanket wouldn't have been enough. She'd wanted to take him to bed. Have him tie her up the way she'd tied up Jamie, and fuck her until they were both sore. She wanted to know what it would feel like, with him. She couldn't figure out how to tell him, then.

"About last night—" she said. She let go of his hand. "Sorry I was so drunk," she said. "I'm sure we made some bad decisions."

"Don't mention it," he said, looking away.

"Did you lock the house?" she asked.

"I shut the door." He was trying to make a joke.

She smiled and got out of the car without touching him again. If they got together, they'd break up, and then she'd be out a place to stay as well as a friend, she reminded herself. She'd been through that before. Knowing it didn't make her want him less. She might have already fucked it all up, with last night. Attraction, by its nature, is unstable. Sooner or later, you settle into a lower energy state. The nervous spark goes away, and the love gets more and more efficient until you barely notice one another. Or, as happened more often in her relationships, things got awkward and that meant not seeing one another again.

"See you soon." She waved.

The street was empty. The guy was gone. Still, Kate looked around to be sure as she walked to her car, a silver 1999 Focus she called Focahontas. Her finger cymbals were still on the sidewalk. Kate picked them up and got in her car. She took off her TJ's shirt and tossed it into the back seat, along with the cymbals. It occurred to her that she should call home, call her parents or her brother and see whether there were any zombies in the suburbs of Madison. She talked herself out of making the call. No time, she couldn't find her Bluetooth headset, and what would she say, anyway? She wanted to drive forever. Go somewhere safe, if there was anywhere safe. She wanted someone to take care of her. She might as well see Walter.

The car radio was broken, and had been for several years, so she tried to use her driving time to meditate. Instead she got lost, something she did regularly, and nearly always in the warehouse district. She finally found 880, and drove towards the airport. Nothing looked amiss: people were out, traffic was normal, pedestrians were walking around. Nobody was eating anyone else. She thought about texting Michael and telling him as much, but he must have seen it for himself. The lack of zombies. She needed to clear her head; get away from it all.

Nearing the Coliseum, she remembered that she was looking for a Holiday Inn—that was the meeting place for the Zeppelin tour. She and Walter had laughed at that when he'd first brought it up. The company offered something so extravagant and expensive as Zeppelin rides, and they couldn't even run a shuttle from the parking lot of a Marriott.

She saw Walter standing near the hotel's front door. The sun was out and it was a beautiful spring day. The smell of the breeze alone was enough to make one feel lighter. She parked her car and walked over to him. Walter was fiftyish, starting to lose his hair. He was dressed in a suit, as always. Probably something name brand, an Armani or Brooks Brothers, Kate couldn't tell. She'd met him after answering his ad on Craigslist a few months earlier.

"You won't believe the evening I had last night," she said in greeting. She kissed him on both cheeks, European style, then thought better of it. Her headache must be due to last night's booze, but she didn't want to pass on a cold if she was getting sick. The first time Walter had kissed her, she'd caught a cold but hadn't realized it yet. She'd felt guilty once she developed symptoms. But when she saw him a few days later, he hadn't caught the cold, so she figured he wouldn't, and she let him kiss her. High on DayQuil, she didn't cough or sneeze, so she hoped there was no harm. For all she knew, he'd given her the cold in the first place.

"You having fun again without me, Katie Kay?" he asked. "Let's walk."

She slipped her hand in his pocket as they strolled through the parking lot. "Not so much fun as I would have had *with* you." In his pocket there were some crisp folded bills. She withdrew them, and pocketed them without looking. That was part of their deal.

"How have you been?" he asked.

"Times is interesting. Michael had a party last night, got kind of wild, but I wasn't about to miss out on seeing you." As soon as she'd said it, she wondered whether it was impolite to talk about parties that the other person hadn't been invited to. Walter knew who Michael was, though they would never meet; Kate talked about her friends. She remembered that she'd forgotten to put on lipstick. It was a bit common to put it on in public, but maybe Walter wouldn't mind. It wasn't as if they were eating at a fancy restaurant or anything. She found a tube in her pocket and ran it over her mouth.

"Is that code for a hangover?" There was concern in his voice, as well as real affection. Kate often had the feeling that he was going to ruffle her hair, or fake punch her on the arm, one of those *Leave it to Beaver* kind of gestures, but he never did.

"A little," she said, telling the truth. She wished she were drunk again. She shouldn't have left the house. It was too late to go back. "Also I hooked up with my belly dance instructor. She made the first move. I'd never been with a woman before. She has a tattoo of an Ouroboros around her hips." Kate nearly said *had a tattoo* but checked herself in time.

He raised his eyebrows. "Put your hand back in my pocket and tell me all about it," he said. "I didn't know you did belly dance."

"Let's just go get a room," she said on impulse. "Hang out. Order up room service. It doesn't have to be here; we can go somewhere else. I just need to see you. Take it easy," she finished. She realized that she had failed to run away.

"I've been planning this for weeks, darling, you know that. You can see me just fine while we cruise the friendly skies."

It had been worth a shot. She thought of the money in her pocket. She could live on her Trader Joe's pay just fine, but the deal with Walter offered something else. Still, she had a few hundred in her bank account, which would not get her very far, and only as long as there was still electricity and ATMs worked. Where, really, was she going to run to? She couldn't bring herself to tell Walter about the zombies. He'd think she was crazy. She wondered if she was crazy. It would explain a lot.

"There's a shuttle that will pick us up in twenty minutes or so," Walter said. He led her towards the edge of the parking lot.

Kate gave him an embellished account of the previous night as they waited, out of habit, including the part about tying Jamie up, at her request, but skipping all of the zombie business. It was easier than coming up with something out of her past, and it made him happy. They stood between two parked cars. His pocket was empty now, but the lining was smooth and thin. High thread count. No underwear. She fingered his penis through the lining as they stood. He made an appreciative noise, and she could feel the first stirrings of an erection. It made Kate feel awkward, being in public like this, but it was also kind of fun. And fun, she knew, was what she provided. She touched him, thinking of how she'd failed to touch Michael. She should have pushed Michael away when he first started; should have known what he was trying to do to her, but she couldn't. She hadn't wanted to.

"I've booked a suite for us at the Claremont for tonight," Walter said. He kissed her neck. "Dinner, and a professional massage at the best spa there is, how about it? The wife's out of town."

Kate took her hand out of his pocket. He might have meant that he would stay overnight with her. They'd never woken up together before. On another day, she might have accepted, out of curiosity. "Oh. I've kind of got plans after this," she said. She wanted to go home.

"I mean I have class. I'm really sorry. Forgive me." She'd told Walter she was a college student. In poetry, for an MFA at the prestigious Mills College in Oakland. She figured that sounded romantic; the truth was that she'd moved to California to work for a year and qualify for in-state tuition, and that had been almost four years ago. He'd recited the whole first stanza of "The Canonization" by John Donne before she'd realized he was quoting a poem; she'd Googled it later. She'd also told him that MFA stood for "Master of Fucking Around." But maybe she should tell him what she really was: crew at Trader Joe's, doing stock and running registers. Her largest drawer, on a Saturday before Christmas, was almost eight grand, three of it in cash. Not that three grand in unmarked bills would get anyone very far, but that she was trusted with it. She kissed his neck.

"Dear, you tease," he said. He put an arm around her.

"And you like it. How about I do you like Bloom, while we stand here." Kate put her hand back into his pocket without waiting for permission. She worked him efficiently; she knew his buttons. He gasped when he came. Kate enjoyed that; enjoyed her power over him, and the way he wanted to give it to her. He'd have to get the trousers cleaned.

"Zeppelin tour, over here," a voice called. It issued from a perky figure holding a clipboard; she introduced herself as one of the pilots.

They held hands as they walked to join the group. Walter favored his left leg, avoiding the wet spot. Kate didn't say anything, but exulted secretly. Hand jobs always reminded her of that Yeats poem. Mad fingers playing on a place of stone. Or something like that.

They were the last ones aboard the minibus, which took them to the north field of the Oakland airport. She looked out the window as they drove, conscious of Walter's arm on the back of her seat. It was a clear day, and she saw no signs of zombies. She wanted very much to believe that there was no such *thing* as zombies, and therefore she wasn't a bad person for abandoning her friends. Other people in the minibus were chatting, looking forward to the Zeppelin ride.

The minibus parked. Walter got out first, and held his hand up for Kate. He liked to play the gentleman. Kate took his hand as she stepped out, not because she needed it, but because it would please him. He offered his hand to all of the women, and several took him up on it.

The Zeppelin was smaller than Kate had expected, with a tiny cabin underneath the white blimp of a hull. A three-step staircase had been set up so that everyone could board. There were scarcely a dozen passengers, plus a flight attendant and two pilots. Two women stood side by side, their pinkies interlaced, necks craned, looking up at the ship. A girl with pink hair was telling a story to an older man. A silver-haired couple stood in their Sunday best; the old guy even had a carnation in his lapel. These people all smelled nice. Kate told herself that she wasn't being stupid and selfish; that this wasn't exactly the wrong thing to be doing. She boarded with the rest of the group. The cabin had a single row of airplane seats on either side, as well as a cute little fake-leather loveseat in the back for when they were at altitude. There were lots of big windows, like the viewing car on a train. This was going to be cool. Sure, she would have to go home and deal with the zombies, afterwards, but she could let down her guard for a while.

Kate sat behind Walter, watching the ground crew handle the ropes. She examined the cute little safety card that detailed the two rows of seats and the two exits, with a few standard safety rules about seatbelts and following crew instructions. "Passenger Briefing" was translated into German as "*Passageierbelehrung*." German was *so* not one of the sexy languages.

"Hi! So I need you to pretend to pay attention during the safety instructions," said their flight attendant, a boyish figure with spiky black hair straight out of anime. He introduced himself as Matt.

The Zeppelin was truly novelty transportation; it would go in a circle around San Francisco, and land again where it started. As they took off, Kate was astonished at how quiet the ship was. Sure, there was the buzz of the engine, but they might as well have been on a lawnmower for all the noise it made. There wasn't the pressure of a normal plane, pushing you into your seat. She felt like she was floating. The airship would reach a cruising altitude of about 1,300 feet and circle the bay for an hour. Walter had said it was almost eight hundred bucks for the two of them. "Eight as in great," he'd written in the email. "Pity there aren't Royal Air Force codes for numbers, like 'A as in Alpha'—'Seven as in heaven?'" The tickets were more expensive than *she* was, she'd thought. She hadn't counted it, but she knew she now had at least three hundred dollars in her pocket. Part of her did wish that he'd skipped the Zeppelin ride and just given her the money, but, still. She wasn't *that* kind of girl.

And, more importantly, it was a Zeppelin. The only passenger Zeppelin in operation in the entire States, which was pretty cool. This would be a nice way to impress anyone, Kate thought. They would circle over the city, the Golden Gate bridge, Alcatraz, and Angel Island, and be back on the ground in time for a late lunch. Through the window she could see the coastline of San Francisco, and the rolling green hills of Marin to the north.

After they'd reached cruising altitude, and Matt told the group they could leave their seats, Kate and Walter found a spot standing at a window facing south, looking out at the water, with the shoreline of the peninsula stretching beyond. Walter put an arm around her and kissed her ear. She liked that he wasn't afraid to make public displays of affection. He said he had an open relationship with his wife; she'd even talked to a woman on the phone who'd said it was fine with her.

"Up here, it seems so peaceful," Walter said. "Quiet."

Kate leaned into him. He was warm. For a while, at least, she was powerless. Safe, and contained. The world would have to take care of itself. She tried to relax into the feeling.

"This is nice. It's good to get away," she said. She decided that perhaps she hadn't sounded appreciative enough. "All my friends will be jealous when I tell them where I was. *If* I tell them," she said.

"And what *will* you tell them?" Though their relationship was semi-secret, Walter had said he didn't mind if she talked about him with her friends. He'd told her that she probably would have done it anyway. Which made her want to keep it secret. Maybe he'd done that on purpose.

She let out a sigh that she hoped sounded romantic. She leaned close and spoke in his ear. "I guess I'd say my sweetie took me out on a Zeppelin ride." She almost said "sugar daddy," but changed her mind. Walter was charming in his way. He always smelled good, and he kissed well, and when she was with him she felt safe. If she wasn't careful, she'd start having real feelings for him. She wouldn't tell him, though; he wouldn't like that.

He put an arm around her. She'd said the right thing, then. She had no intentions of telling anyone about what they did together. Only her brother Jacob knew anything about him. She didn't like to think of herself as the kind of girl who would do what she was doing. Over coffee, on their first meeting, Walter had made clear his proposition. It wasn't like anything she'd done before. She was curious, and at the same time she wanted to run and tell someone. She knew that if she had, it would have been funny, and she would have had to turn him down. Walter gave her the impression, maybe purposefully, that he was lonely. And though she'd agreed to do what he wanted, he still insisted on a courtship period of sorts. Lingering glances, holding hands at the movies. Nice restaurants. Museums. He was the only person Kate knew who actually went to theatre and opera. She went with him when he asked, but after the first few times she stopped being impressed. She'd excuse herself during the intermission and walk around, watching the old men checking her out. She'd thought about chatting them up. For the amount of money Walter spent on dinner and a show, she could throw a huge party, or go gonzo at her favorite bookstores. But she did enjoy the time with him. He made it easy.

So when he finally kissed her after dinner, she let him take her to a hotel. He'd booked the room in advance, she realized, which was a disappointment. After that, they still did cultural stuff, but it usually ended in sex. They were discreet: hotels—the kind with a minibar and name brand shampoo. They never stayed the night. His wife went out of town regularly, and Kate had worried about what she'd say when he finally invited her over. She found the thought of going to his house skeevy, but he never asked, and then she started to wish he would so that she could turn him down. It was one thing to fuck a guy, and it was another to sleep next to him. Asleep, she might fart or snore or steal the bedclothes. He might. They'd both have morning breath. She'd have to trust that he would find it charming, or at least not mind too much. It was like that old joke about the woman who wants to ask her boyfriend to help pay for her birth control pills, but she doesn't know him well enough to talk about money.

"So what are you reading?" Walter asked. Not, "Have you read anything lately?" but "What are you reading?" She liked that.

"*The Firedrake*, on your recommendation. Turns out it's not about dragons at all. I was telling my brother about it and he made a joke about how drakes were really just male ducks. As in, 'I thought this dragon would be a little scarier. That it wouldn't *waddle* so much.'"

He smiled. "But do you like it?"

"Oh, yeah. Once I got used to how short the sentences are."

They talked about the novel for a while, and then about reading and storytelling. He knew a lot, and liked to talk about it, but he also liked it when Kate came up with stuff. She wished she were in school full time, not just because it would give her more to crib from, but because she found books fascinating. She'd taken a few classes, and still wanted to get her degree in literature, though she knew it would largely be useless in terms of getting a job. Even in-state tuition was steep. She'd vaguely hoped she could get Walter to throw down for it, if things were still going well by the fall. She was waiting for him to offer, though she wasn't sure she'd accept it.

On the intercom, Matt was keeping up a steady patter about the landscape and the features of the airship. "The hull is only 2,200 pounds, and the entire ship is kept alight by the second lightest element in the universe, helium."

"He, he, he," Walter said.

"What do you take me for, a chemistry major?" Still, she smiled. Kate was grateful for the relative quiet. The view distracted the other passengers, who were talking and gesturing at the landscape. Kate and Walter made their way back to the loveseat in the rear of the cabin. The conversation of passengers around them was calm, almost somnolent, punctuated by little gasps and exhalations of awe. Kate realized that she hadn't slept much. She rested her cheek on his shoulder.

The hills of Marin were in the distance, and soon they were looking out at ocean and islands, bridge and city. San Francisco. It was beautiful. Adrift, Kate found herself thinking about how it had felt last night. Michael's fingers, surprisingly gentle. How much she'd needed to come, and how easy it had been. She thought about Jamie's warm nipples in her mouth. How patient Jamie had been. She rewound to the beginning, in Jamie's car, and wished she were back there again. She'd take Jamie somewhere else, somewhere safe, and none of the other events of last night would happen. No one would turn into a zombie. She wouldn't hook up with Michael. It would be like every other day. Kate didn't sleep around normally; she preferred her adventure and drama to come from movies and books. She liked Walter because he was drama-free. Mature. The sex was pretty good; almost as good as he thought it was. She liked being with him because she was in control. He wanted her more than she wanted him. He couldn't hurt her.

Kate became aware of how long she'd been quiet. "So it's St. Peter's day off," she said. "Jesus is filling in at the Pearly Gates, and this old man comes up in the line. It's near the end of the day, and he's tired of the normal question-and-answer that Petey always does. Instead Jesus says, 'Why do you think you're here?' It's kind of like what the cop says to you after he pulls you over. Old man says, without skipping a beat, 'I am merely an old carpenter. I have been looking my entire life for my long-lost son. I have looked everywhere in lands known and unknown. People have said he would be here.' The old man is obviously emotional. Jesus is affected; everyone knows that Jesus must have daddy issues, what with a mom who swore she was a virgin. Jesus looks closer at the man's face. His nose looks awfully familiar. Jesus drops to his knees and says, 'Father?'"

"Wait," Walter said. "Before that, Jesus says, 'What does your son look like?' Old man says, 'He has holes in his hands.' Jesus says, *I have holes in my hands.* Old man says, 'And he has holes in his feet,' Jesus says, *I have holes in my feet.* Jesus drops to his knees and says, 'Father?' and the old man says 'Pinocchio?' That was one of my mother's favorite jokes."

"It's funnier your way." Neither of them laughed. She tried to think of another joke; she'd told Walter all of her good ones already.

"Honey? Are you OK?" a man said, loud enough to make her turn and look. "Honey?"

The pink-haired girl sat on the floor. She was no older than Kate, and she had long nails the same color as her hair. She was skinny enough that you might think she was a dancer, or an anorexic. Kate would have tried to befriend her if they'd worked together, or frequented the same coffee shop: she looked like a nice girl. Perhaps she was here with her sugar daddy, too. He squatted near her, reaching down a hand to help her up.

"Rebecca?" a middle-aged woman said. "Sweetheart?" Kate hadn't realized the woman was with the girl and the man. That explained everything; they were a family. She calculated what it would cost for the three of them to be up in the Zeppelin. She had a working-class disdain for rich people. Kate's own folks considered McDonald's a sit-down meal.

The girl let out a low moan. It was the same exact moan as Jamie's, when things went bad. Kate's mouth went dry. This couldn't be happening. She looked around the airship cabin. Windows, windows everywhere, but a drop of a thousand feet. She wasn't going to get out of this.

"Something's happening," the girl said. Jamie had said something like that. So had Cameron, Kate thought.

The girl's eyes were white.

"Honey. Let me help you up," her father said.

"No," Kate said. "Don't touch her." She moved towards them. Too slowly.

The girl took his hand and brought it to her mouth. She bit the side of his palm. He yelped. She'd drawn blood. She lay on her back in the aisle, looking at her hand as if it had betrayed her. Then she smiled, and licked her lips. The whole cabin was watching by now, their chatter ceased.

Kate cursed. She should never have left home. Abandoned Michael to deal with their friends. She'd been a selfish asshole, running away as if none of the zombie business had been real. She angled towards the flight attendant; pulled him a few steps away, trying to be discreet. "We need to land this airship," she said. "If we can get everyone off the ship quickly, we can avoid making a scene." The cabin was small; there was nowhere to quietly stash a zombie. Perhaps they could tie her to a chair.

"We're on our way back," the flight attendant said. Below the ship was nothing but ocean and rocky islands.

"How soon?"

"Twenty minutes, maybe a little less. We can't just land anywhere, you know. It takes a landing crew, a big flat space."

"You understand that this is a serious medical emergency?" Kate said, trying to keep her tone even.

He ran his fingers through his pretty hair. "What?"

Kate took a deep breath, wishing Michael were there. Then she stopped wishing that and started wishing she'd never left the house. She sat next to the girl, who parted her lips and flicked her gaze over Kate, sizing her up. The girl moved her mouth, as if trying to work out what to say. She propped herself up on her elbows, jutting out her breasts. Already her movements were jerky and unnatural.

"Excuse me," Kate said. "I don't want to do this, but it's best for all." She straddled the girl, who let out another moan. Kate put her hands on the girl's forearms, trying to judge whether she was more afraid of being bitten or scratched.

"What are you *doing*?" the middle-aged man who wasn't the girl's sugar daddy asked. "Get away from her."

"It's going to be okay," Kate lied, smiling at the parents. "You have to trust me." She turned to Walter. "Give me your belt."

He stood in the aisle. "Kate? What's going on?" Walter put his hands in his pockets and then took them out and put them on his hips.

"She's not in her right mind. We need to help her." Kate looked to the group of watching passengers. She didn't want to be doing this. "Please, you have to believe me."

"How dare you insult my daughter?" the woman said, raising her voice. "She's Phi Beta Kappa!"

"She's going to be a zombie," Kate said. "Walter, that belt, please."

"You're not doing *anything* to my daughter," the man said. "What is this spectacle about? Rebecca, you stop this right now."

His daughter bared her teeth and started humping Kate.

"Oh, Jesus," Kate said. The girl's pubic bone was positioned exactly right. She shifted her weight onto her thighs, over the girl's hips, hoping to still the girl's movements. Kate tightened her grip on the girl's forearms.

The girl's mother broke the moment. "Rebecca, honey, do you have something to tell us?" Her voice had lost its anger. "Because we'll love you, no matter what, you know that. Your cousin came out, and everything was fine, remember? Have you been together long?" She smiled at Kate. "What's your name, love?" Her smile was meant to cover her panicked tone, the way that women hide things.

"Wish it were that easy," Kate said. "I mean, not to imply that your daughter's easy." She willed herself not to blush. What *was* she doing? She shifted to kneeling, her shins on the girl's thighs, creating a safe distance between them. "My name is Kate."

"Alex, and my husband is Jerry."

Kate did not reach up to shake Alex's proffered hand. The zombie licked her lips. There was blood on her teeth. This couldn't go on. Kate took another look around the cabin. Even the cockpit had no door. There was nowhere to put a zombie. But there was another door. The *bathroom*, she remembered.

"Walter, please," she said. "Your belt."

From behind Kate came a familiar sigh, and a familiar sound of a clasp unfastening, and leather sliding against fabric. "Anything for you, honey. But if you think you're scoring points with this coming-out story, it isn't doing anything for me." He was joking, from his tone of voice, but also concerned, and confused.

The girl exposed her neck, the universal submissive gesture. Kate had a distinct urge to see what that pale, perfect skin would taste like. She pushed the thought away. Then reconsidered. She was missing something important. Then she saw it. The zombie's skin was unbroken; there were no obvious marks. The girl turned her head, showing off the other side of her neck. The skin was unbroken. Kate looked at the girl's arms and hands. There were no marks.

The father had his bitten hand in his mouth. He was drooling blood into a Kleenex. He gripped the back of a chair with his other hand. He seemed like the kind of guy who would faint at anything worse than a scratch. How long had it taken with Cameron? Ten minutes? They'd been on the airship longer than that, so if the girl *had* been bitten, earlier, maybe it was a matter of metabolism. Maybe girls could hold out longer. But that didn't entirely explain how Jamie had taken hours to turn. Jamie hadn't had any bites, either. There had to be more than one vector, unless it was airborne. Kate wouldn't let herself consider that possibility. Was it an STD? Then why hadn't Kate gotten it herself? Perhaps some people were immune. Kate hoped she was.

"Is she OK?" a woman asked. As if given permission by the comment, everyone else in the cabin had something to say.

"What are you doing? Why are you sitting on that poor girl?"

"Are you bleeding, sir?"

"You should tie her up."

"Throw her out the window!" Everyone had an opinion.

"Oh, look! Alcatraz," one woman said, distracted by the view.

"You know, I hate to say it, but her family could sue you, child," a man said. "Good Samaritan laws aren't as strong as they could be. My firm would be available to represent you if necessary. Your father here can serve as a witness."

"Everyone please calm down and return to your seats," one of the pilots called.

Kate couldn't take it anymore. "Simon says everyone take one giant step back," she said in a threatening voice.

The group stood back, except for Walter, who said, "Mother, may I?" He wasn't one to leave a straight line lying on the table.

"No, Daddy," she said without thinking. She'd meant to call him "Daddy" for some time now; he'd hinted that he wanted her to, but she'd held off, never sure if he didn't actually mean the opposite. "Tie her hands for me," Kate said. She considered the mechanics of the situation. "Slip the belt in behind her knees, then raise it up to above her waist and cinch it around her hands. Got it?" Kate looked at Walter to make sure he understood. "You have to trust me."

He winked. Maybe this was turning him on; maybe he thought this was a stunt. She could feel Walter working the belt up behind the girl's thighs. Kate moved to give him room. He tightened the belt over the girl's hands, latching it at the loosest hole. Walter was a trim enough man. Then he grazed Kate's ass with both hands. At least she hoped it was Walter's hands.

"If everyone could please be seated," the flight attendant said in a weak voice.

The girl moaned, and Kate sat gently on her rib cage, holding her elbows. "Sorry," she whispered to the girl. The universe was telling her she shouldn't have left the house. Everyone there might be zombies already. She'd have nothing left to go home to. Dealing with this situation wasn't going to make amends for abandoning her friends, but she had to do something if she hoped to see them again.

"What are you doing?" the girl's father said. "I'll sue you for all you're worth, child, you and your father." The girl's mother started crying.

"Someone open the bathroom door?" Kate said. "We can put her in there. Just for now, until we land, and we can radio for an ambulance to meet us."

"Just let her up, so that she can sit down," her father said. "She's not hurting anyone." He put his bitten hand in his pocket, and wiped the blood from his lips onto the sleeve of his sport coat.

"Throw her out the window!" a man said.

The bathroom probably couldn't be locked from the outside, while a seatbelt would hold the girl but not keep her from biting someone else. Throwing the girl out of a window was beyond considering, although they did open. Kate took a breath to explain.

"You're not sticking her in the bathroom," the girl's father said. He was distraught, one arm around the girl's mother. "We don't even know what's wrong with her. I don't *think* it's an overdose."

"Um, if everyone could please return to your seats and fasten your seatbelts for landing," the flight attendant said again.

"You're kidding," Kate said. She half-rose from the zombie, then turned the girl face-down. The zombie drummed her toes on the floor. She turned her head to the side; her tongue protruded. It was already turning gray. Soon the only pink on the girl would be her hair and nails.

"Sorry," the flight attendant said. "FAA regulations. If you can get off of the girl, perhaps she can be seated."

Kate grew angry. She turned to the flight attendant. "You people don't know what you're dealing with here."

"Do you?" the girl's father snapped. "Show some respect. I ought to show *you* the back of my hand."

"Which hand, the one she bit?" Kate couldn't stop herself. She looked to Walter, who shook his head. The girl's father outweighed Walter, and the fight would not be in his favor. The girl's father grabbed Kate's hair, pulling her to her feet. Kate struggled, her vision blurring from the pain. "Ow, fuck," she said.

The man let go, looking ashamed. Kate fell into the aisle.

The zombie rolled onto her back and sat up. She shook out her pink hair.

"If everyone could please be seated," the flight attendant called. No one moved.

"Really, the bathroom is the best option," Kate said. "We need to contain her. She's not in her right mind, and it's not her fault. Something is really wrong. She *will* bite others. I've seen it happen, and it'll happen to you, too, sir. That's how it's transmitted." She could hear the pleading in her voice. She didn't want to be the one in charge of dealing with the zombie. "And you'll turn into what she is. Think of all of the other people that she'll bite. They'll all sue you, if they somehow don't get sick themselves."

"Sure, in a bad movie," he said. "Just leave her alone. I'll help her."

Outside the window Kate could see the cranes in the Oakland port that had inspired the walker robots in *Star Wars*. The ship was over land now, at least, so if they crashed, they probably wouldn't drown. The Oakland/Berkeley hills were in the distance, to the east. To calm herself, she looked for the hill where she lived. She could never tell which one it was. "We should call for an ambulance to meet us on the ground," she said. "Until then, it won't make a difference to her where she is, and it *will* make a difference to the rest of us. But I need help moving her." She looked to the ground. Too far to jump.

"Please sit," the flight attendant said. "We can't land until you're all seated. Don't make these good people wait." A few people had seated themselves as far as they could get from the zombie. No one would meet Kate's gaze.

"If you could just sit, please, miss," Matt the flight attendant said, leaning over the zombie. "In your seat, that is. I'll call for an ambulance to meet us on the ground."

"Ground," she said. He voice was dark as grave soil. The zombie smiled at Matt. She flicked her gray tongue over her lips, and raised her chin. She reached for him. He took a step back.

Kate had a bad feeling about all of this. "Walter?" she said. He'd seated himself already, and beckoned to her.

"Saved you a seat."

Kate stood.

"Come along, honey," the zombie's father said. "Stand up, please, Rebecca." The zombie kept gazing at the flight attendant. She let out a moan, huskier than before. The flight attendant blushed.

The father went to untie the belt around his daughter. "We'll just take this off," he was saying. The cabin grew quiet.

"Maybe you should leave it," the attendant said.

"Leave it," a woman called from the back of the cabin. Several others joined her.

"She can't very well stand up with her hands tied," the father said. Still, he paused. "We'll just get you a seat near your mother, there," he said softly. He pointed to his wife, and the woman shrunk in her chair. He brushed pink hair from his daughter's face, tucking it behind her ears. Then he did it again, with a smile that did not reach his eyes. She bit his wrist. He screamed, wrenching his hand away.

"Walter!" Kate hissed. She held out a hand towards him, and took a step towards the front of the cabin. Walter undid his safety belt and caught up with her.

The zombie giggled. She opened her mouth for another bite. Her father screamed again, and backed away. He sat down hard on the floor. Abruptly, the zombie turned back to the flight attendant. She started to get to her feet, leaning on a hand still secured with Walter's belt. There was a loud *crack*, as if she'd dislocated her shoulder, and she fell.

The flight attendant called towards the cockpit, over the noise in the airship. "I can't get them to sit. Can we still land? We're going to need an ambulance; there's a medical emergency."

The zombie crawled on her belly towards the flight attendant, inching her hips along the floor. One shoe came off, revealing a blue sock and a gray ankle. Whatever had happened to her injured arm had made it a few inches longer than the other; with her hands tied to her hips, one elbow stuck out. As she wormed along the floor, Walter's belt was pushed down past her hips, onto her thighs. She dragged her hands behind her, one arm flopping. Then she noticed that she could move her arms. She braced her hands against the floor and raised her upper body. There was an audible crack as she pushed herself up. She looked to be doing yoga, the Cobra pose, but she was lopsided. She struggled to pull her legs under herself, and came up to kneeling. The flight attendant took a step back and bumped into the wall. The zombie smiled up at him, reaching for his trousers. She licked her lips. He screamed and twisted away.

There was another moan. The zombie's father. He sat on the floor, holding his injured wrist. He shook it, making his fingers flop against the floor. The movement created a tinny sound, echoing throughout the airship. It must hurt, the way he was bashing his hand, but the puzzled look on his face suggested that perhaps it didn't.

The flight attendant screamed again. He looked to Kate, beseeching.

It was hard to turn away. Kate led Walter to the bathroom. She shut the door behind them, then turned the lock. She could at least save him. It was cramped inside; they both had to stand, but there was a large window, and a high ceiling. Their faces were close. They were both sweating. Inexplicably, he had a hard-on.

"Honey," he said. "I'd love to join the Mile High Club, but do you really think this is the time?" He kissed her neck anyway, and hugged her close. "What the hell is going on?"

"Shh," Kate said. She looked out the window. They were still too high to jump, even if they could get the window open. "They're all going to be zombies soon, and so are we unless the pilots manage to land this thing. And we're not a mile up, my heart. Not in a Zeppelin. Not even close. There are some things I need to tell you."

"That girl—" he said.

Kate put a finger to his lips. "Shut up," she said. She pressed her ear to the thin door. Through it she heard the girl zombie moan. Her father moaned. A voice screamed. Then another. Kate watched the ground below, wishing it were closer. This couldn't possibly be real. Maybe it was a dream, or a hallucination. She pinched herself. Her fingernails left a mark.

Someone started giggling. Then screaming. "Something's happening," a male voice said.

"*What's* happening?" Walter asked. "Don't fuck with me, Kate. This is surreal."

There was a knock at the bathroom door, fast and frantic. Walter reached for the handle. Kate grabbed his hand.

"We can't," she said.

"Help!" a woman's voice squeaked. She was breathing fast. "Let me the fuck in," she whispered. "They're *biting*!" She knocked again. A *thud* followed, as if she were hitting something soft yet solid. Then more screams.

Kate reached for the door handle. She couldn't let this happen to *everyone*. Walter grabbed her hand.

"I changed my mind," Kate said. "We have to let her in."

"She won't *fit*," Walter said. Already the two of them barely had room to stand.

"She's going to turn into one of *them* if we don't let her in."

Walter pushed Kate onto the toilet. There was no lid. "Honey, you had better start explaining."

Kate glared at him. "You are alive because of me. Just remember that." She stood. "Jesus, I wish there was a portal on this door."

"You mean a porthole? Portal *means* door."

"I mean a viewfinder hole, like in apartments. Damn it. Damn you. We could fit one more in here." Kate opened the door, pulling in a woman, the first unbloodied limb she could grab. Walter was pushed onto the toilet. Kate shoved the woman towards Walter, then leaned on the door to close it.

"Let me in," a man's panicked voice said. Four fingers scrabbled inches from Kate's face. The skin was unbroken, not gray or bloody. But there was no room.

"I'm sorry," Kate said. She closed the door on the fingers, again and again until their owner retracted them. It was the hardest thing she had ever done. She locked the door, and turned to the woman. Fortunately, she was small. Still, the three of them barely fit. Walter had to stand on the toilet; they were lucky that the ceiling was high. It wasn't like the sloped ceiling in an airplane bathroom; they were in a gondola.

"Are you bitten?" Kate demanded. "Did any of them bite you?"

The woman was breathing fast. "No, nobody bit me. But my partner is out there," she said. "You have to help me. That guy who was yammering earlier, there's something wrong with him. He was coming after me, like a zombie. And the flight attendant is down. The girl is," she shuddered and then pulled Kate into a hug.

Kate realized that the woman wasn't going to say, "The girl is eating him." She patted the woman's back, trying to make her let go. The counter pressed against Kate's hip, and the grab bar pushed into her side. The room was so very small, so very full.

There was a loud knocking at the door. Then a scream, close by, and a moan further away.

"Let me in," a female voice said from the other side of the door. "Christine! Let me the hell in."

"Nora!" the woman shouted into Kate's ear. She tried to move Kate away from the door, but Kate stood her ground, hating herself for doing it. If they opened the door, they might not get it closed again.

"Please!" the voice said again. "If you love me, you'll open this door. Now!"

"My wife's out there," the woman said. "We have to *make* room."

Of course, Kate thought. No one came on a Zeppelin ride alone.

"There's no more room," Walter said. "Like you said before, when there wasn't any room. There's still no more room, in fact, there's less room now than there was when there was no room before. The foot's really on the other shit, now, huh, Katie? Gonna change your mind again?" His voice was dead serious, and Kate saw that he could kick her out if he wanted to.

Her back to the door, Kate could feel someone pounding on it. The plastic was so thin.

"Move aside," the woman said softly. "Please. I'll ask once."

Kate shook her head, hating herself. This close, she could see the crow's feet around the woman's eyes, and the remains of maroon lipstick feathered over her lips. She had a strange impulse to kiss the woman.

"Sorry," the woman said. She slapped Kate, surprisingly hard. Then again, on the same cheek. Kate lost her balance from the force of it. Time slowed. Her face stung. It had been years since anyone had hit her, and padded weapons and bamboo swords didn't count. She'd never been slapped on the face. She put a hand to her cheek, trying to understand why she was so turned on.

The tiny bathroom was a bedlam of bodies. Kate was lifted onto the toilet, and Walter took her arm to steady her. Kate held her cheek. It was hard to think.

The woman opened the door. Hands reached into the bathroom. It was loud outside.

"Nora?" the woman shouted. One of the hands waved. The woman clasped it and pulled. The hand was followed by sleeves, and a shoulder, then a head, torso, and another arm. In her other hand Nora held a fire extinguisher. The bottom end of it was coated in blood.

"Make room!" Nora said. She was fortyish or fiftyish, and slender.

"Let me in," someone else said. "Let me in! Bastards!"

Kate was pressed against the wall. She was trying not to step into the toilet bowl. She found Walter's hand and held it. He squeezed her fingers. She watched Nora use the fire extinguisher to beat the hands reaching into the bathroom. Their owners screamed and begged. Blood ran down the door. A small and selfish part of Kate was grateful that she was trapped, and not the one beating back the hands. It wouldn't be Kate's fault if the other people pushed their way in.

Finally the two women pushed the door shut, and locked it. Then they embraced, the fire extinguisher between them. After a moment, Nora pulled back and slapped Christine, leaving a bloody handprint. Kate understood where Christine had learned to slap like that.

"Don't ever leave me again," Nora said. She rinsed her bloody hands in the sink. It was impossible to see whether she'd been bitten. They were crammed into the room back to back, belly to belly.

"I'm sorry," Christine said. "I got scared."

Nora cupped Christine's face. She tried to wipe away the blood but only smeared it. "Oh, honey," she said. "Look at you." She hugged Christine close, then kissed her. Christine returned the kiss, opening her mouth. Nora worked one hand under Christine's shirt. She let go of the fire extinguisher, which landed with a thud on the floor.

The screams from the cabin grew louder, and more frequent. So did the moans.

"What now? Kate?" Walter whispered.

"We drift," Kate whispered back.

"*Drift*?"

"Until we land. Maybe there's an autopilot, or the pilots can fend them off. But we should come to ground eventually; we've been losing altitude."

"*That's* your plan?" he asked. "The wind's inland, east. We could wind up in Lake Tahoe."

"Gives a whole new meaning to Donner Pass," Kate said. She tightened her grip on Walter's hand. "We're only a few hundred feet up. We'll probably land in the Oakland hills."

"So long as the wind doesn't change."

They fell silent. The two women had gone way beyond the kiss of reunited lovers. Nora was unzipping Christine's pants. She knelt, and Christine gasped, bracing herself on the metal handrail. Kate couldn't stop watching them. She found herself thinking of Jamie, how wet she'd been. The feel of her own cheek sliding lubricated against Jamie's thigh. The likelihood that the Zeppelin would land safely and that they would get out alive seemed distant. If they were going to get eaten, or turned into zombies, there were worse things to do with their last few minutes.

Kate reached for Walter's crotch. She traced the outline. It wasn't like him to be hard again so soon. He brought her other hand to his mouth, and put two of her fingers in. She could feel his hard palate under her fingertips, his tongue against her fingernails. She leaned against the wall, trying to keep her balance.

There was a thud at the door, then another. "Let me in," a male voice was saying over the screams and moans. The man hit the door, then again. The impact was visible. Kate tried to ignore it. There was nothing they could do. The door rattled, but held. Finally the man screamed, and the pounding ceased.

Christine's pants were around her ankles. Nora was using both hands and her mouth. This close, Kate could smell the woman. It was strangely intoxicating. Walter's hand was on her thigh, moving upward.

"Something's happening," Nora said.

chapter six

Traffic wasn't too bad as Michael made his way home, using a shortcut through Emeryville to avoid the maze where the 80 and 580 and 980 freeways messed around with each other like a high school group of friends, everyone hooking up with everyone else. He debated whether he should call or text someone at home. Maybe Audrey. Or Henry. Probably not Natalie. Just to see how things were going. Only the three of them had stayed over, he was pretty sure. Not counting the zombies. He wondered if he should even go home. He had half a tank of gas, and a five-dollar bill in the glove compartment. Not like he'd get far. He'd been stupid to leave in the first place; he could blame it on making decisions before he'd had any coffee, but he knew that it was just Kate who'd made him leave. He'd done what she wanted, even though they both knew that it had been wrong.

He turned on the radio. Flipped through hip hop, old hip hop, and that morning talk show on the rock station that seemed mostly to be about embarrassing things that could happen during sex. People called in from all over to confess. Now, though, the girl was reading the sports update. Funny, in the Bay Area, it was always girls and gay guys who did the sports. Michael listened for a while, then changed it to NPR during the commercial break. It was a pledge drive. The gift this hour was a wine-tasting for four people.

Michael flipped through the channels again, disgusted. He expected at least NPR to understand the zombie uprising. That phrase was taking shape in his head. It was silly: to call it "the zombie uprising" made it sound like a civil rights rally. As if the zombies were storming the capital chanting "Power to the People!" Everyone knew zombies couldn't chant. They'd be moaning "Brains!" on the Capitol steps, and that would be a different statement entirely. As a fan of zombie movies, Michael had always planned on having a plan for when the zombies came. He didn't own any firearms. Still, he fancied himself smarter than the average dude in a zombie movie. He wouldn't go spastic. He could board up the doors and windows, except there were too many of them at his house, even if he could find enough wood. Why did houses in zombie movies always have lots of plywood lying around? Maybe it was because the zombies always hit in the country; people actually built things in the country, since IKEA was too far. Michael decided that he had to get his friends out of the house, and go somewhere defensible.

He stepped on the gas. Again he thought of calling someone at home, but didn't want to wake them if they weren't already up. There were no signs of zombies as he drove, which should have been calming. But he knew what he'd seen.

His neighborhood was quiet. Parked cars crowded the street and the driveways, just like normal. Michael parked his car, nearly forgetting to set the parking brake against the hill. Still, he looked around before getting out. Cameron's car was parked in front. He hurried to his front door, finding it unlocked.

"Hello?" Michael called softly. He turned the knob and let the door swing inward, not wanting to lean in without a sight line and get his face torn off by a zombie. If they'd gotten loose. That was a big *if*.

"Hello?" he called. "Guys? Morning."

A low moan answered. Michael was flooded with guilt. He couldn't have been gone for more than half an hour. His friends had been fine when he left, sleeping like angels with hangovers.

They probably got curious, and had to investigate the zombies they'd so carefully contained last night. Had they learned *nothing* from the movies?

He debated what to do. If his friends had all turned into zombies, he should go get help.

There was the sound of footsteps. The entry hallway was empty, and so was what he could see of the living room and kitchen. Michael stepped outside and shut the door, leaning against it. Containment was the most important thing with zombies. He should check that all of the windows and doors were shut. Yeah, because zombies *never* broke windows.

A scream came from inside. Definitely human, and a girl's. That meant someone was still in danger. Michael's knees grew weak. He understood what he had to do. He opened the door, went inside, and searched for the nearest weapon. There was an umbrella jar in the hallway. He took out an umbrella, and held it in front of him.

"Hello?" he called.

A zombie turned the corner from the hallway. Cameron. His skin was gray, and his mouth and cheeks were dark with blood. Fresh blood. He wore a grin, as if this was the funniest joke ever.

"Dude," Michael said. He took a step back. "Dude?" He poked Cameron with his umbrella, intending to stab him.

Cameron batted aside the umbrella. He looked Michael up and down.

Michael backed up slowly into the kitchen, aware that walking backwards was a sure way to get brained. Maybe he deserved to be eaten by this zombie, he thought. Maybe this was all his fault.

Cameron raised his arms and followed. He moved slowly, as if he enjoyed the chase. Michael tripped over something—a kitchen chair, he saw as he fell—and landed on his ass, bashing one elbow. His back tensed from the impact. His elbow had to be broken. "Cameron, please," he said. He crawled backwards, desperate. Cameron leaned down and put a hand on Michael's leg, and Michael felt his bladder let go.

There was the crack of a whip from the living room.

"Cammy!" a female voice called. "That's enough, now."

Cameron dropped his hands to his sides. He wore a look of doggish disappointment.

Michael was astonished. He was afraid to say anything, afraid to even move. The part of his mind that liked to make irreverent comments told him that he was lucky that he hadn't shit himself. Yet.

"That's a good boy, Cammy." Michael recognized the voice as Audrey's. "Now go sit down," she said.

Cameron went to sit on the chair Michael had tripped over. It was lying on its back, legs sticking up like a dead insect.

"Wait, hon," Audrey said. She leaned over and righted the chair. "Now go ahead."

The zombie sat. The muscles under the skin of his face moved like stoned rats under a blanket, until his features formed a smile. He rested his face in his hand, his elbow propped on the table in the gesture used by tired children and people who suffer from unrequited love. He picked up a half-full glass from the table and drank. Last night's whiskey and soda spilled from his mouth, but he swallowed most of it.

Michael found his voice. "What's going on? Audrey?"

She smiled down at him, and it was a smile not unlike the zombie's—it seemed to take effort, and had an artificial feel to it. "Fuck you," she said. "I cleaned up your mess." She took in the state of Michael's pants. "Well, most of your mess," she added.

Michael didn't know where to start. "Where's Natalie and Henry?" he said. He cradled his elbow, which still throbbed, but less so than before. Probably it wasn't broken. Probably he'd just landed on his funny bone.

"They left. Went home. This morning. I told them it was all a big joke last night."

"They believed you?"

Audrey shrugged. "They were all hung over. And I told them I'd been in on it, and now I had to clean up."

"So of course they left, before you could ask them to help clean." Michael understood. "But why'd you try to clear them out in the first place?" It didn't make sense that she'd say that. Or that they believed she'd *offered* to help clean. But they had all been really messed up last night, not thinking straight. Had they really been watching zombie movies?

"You have to admit it *was* more entertaining than the average party. Even *your* average party." Audrey said. "And you know as well as I do most of our friends are useless in an emergency. I had to get them out for their own safety." She squatted down on the floor in front of Michael, still holding the whip in her hand.

"I was awake when you and Kate left, this morning. After everyone left, I went to check on Cameron here. I was thinking about how, last night, when I switched my whip, how he listened. And he looked so sad there, tied up. He recognized me. So after everyone woke up, and I cleared them out, I untied him. I had to. Also I found this in your bathroom in the hallway."

She stood and retrieved something from the counter, and Michael realized that both he and Cameron were watching her ass. She dropped a book on Michael, and he caught it. It was his battered copy of *Passage of Darkness: The Ethnobiology of the Haitian Zombie*, by Wade Davis. He'd ordered it online, used, and it had arrived signed by the author, mysteriously inscribed to Kelly, with best wishes. Davis had handwriting like a high school girl.

"This seemed like the most useful of your reference material. Zombies respond to whips," she said. "Presuming that our friend here is actually a zombie. So I looked up whips in the index, and it turns out that they're used in Haiti to, like, call spirits and shit."

"Haitian zombies are more about punishment for people who've broken the laws," Michael said. "The process involves poisoning them so that they appear to be dead, taking the spirit or *ti bon ange*, and then resurrecting the body and making it work the fields." Michael became aware that he was slipping into lecture mode. The wet spot in his pants was starting to cool. He was still sitting on his kitchen floor. His head spun. "What about that belly dancer zombie, Kate's friend? Where's she at?"

"Still tied up, I think. Cameron's kind of got the hots for her," she turned to address the zombie, "which is awfully *rude* if you ask me, trying to get with another girl right in front of your girlfriend."

"You guys are back together?"

"Sort of," Audrey said. "You have to admit, he listens better now than he ever did." She cracked her whip. "Cameron, go wash your face," she said.

The zombie stood, obediently went to the sink, and fumbled the handle until water came out. He leaned down towards the tap, bonking his chin on the spout.

"Ketchup," Audrey explained, standing up to help Cameron. The bottle was still on the kitchen table, the top coated with dried ketchup crud. "Zombie, you're getting it everywhere. And this water is cold." She fussed over him, splashing his face.

"Water," Cameron croaked. His voice sent chills through Michael. That was Helen Keller's first word.

Michael realized Audrey had probably said *baby*, not *zombie*. He stood up, still shaky. His clothes were in his room, down the hall. He wanted dry pants. "Ketchup?" he asked.

Audrey brushed Cameron's wet hair from his face. He smiled at her, water running over his bitten lip.

"You said we were going to take them to the hospital," she said. Her voice was quiet and even, like she'd rehearsed this. "But we didn't. And now look what's happened to him. I know we were all fucked up, but still. You're the most responsible, even drunk and stoned. It was *your* party."

Michael took a step back, understanding. Something moved in his bowels, and he tightened his sphincter against it. "You did this to get *back* at me?"

"Did it work? I was a little bummed that Kate wasn't with you when you came back, so she could be part of it, too. You've got a thing for her, don't you?" Audrey dried her hands on her tight skirt. Her skin was pale against the black leather. Her nails were bitten short; all of her fake nails had broken off. She gestured towards Cameron. "I *wanted* to get back at you. At someone." She turned to the tap and put one hand in the water, then brought it to her face. Michael saw then that she was crying.

"And now we're even," she said. "Except you still have to help me get him fixed."

Cameron lowered his head towards Audrey's shoulder, as if to kiss her. Less than twelve hours ago, the gesture would have been romantic. She stepped back, and switched her whip. "Wash your hands, baby," she told him. He obeyed, putting his hands under the tap and halfheartedly clapping them.

"Excuse me. I'll be right back," Michael said. He very much wanted a shower and a shave, but there wasn't time. He found that his bathroom was strangely lacking any evidence that the previous night's scene had happened. Except for the bloody towel, and a length of rope still tied to the shower door. They should have used the handcuffs Cameron had brought. But then again, who knew how easily they'd come apart.

He kicked off his sodden pants and boxers, then emptied his bowels into the toilet. He washed his hands, used a clean towel on his legs, applied deodorant, and put on fresh clothes. He moved quickly. He thought about calling Henry and asking him to come back and help deal with the zombies, but he didn't want to endanger anyone else. Plus, Audrey would brag about how she made him piss himself.

He found Audrey sitting at the kitchen table reading the book about Haitian zombies, the whip on the table. Cameron sat nearby, watching her. She pursed her lips while she read, mouthing the words. She didn't look up when Michael entered the room. He thought about going to the liquor cabinet and pouring a drink. Just one, for his nerves, but maybe that wasn't a good idea.

"Hey," Michael said. "Audrey?" He wondered if he should go give her a hug, or something. There was a new distance between them. It felt a little like after they'd first broken up, not that they'd been together for very long. Audrey wasn't as good in bed as she thought she was, and she tended to be the one who initiated her break-ups.

"How do you want to do this?" Audrey asked. "Do you think we should go to Kaiser, or Alta Bates? Cameron's got no insurance. He was waiting until his ninety days at TJ's, when it kicked in. We were going to go to this indoor skydiving place once we both had insurance. You know, just in case. Do you know if Kate's friend has any insurance?"

"No, I don't know," Michael said. "I could check her purse, but I doubt it. I'm not sure she even had a purse. Hey, but maybe this is weird enough that the hospital won't charge for treatment. All of the residents could publish papers on it."

"And it'll turn into an episode of *House*, with wackier and wackier theories and tests until he looks like he's at death's door," Audrey said. "Just as long as they figure it out in time, and cure him. He's not really dead. Not like movie zombies." She looked up from her book, and smiled. "It says here that if a zombie is fed salt, he remembers who he is."

Michael grabbed the book, vaguely remembering reading that but not daring to believe it would be so simple. Sure enough, the book said that salt would do it. He grabbed the shaker, wanting so much for all of this to be over, and laughed, giddy with hope. Audrey laughed with him.

Cameron opened his mouth when Audrey told him to, flicking her whip, and Michael shook the salt over his ruined mouth. Salt went everywhere, onto Cameron's face and shirt, onto the table and the floor. Cameron moaned, and coughed and blinked. He stuck out his gray tongue and brushed at the salt with a clumsy hand. Surely some had gotten down his throat.

"Do you think that was enough? How long is it supposed to take?" Michael asked. He looked at the clock on the microwave. It was eleven thirty.

"Yeah, I already tried it," Audrey said. "Before you got here. It's supposed to be instantaneous. The zombie wakes up and remembers who he is."

Cameron licked at the roof of his mouth like a dog given peanut butter.

The shaker dropped from his hand, thudding on the kitchen floor. "You already *tried* it?" he said. "And you let me get my hopes up? You *bitch*." He wanted to hit her, and kicked the table leg instead. He regretted it immediately. It took real effort not to double over from the pain. After a moment it dulled to a mere throbbing, and he flexed his toes inside his shoe to check that they weren't broken.

Audrey pursed her lips, but didn't laugh. In the space of maybe fifteen minutes she'd scared him half to death, and then crushed him. Was she operating out of grief and shock, Michael wondered, or was this some kind of a power trip? He sat down at the table.

"I just wonder why doesn't the salt work if the whip does?" Audrey said after a while. There was sorrow in her voice, and regret. "I guess I wanted to see someone else try it, just to show that I wasn't crazy, but I should have explained. That was really mean of me. I'm sorry, Michael."

Usually it wasn't hard to forgive Audrey; she'd put a dent in your car, or finish the ice cream you'd been promising yourself, or fuck your friend and make things awkward, but she was always charming and contrite after. This time, though, she'd crossed a line.

"And I'm sorry for frightening you earlier, when you first came in," she said. "It's inexcusable, I know. That was just because I was angry at you for leaving, and I'd almost convinced myself that you weren't coming back. Where's Kate?"

Now Michael was embarrassed. "I'm sorry I left, too. It'll be funny after all of this is done. You know, the way it's a tragedy when you get pulled over and have to walk the line and say the alphabet backwards, but then it's funny later, if you don't go to jail. Kate asked me for a ride, and I did it." It sounded silly as he said it. What was more important than being with your friends when they needed you? "She said she had to work, but she could have called in. Being late on *rent* would be vastly preferable to being, well." He wouldn't allow himself to finish that thought.

"She wasn't scheduled for today," Audrey said.

"She wasn't?" Kate wouldn't lie to him, Michael knew. He was pretty sure. Audrey might, though. She didn't have Kate's work ethic.

"I remember this shit. It was Cameron and me and NGNCNF on the schedule for today, plus Sandra. Obviously we're not going in. The drama mamas will have to deal." The latter was Audrey's term for everyone she didn't like.

"NGNCNF?"

"New Guy Not Cool Not Funny. Actually he's pretty cool, and he teases back."

"You're such a hazer." Still, that was how Audrey had endeared herself in the first place when Michael had started at Trader Joe's. She'd been the first of the group to befriend him. Now he wasn't sure if she was still his friend. Michael reached over and turned the book in Audrey's hands to show the cover. He was careful not to lose her page. "*The Ethnobiology of the Haitian Zombie*," he read. "This is probably not the right manual. We're not in Haiti, for starters. And he's not a Haitian zombie. Haitian zombies are way more complicated. Here in the States, we have the post-Romero zombie. Maybe that changes things."

Audrey wasn't listening. "Maybe we could take them to a *bokor*, like a Voodoo priest." She took out her phone and typed in "San Francisco bokor." The results included a LinkedIn profile for one Janine Bokor, and the Bokor National Park in Cambodia. "Maybe Voodoo San Francisco?" she said. The results this time were for nightclubs and hairdressers. "I guess not so much," she said. "Damn."

Michael and Audrey both looked at their zombie, as if he might provide the answers. Cameron's gaze was focused on Audrey's breasts.

"Do you have a T-shirt I could borrow, at least?" she said. "Maybe some pants? Or would Kate have anything?"

"Sure." He went to his room and fetched a few items that might fit her. Then inspiration struck and he took out his whip. It wasn't huge or showy, but he'd gotten it at a good price, and taught himself how to use it from videos on YouTube.

Walking past Kate's door, he stopped to listen. It was quiet. He knocked. He ought to let Kate's friend out. "You OK in there?" he called. "The safe word is juniper berry." It wasn't, of course, and who knew if Kate and her friend had even been using a safe word. Michael doubted they'd even needed one.

There was a moan from inside the bedroom. Michael set down the clothes he was carrying, and turned the doorknob, hoping hard that the zombie was still tied up. He opened the door a crack, and peeked in. The room smelled of cigarette smoke. The curtains were drawn, and one lamp threw soft yellow light. Kate's friend was seated on the bed, a cigarette in one hand. She'd managed to get free of the rope. Her wrists must be abraded, but it was too dark to tell. Michael had a terrible suspicion that they had left this woman tied up all night. She'd call the cops, and he'd go to jail. It would all be his fault.

"Are you all right?" he asked. He couldn't remember the woman's name now, and he felt bad about that, too.

She looked up as he spoke. Her eyes were clouded over. Definitely still a zombie, Michael saw. Part of him was relieved. She was naked. She stood, and as she came towards the light in the hallway, Michael saw that even her tattoos looked like they were losing their color. Her skin was so gray. She stood, letting the cigarette drop to the carpet. She raised her arms as if she wanted to be embraced. But she didn't swing that way, not if she was banging Kate last night. Michael froze, unable to look away and simultaneously unable to do anything about the burning cigarette, which now smelled like burning plastic. What were the carpets made out of, polyester?

The zombie raised her arms, not forward like he expected, but to the sides. Her arms writhed like snakes. The ripple moved out from her shoulders to her elbows, her wrists, and her fingers. The skin around her wrists was torn, with scabby bracelets of black blood where the rope had been. Her hips swung around, to one side and then the other. She took a step forward, and Michael stepped backwards. The zombie wore a stage smile, big and brilliant. There was no music, but she kept time, stepping forwards. Knees bent, she rocked her pelvis back and forth. The motion was sharp and practiced. Beautiful, in its own way.

Michael backed into the hallway. The zombie danced towards him. She shook her shoulders, jiggling her tits. Then she cupped her breasts in her hands. The flesh was firm, even if the skin was gray. She looked down at her chest, then up to Michael, presenting her tits. It was the clearest offer he'd ever gotten, and he was embarrassed that it was having an effect on him. The zombie bared her teeth, pinched her nipples, and took a step closer.

Michael remembered the whip he held. He swatted the air with it, producing only a swishing sound. He did it again, harder, and got it to snap. The zombie stood still. Then she reached one hand down to her pubic hair, and gave it a little tug.

There was a moan, loud and close. Definitely from inside the house. But the zombie's mouth hadn't moved.

Without looking away, Michael called out, "Audrey, you guys okay?"

"Yeah." She sounded bored.

The zombie was working two fingers between her legs. In and out, in and out. Then she licked her fingers. It was as compelling as it was gross. Michael could smell her, and she smelled like a normal girl. He wondered if she was actually dead, or one of the walking dead, or just infected with something and still alive. And how exactly did the transmission of zombieism work? She already liked being tied up, at any rate. If he had sex with her but didn't let her bite him, could that be safe, if he used a condom?

He wanted to forget he'd ever had that thought.

"Stop that," he whispered. He said it again, louder, and cracked his whip again.

The zombie's hands stopped moving, but stayed where they were. She looked Michael up and down, then settled her gaze on the whip.

Another moan came from nearby, louder than before. They sounded like they were coming closer—Michael looked around, trying to figure out where the sound was coming from. Once, when he'd heard the soft, please-change-my-battery beeping of a smoke detector, he'd had to go through the whole house to find the one that wanted attention—but the moans seemed to be coming from Lena's room. He'd found Lena by advertising a room for rent on Craigslist, and in their first conversation, she'd said that she didn't want to live in any of the neighborhoods where she could afford to get an apartment on her own. Oakland had a bad reputation, but parts of it, including the hills, were really upscale. Safe. She'd moved here to be safe. She'd been out last night, and usually spent weekends at her boyfriend's. She was a perfect housemate. But maybe she'd come home in the middle of the night and gotten bitten, though surely he would have woken up.

The zombie whose name he couldn't remember moaned then, and Michael was reminded of someone clearing their throat to get attention. She cupped her tits, moaning again. There was an answering moan from somewhere else, somewhere nearby.

"Cut that out," Michael said. He cracked his whip. "I mean it, drop your hands."

The zombie obeyed. Part of Michael liked that, and he was disgusted with himself for it.

"Stay there," he told the naked zombie. If zombies could look petulant, this one was doing it; one hip pushed out to the side. He shut her inside Kate's bedroom, wishing there was a way to lock it from the outside.

"Hello?" he said, quietly so that Audrey wouldn't hear. Kate's friend moaned, and someone moaned back. Brandishing the whip to reassure himself, he opened the bathroom door. The room was empty. So was his bedroom, which he checked even though he'd just been there. It didn't seem right to snoop in Lena's bedroom without at least trying to make sure that the noises weren't coming from somewhere else. He even checked the hall closet, which no one could fit inside without curling up on a shelf, and even then they'd have to pull out a bunch of sheets and blankets to make room. Finally he gathered his courage, and opened Lena's door a crack. It was dark inside. He wished he'd brought a flashlight. He could imagine reaching inside to flick the light switch, and being bitten.

He meant to ask if there was anyone there, but when he opened his mouth, his voice was gone. He cracked the whip instead. A feminine moan answered.

Michael felt a compulsion to see what was inside the room. Before the zombie just tumbled out. It sure did sound like there was a zombie in there. Without expecting that he would do it, Michael kicked at the door. It swung inwards.

Michael didn't believe it. He didn't *want* to believe it.

Natalie and Henry were zombies. They wore their costumes from last night, which now felt sickeningly inappropriate. Natalie had abandoned her hat, and Henry had lost his wine bag on its IV pole. His hospital gown was dashed with wine stains, or at least Michael hoped it was wine. Their eyes were clouded; they reflected light like a cat's.

His friends moved towards Michael.

"No," he said, finding his voice. He fell backwards in shock, thinking as he fell that he was fainting. His friends would eat him. This time, nobody would save him.

He landed on his ass, and the pain brought him into focus. The whip was a lump underneath him; he'd fallen on it, and he groped for it as he scooted away from the zombies. He grabbed the whip by the middle, and found his way to the handle. After a few flicks he managed to make a noise with it, without hitting himself. The secret really was in the wrist, like so many other things. "Back up," he said, trying to sound authoritative. "All you zombies, back the fuck up."

His friends stayed where they were. Michael scrambled to his feet. He reached inside the door and turned on the light, needing to make sure he wasn't hallucinating. Maybe he was. He wanted very much to be hallucinating. His friends looked terrible. The

light reflected from their cataract eyes, and all of the color had
left their skin. Their faces were gray, with black shadows, as if the
scene were a photo he'd put into grayscale in Photoshop. They
were all looking at him with an unpronounceable hunger. Actually
it was a lot like the faces you see in porn, but with less certainty of
their course of action. It was as if they couldn't decide whether to
fuck him first, and then eat him, or the other way around. Except
that probably wouldn't work as well.

Michael shut the door, quickly. He stood in the hallway, still
holding the whip. His breathing sounded very loud in his head.
The doors didn't lock from the outside.

He wanted to go lie down. Except that he also wanted to get out
of the house. He wished Kate were there. She'd think of something, or at least she'd be a rational person who wasn't trying to
fuck with him. Damn her for leaving. He hoped that she'd gotten
turned into a zombie, then he changed his mind.

He started towards the kitchen. He stopped. Maybe he shouldn't
tell Audrey that he knew about the zombies in the house. What
would have motivated her to lie about them going home? It hadn't
entirely made sense when she said it, but he'd wanted to believe it.
But *why* would she lie like that? Audrey was an odd character even
among their friends, most of whom were already a few standard
deviations from normal. Could she have woken up with them
gone, and just *thought* that they'd left?

Michael shut himself in the hall bathroom to think about it. He
needed to use the toilet again, and counted himself lucky that he
hadn't soiled himself already. If he didn't do what Audrey wanted,
she could sic her zombie on him. She'd done it already, just for
effect, but maybe she wouldn't stop Cameron next time. He
supposed that he could sic Kate's friend the zombie on Audrey's
zombie, but that didn't seem fair. They should work out their
miscommunications like adults, without making zombies fight for
them. He'd figure something out. He had to. What would Romero
do? Probably kill them all, he thought.

He took out his phone, and ran the tap to cover the sound of his talking. He called Kate.

"Hello?" Kate said. It was good that she'd answered; she didn't usually answer while she was at work. "Michael?" Her voice sounded like she was in a small space. Sometimes she answered her phone while she was in the bathroom.

"Kate. Oh, Jesus." Michael tried to decide what to tell her first. "They respond to whips," he said. "The zombies. When are you coming home?"

"Whips?"

"Yes, whips. Remember last night, with Cameron, when Audrey smacked herself in the face with the whip, and Cameron paid attention?" Kate was silent. Michael heard a guttural moan. "Kate, what's going on? Are you OK?"

"Long story," she said in a faint voice. "How does the whip thing work?"

"You just snap the whip, and the zombie will do what you say. They're not very smart, like, Audrey told Cameron to go wash his face and he stuck his whole head under the tap. I think it was the sound, or something, like it's a certain wavelength that they respond to. Or maybe the gesture of raising a hand over your head, I don't know. I've got a book but it doesn't explain everything." Michael thought about what he was saying, and how it probably didn't make any sense. "When are you coming back?"

"What was that? You cut out after…" The phone went quiet.

"Damn network," Michael said. "Hello? Kate? Aw, damn."

chapter seven

K ate shook her phone in frustration, as if that would do anything. Network coverage was sometimes spotty with iPhones. She'd gotten one after she started seeing Walter, when she decided she could afford it. Normally she wouldn't answer her phone when she was at first base, Walter's hand under her shirt, but this wasn't normal. They were in the bathroom of a Zeppelin, and the woman on the floor had said, "Something's happening." Kate put Walter's hand in her mouth and bit down an SOS—dot dot dot dash dash dash dot dot dot—hoping that he'd at least understand that much Morse code. He turned his head towards Kate. In his profile Kate noticed the beginnings of a second chin.

Nora moaned. She threw back her head, shook her hair, and then dove back down. She had a really long tongue. And she seemed to be using it to good effect, judging by her wife's reactions. Christine was leaning against the wall, legs spread, her eyes closed and her own tongue protruding from between her lips. She had pubic hair on her thighs.

"Whip?" Kate whispered. "We need a whip. Michael told me that it works."

Walter blinked. "What?" Kate had told Walter about Michael's predilections. Near the beginning of their relationship, by way of explaining her living circumstances, she had made up a story about the Puerto Rican cleaning lady discovering Michael's whip, and running away screaming. Walter had been properly amused. He wasn't sharp enough, or mean enough, to ask why they had a cleaner; twentysomethings in Kate's income bracket cleaned their own places. But Walter had alluded to girls he'd been with in the past who were doing it because they needed the money, and how unromantic he'd found that attitude. So Kate pretended she had more money than she did. She wanted Walter to think she was spending time with him because she liked him, not because she needed the money. In return, if he thought she was lying, he didn't call attention to it. They'd negotiated this entirely through subtext, and Kate wondered occasionally if she was completely misinterpreting him.

"That's not what I mean," she said.

He pinched her nipple, and thinking became difficult. She pushed his hand away and brandished her phone. Through the fog of last night, she remembered Audrey flicking a whip. It started to make sense, and Kate was upset that she hadn't remembered sooner. It might not work, but at this point, what did they have to lose?

"I don't even have a belt anymore," Walter said. "Good fucking luck." He unzipped his trousers and brought out his dick. It was bright pink, and hard. Kate was embarrassed, and turned on. His smell, like fresh bread, mingled with Christine's smell. He stroked himself, pulling back the foreskin to expose the head.

"What are we *doing*?" Kate asked.

"What does it *look* like? I've seen movies. I know we're going to die." He turned to face her, kissing her ear. She thought of leaning forward, tasting him one last time. That skin was always so soft, and so sensitive. She put a hand on him, and he made a noise in his throat. She opened her mouth to say something, and stroked his dick instead. She felt cheap. So easily manipulated.

Her phone rang again. It was Michael. She answered. Walter went back to stroking his dick. Outside the bathroom door, someone started whimpering. The buzz of the engine wasn't loud enough to cover the noise. Through the window, the hills were growing closer, but they were still too high up to jump.

"Hello?" she said into the phone. There was no one there. "Damn."

Her phone vibrated. It was a text message from Michael. *Whips*, he'd written. Another text came in while she was looking at the first. *Help*, it said. *All zombies here except Audrey.*

"Damn," she said aloud. It was her fault. She had to get back home, but how? Her brain felt like it was full of cotton. Soft, silky cotton. She found herself watching the women fucking. Nina? No, Nora. And her wife, who looked like she could be in porn. Not mainstream porn with Jenna Jameson and her duck lips full of collagen, but honest, femme-positive porn made by women, with real bodies and real reactions. Kate was envious, both of Nora's skills and of her wife in receiving them. She was supposed to be doing something, but it was hard to remember what.

Nora moaned, deeper than before. She leaned against Walter because there wasn't any room to lean against anything else. She shuddered. Christine opened her eyes, which were unfocused. Nora started to take off her shirt, getting tangled.

"Honey?" Christine said. She leaned over to help Nora.

"Something's happening," Nora said through the shirt. Kate felt a muscle tense in her back. "No," she said. She looked at Walter, who still had his hand on his dick. He was closer to Nora. "Step on her. She's turning."

Walter's puzzled expression turned to fear. "Turning?"

Nora managed to get her shirt off. She wore a lace bra, the material between her breasts yellowed with old sweat. Still, she had nice tits, small but firm.

"Walter!" Kate said. "We have to do something."

Nora reached around to fondle Christine's ass. She buried her nose in Christine's pubic hair. The gestures might have been arousing, or tender, if it wasn't becoming clear what would happen next.

"You have to get away from her," Kate said. "Walter, you have to tie her up, or sit on her or something. And where am I going to get a whip?" She and Michael had managed to tie down a zombie last night, but this was hopeless. If Michael were there, they'd stand a chance. From his texts, though, he might be dead at any minute. She glanced around the interior of the bathroom, close to panic. She focused on her breathing, tuning out the moans from inside the room and the moans and screams from the main cabin.

I'm going to my safe place, she thought, though she'd never admit to anyone that she had one. It was Lake Merritt, a three-and-a-half mile estuary in Oakland, where she liked to jog on a sunny afternoon, as long as it wasn't too hot outside. In her safe place, there were no zombies, and she ran because she liked the feeling of it, and even though she'd done it a number of times, the scenery changed often enough to instill anticipation of what would happen next. The aviary, for example, with lots of pigeons and gulls and squealing kids with bags of bread in their hands. Running, she dodged goose poop, uneven sand and grass. Light filtered through the trees alongside the trail behind the Children's Fairyland, with its brightly painted Alice in Wonderland play-ground. She and the other joggers wore headphones, everyone in their own safe places. She'd pass the tiny Asian women jogging in jeans, lots of people walking on the path or lying around on the grass. Her favorite were the delicious-looking young men in their tracksuits, the sweatshirts unzipped. Those men always ran too fast; she could only get a good look at them if they were running the opposite direction. Maybe she should have tried to meet one of them, faked an injury or just started talking to get the attention of a particularly cute one. Some were students, surely, but most were probably career guys, and single. Stable. They'd be good listeners and they'd make her laugh. But if Kate tried to jog with them, they would surely run faster than her. The relationships would never work out.

Christine let out a scream that brought Kate back. Her fingers were in Nora's hair, her knuckles white with effort, pushing Nora's head away. Nora's mouth, Kate saw, was bloody. It was happening.

Christine fainted, slumping against the wall and sliding towards the floor. Nora went for Christine's belly. Part of Kate felt like it came loose. If she lived, she would see this scene over and over in her dreams. If she were lucky enough to live. Why did zombies always go for the belly? Because it was soft and boneless? Maybe, but the belly was the slinkiest part of a person. Christine's guts, ripped open, smelled like shit. And zombies were supposed to go for brains.

Kate realized she was still holding onto her phone. She stabbed at it, trying to call Michael, and found herself in the App Store. She was ready to cry, poking at the keys, when she saw something that said *Indiana Jones*. She came to understand that it was an application that would make a whip noise, along the lines of the light saber noise that everyone had. She pressed the button, hoping against hope. It wanted ninety-nine cents. She ground her teeth with frustration. The money wasn't the issue. She selected the app and hoped that the phone would recognize the credit card associated with her account. She'd die if she had to call customer service and wade through their system, however friendly the robot operator was. Walter was whimpering, his dick still in his hand. It had gone soft. He sounded like he was saying, "Wha, wha, wha?" Each iteration rose in tone, like a question or a Valley girl's intonation, and not the Silicon kind of valley, either.

Christine opened her eyes, looking at Kate, and mouthed something. Perhaps it was, "Something's happening," just like all the other zombies had said. Or, "How could you let this happen?" She put her hands in her wife's hair, pulling her head up, and Nora acquiesced to the tug. The women considered one another for a moment. Christine seemed to be beyond frightened, in that cold accepting place Kate had been in once, when she was really high, in the family car in the school parking lot, waiting for the cops to come along and arrest her for being really high. At a certain point, she knew, you stop dreading the inevitable and hope that it'll happen sooner, so that you don't have to hang out dreading it anymore. Eventually, she'd gathered herself together enough to drive her friend home, then herself, though she'd forgotten to put the bag of grass away in the glove compartment. Her brother had noticed it on the dashboard, the next morning. Probably he took it, which was OK because then they both had a secret. She'd sobered up after first period. Jazz band. Kate held onto the memory; maybe things would still work out.

The app was still downloading. Christine guided Nora's head back to her guts. The expression on Christine's face said, *I'm doing this for you*. It wasn't clear to Kate who Christine was doing it for. Nora obligingly bit into Christine's small intestine, yanking out a length of it. It was very long. The woman contained multitudes. Christine screamed and passed out again. That was the difference between zombies and people, Kate realized. Zombies were all id and no ego; entirely focused on the pleasures of the flesh. People could plan for the future. But this was Christine's plan?

Walter vomited then, small yellow chunks that splattered the floor and the zombie. She didn't notice. Kate held her breath, her stomach already rising.

"Walter, we need to get them out of here," she said. But how? Fingers scrabbled on the other side of the door. Even if they could get it open, how could they push the women out without letting others in? Probably everyone outside was a zombie by now. Walter heaved again. They were trapped.

She screamed at her phone, ready to throw it. Finally the application finished downloading. She opened the app, praying out loud that she'd heard Michael correctly, and that this whip sound, if she could make it work, would actually do something. There were a lot of contingencies, but she was desperate. If there was anything she'd learned from zombie movies, it was that everyone was on their own. The cavalry wasn't coming, or if it did they would kill you first and ask questions later.

Christine's eyes opened. They were white. She moaned. Nora dropped the intestine she was chewing on, as if it had gone bad. The goo draining from Christine's gut was already slowing. She'd finished turning. That was fast.

The two zombies turned and looked first at Walter, and then Kate, deciding who to eat first. Walter was closer, and they moved towards him almost in unison, each grabbing a trouser leg.

Kate screamed. She brought her phone down to strike the closer zombie's head, and right before the impact she heard a tinny whip sound. The zombies both held still. Kate brought the phone up and down again, hoping she hadn't broken it by whacking the zombie. The whip sound was louder this time. The zombies looked at the phone.

"Back up," Kate said. "Back up, now." If this didn't work, she was dead.

The zombies moved a tiny bit back. There wasn't really anywhere they could go.

Kate felt a rush of relief so strong she started laughing.

"What the hell?" Walter said. He'd found his voice, though it sounded strangled.

Kate couldn't stop laughing. "Whip it," she said between giggles. "Whip it good."

"Kate?"

She bit her cheek, trying to collect herself. She took a small breath. The tiny room smelled of vomit and shit. Had one of them shit their pants, Kate wondered, or was it just the zombie's intestines? Somehow that was funny, too. Old jokes came to mind unbidden. "What does the vegetarian zombie eat?" Kate said aloud. "*Bran*. Or maybe *grains*, I'm not sure."

"Are you OK?"

"And who does the baby zombie eat while his mother's at work? *Gran*."

"Get ahold of yourself, dear." There was an edge of panic in his voice, but still he sounded calmer than before. A little patronizing, even. Almost back to normal.

"It's the whip," she said, regaining control. "My friend Michael told me that zombies respond to the sound of a whip. I don't know why, but I certainly don't know why this otherwise perfectly normal couple turned into zombies in the first place. These are *real* zombies; there's no reason why they'd behave like movie zombies. It isn't like Romero invented zombies out of whole cloth. Or whole flesh, or whatever."

"Whip," Walter echoed. "So there's an iPhone app for fighting zombies. Interesting." Usually when he said that something was interesting, he thought the opposite, or he didn't understand it and didn't want to say so. It was one of those words that could mean anything. "You have real *chutzpah*, Katie."

"*Chutzpah?*"

"That's the one about the kid who kills his mother and father, and then throws himself on the mercy of the court because he's an orphan. That's *chutzpah*." His thigh was warm against Kate's.

"That's not a very good joke."

"I think it's from the Bible." Walter seemed to be recovering. He put his dick away and zipped his pants. They were loose around his waist. That gave Kate an idea. Both of the zombies wore belts. If she could secure their hands, that would at least slow them down. Who knew how long the whip would work. And if one of them bit her, it would all be over. Walter wouldn't stand a chance, unless she could distract them long enough for him to escape, and there was nowhere to escape to. There was a steep valley below them, through the window, though they were progressing inland.

Nora moaned. Christine moaned.

"Shush," Kate said without thinking, and flicked the phone towards them, producing a satisfying, if tinny, *whapeesh*. Their cloudy eyes were wet with desire, but they closed their mouths.

"Stand up. Hands up," she said, using the whip again. They obeyed, looking for all the world like sheepish arrestees already thinking about their phone call. A friend of hers had called his grandmother, after he'd been arrested. What an awkward conversation that must have been. With both of the women standing, there was a tiny bit more space in the bathroom.

"Here," Kate handed Walter the phone. "Just do what I did, if they get excited. I'll get their belts first." She wanted to hurry, before the zombies moved again. She leaned forward, inadvertently elbowing Walter.

"If you say so. You're driving this bus," Walter said. He looked at the phone in wonder. Shock, Kate realized. He must be in shock. Which meant that she must be, too, but she didn't have time to worry about it. Except maybe it meant that her decision-making was clouded, and that moving towards the zombies wasn't the right thing to do. But she was already doing it. And it was easier than she thought, even with trembling fingers. Once she had the belts, she wanted to back away, but there wasn't really anywhere to go.

"Give me the phone." She held out her hand, afraid to look away from the zombies. "Hands down," she told them. *Whapeesh*. The zombies obeyed, getting tangled in one another as they brought their arms down.

Kate made Walter hold the phone again while she leashed the belts, one at a time, around the zombies' waists, tying down their arms. They both moaned as she touched them, but they didn't move. Kate worked through the fear. Maybe if they survived this, she *would* take Walter up on that offer of a spa treatment. What else was there to do, if everyone she knew was dead? Probably she wouldn't take the massage, though. She didn't want anyone to touch her.

After she had tied both zombies, she wiped the blood from her hands onto her jeans. The sink was behind the zombies, and she wished she could wash her hands. Probably these women had been perfectly healthy, but you could never be too careful with strangers' blood.

"Now what, MacGyver?" Walter asked.

It must have been his tone, weary and sarcastic. Kate snatched her phone back from him, saying, "Well, now I'll create a steam-powered time machine using only spit and a bicycle, and use that to take us back through time until before I ever met you."

His face fell, and Kate regretted her words. "You got any spit?" she offered, trying to smooth him over.

He nodded, then licked his lips. "Spitful and fancy free."

She kissed his forehead. She would have wrapped her arms around him but didn't want to mess up his suit.

"I'm glad you're here with me, Kate."

She meant it when she said, "Me, too." She knew they weren't exclusive, but she didn't want to think of what would have happened to him, if he'd taken some other girl.

"If I live through this, the first thing I'm doing is going to my chiropractor," Walter said. He wasn't a large man, but he was in an awkward space, standing on half of the toilet, pressed against the wall.

"Do you want to switch positions?"

"What, you want to be on top?"

"Touché." She had to smile at that one. If they could keep a sense of humor, they might survive. "I meant that we could try to sit the zombies on the toilet, and we could stand. I don't know. I guess we could pull their teeth out," Kate said. "But we don't know that this is irreversible, and besides, that's a lot of work."

"And the only thing worse than being bitten to death is being gummed to death."

"*Gran*," Kate moaned. The zombies watched them, swaying as they stood, hands tied to their sides.

"We could call 911," Walter suggested.

"Not on my phone," Kate said. "I need that. Use yours."

Walter put his hand in his pocket and fished around for his phone. Then the room turned sideways, and she fell against the wall. Kate and Walter both screamed. Her phone went flying. There was a scraping sound, as if the Zeppelin itself was in pain. Kate looked out the window. They were landing.

chapter eight

Michael tried calling Kate again, but it didn't even ring this time. He hung up without leaving a message. Then he called back. "Kate, um, call me when you get this. I'm kind of in a situation here, and I could use you. They're all zombies. We need to talk." He hung up.

"Michael, you okay?" Audrey called.

"Fine, be right there," he said. If only the bathroom had a window. There was only a tiny opening on the ceiling for the exhaust fan. It was probably about as large as the ventilation ducts in the cells at Alcatraz that those prisoners had escaped through, except that they'd had months to chip away at the surrounding concrete, which had softened from years of damp sea air. Looking up, Michael was vaguely jealous of the Alcatraz escapees. Sure, they had probably died, but maybe they hadn't, and at least they'd escaped. He was stuck here with Audrey, and now doubted whether she was stable enough to trust, despite her apologies. If she'd known their friends were zombies, and lied about it, that might really be unforgivable. She might not let him leave, though; she could just attack him with her zombie, which wasn't even really *her* zombie, it was their friend Cameron, but Audrey had always been possessive. But he didn't have to walk past her. He could escape by way of the deck, through the master bedroom, and climb the wall to the street.

Michael weighed his options: try to leave, go get Kate and find somewhere safe, or stay to confront Audrey. The moral dilemma wasn't so much that she'd hidden them, even, because that's what you *do* with zombies if you didn't want to—or couldn't—bash their heads in, but that she hadn't said anything about them. She was pushing to get medical treatment for Cameron, but she didn't seem to care about their other friends. Maybe she was in shock; maybe she'd lost it. Not so much that she'd *forgotten* the other zombies, but had been unable to process their existence. Still, he couldn't leave her. She was the only one who seemed to be able to hold her own against the zombies.

In the mirror Michael's reflection still had traces of makeup from last night. He'd been Charles Dickens, but only the white pancake remained. The Victorians never got much sun, what with the smog. He washed his face. Then again. Drying his face with a towel that smelled musty, like it had been used too many times, he thought about whether he could reasonably put on enough makeup to pass for a zombie. Give Audrey some of her own medicine. Probably it wouldn't be that hard; he had enough stage makeup. But the eyes would be a problem. He didn't have the right contacts. And it would take too long.

The smoke detector went off. Michael smelled something burning. He cursed. The zombie's cigarette. He grabbed a bath towel from under the sink, and his whip. He touched Kate's bedroom door to test it for heat. It was still cool, so he opened it. A patch of carpet was smoldering, but it was still small. The zombie was lying in Kate's bed, and had pulled the covers up over herself. Only the ends of her hair were visible. Michael toweled the carpet until the flames were out, then went back to the bathroom and ran the blackened towel under the tap. The wet towel sizzled as he threw it on the burned carpet. He stamped it down, trying to make sure he got all of the embers. The room smelled of damp burning.

"You OK?" he asked the zombie. He knew it was pointless.

She didn't reply, but that was fine, too. As long as she stayed under the covers. Michael threw the window open. Then he brought a chair into the hallway and stood on it to remove the battery from the smoke detector. Hoping that the smoke would dissipate quickly, he closed the bedroom door with the naked zombie safely inside. He wedged the chair under the doorknob, just in case.

Audrey stood in the hallway, with Cameron behind her. "You all right in there? What's going on?"

"Zombie smoking in bed," Michael said, although that wasn't entirely true. "Terrible for your health."

"You're going to *leave* her in there?"

"I opened a window. The fire's out. It was only a little one." He still wanted to throw more water on it, and went back to the bathroom to get a bucket. There was one under the sink, filled with cleaning products. He dumped the bucket out on the counter. Mostly spray cleaners – could those be used as weapons? He set down his whip and picked up a bottle, looking for the warning label. It was all natural, procured from Trader Joe's, like everything else in the house, and it was made of crap like corn and soy and ash. Great if you had kids or pets that liked to lick the floors, but useless against zombies. He did have a container of Comet, which always reminded him of that childhood song: *Comet, it makes you vomit, so get some Comet, and vomit, today*! But that was powder, and impossible to throw without getting it everywhere. And zombies seemed pretty insensate to pain, anyway. He gave up on that line of inquiry.

The sink wasn't quite big enough to fit the bucket under the tap. He cursed. He turned on the bathtub and placed the bucket under the faucet. "Audrey?" he said, poking his head into the hallway. "Is there anything you wanted to tell me?"

"I don't smoke?" she said. She'd found the clothes Michael had dropped on the floor, and was shrugging on a T-shirt over her vinyl dress. He wasn't sure how she was going to deal with the jeans. Michael turned his back and went into the bathroom to give her privacy. That was just like Audrey. She probably thought her lack of modesty was charming.

The sound of water was calming as the bucket filled. He called over his shoulder, "I mean, about what happened this morning? Anything you maybe left out? By the way, we need to put Kate's friend into some clothes before we take her anywhere. Maybe you should do that. It would be less perverted if a girl did it. Although if she's a lesbian, then that doesn't totally make sense." He turned his attention back to the water. When the bucket was nearly full, Audrey let out a surprised shriek, and then a real scream.

"Audrey?"

"Michael!"

His whip was gone. He cursed, then picked up the bucket, which he could at least use to slow down a zombie. It was heavier than he'd expected, and water sloshed from it as he took it into the hallway.

Cameron was humping Audrey, his hips to her ass, his arms locked around her waist. She was trying to pry them off, and elbowing Cameron in the ribs. He didn't seem to notice. Cameron also didn't seem to notice that he was still wearing pants, and wasn't actually having sex. He did seem to be enjoying himself. He leaned forward and kissed Audrey's shoulder with his mangled mouth.

Audrey pitched her upper body forward as far as she could. "Michael, help!" Audrey screamed. "If he bites me!"

Michael threw the water at them. Most of it hit Audrey. She and Cameron both screamed, nearly a perfect octave apart. Audrey's T-shirt, now wet, clung to her erect nipples. Her hair hung over her face. She'd managed to put on the jeans under her dress, not that they seemed to help.

"Sorry!" Michael said. Desperate, he put the bucket on Cameron's head, thinking that at least he could stop him from biting. Cameron humped harder. He was moving pretty quickly for a zombie, or at least the real kind of zombies, not the rager kind you see in movies. Audrey's struggling grew wilder. She kicked and elbowed at Cameron. Apparently he liked it rough.

"Michael, *do* something!"

Michael charged, knocking both Audrey and Cameron over. Audrey's head hit the wall as she fell. She landed in a soggy pile, but at least Cameron was down. Michael wanted to hit him, knock him into submission, but he still wore the bucket on his head. Michael was struggling to stay calm. He sat on Cameron, pinning his arms. "Audrey," he said. "Audrey?"

She didn't answer. Maybe she was playing another trick on him, but Michael had to deal with Cameron first. Cameron kept humping; either he didn't know or he didn't care who he was fucking. Michael wished he had handcuffs, or some rope. Cameron's arms were badly scratched from Audrey's nails, and Michael didn't like the thought of touching Cameron's blood. It was still red, which gave him pause. Maybe the zombies really *weren't* dead. Maybe they could still be saved. In the movies, zombies were always dead, but in the original Haitian sense, they were most definitely alive, sort of. He took off his hoody and used that to tie Cameron's hands. It wouldn't hold for very long, but it was something.

"Audrey?" he said. She lay still. Michael felt close to panic. He didn't want to risk hurting Audrey by moving her, but he didn't have a choice. He stood up from Cameron and picked her up, trying to keep from jostling her spine. He dragged her along the floor down the hallway, carefully, the way you were supposed to move people if you suspected an injury. Cameron growled and sat up. He used his tied hands to knock the bucket from his head. What was left of his lips had started bleeding again. He stood.

Michael dragged Audrey as quickly as he could. The hall bathroom was closer, but his bedroom would be a better option. If they could get there. Audrey moaned, and it was mostly momentum that kept him from dropping her. That was a good sign, though; moaning meant she was close to consciousness. That she was still human. Not enough time had passed for her to start turning, and he didn't think she'd been bitten anyway. He hoped not, at least.

Michael dragged Audrey into his bedroom and dropped her on the floor. He went to shut the door and would have made it except for Cameron reaching inside. The hoody Michael had tied

Cameron's hands with had already come off. Michael pushed the door as far closed as he could. Cameron's gray fingers twitched as Michael leaned against the door, hoping Cameron would get the message. If they could just hole up in the bedroom, he could call an ambulance and Audrey would come around and they could figure out what had really happened that morning and everything would be OK.

The door was thin, and wouldn't hold up to anything beyond a good slamming. Michael had been meaning to get a nice, solid one ever since they moved in, something a bit more soundproof, but he couldn't really justify the cost. Now he wished that he had. And wished that he'd bought a gun, for just this eventuality. Michael knew that owning a gun greatly increased your chances of being shot, and that had always been argument enough. He'd never wanted to own a gun. Except now. Now he really wanted one. Friend or no friend, Cameron had turned on him, and he had to protect himself. Without looking, Michael picked up something from the shelf nearest to the door. It was a cobalt vase he used to store quarters. He beat Cameron's hands with it, showering the floor with coins. Maybe he broke a few fingers. Cameron didn't seem to notice. Michael hit him harder. Cameron opened the door a few more inches. This wasn't going to work.

Michael abandoned the vase and grabbed Audrey, who moaned again. He dragged her backwards as Cameron came into the bedroom. Moving as fast as he could, Michael opened the sliding door onto the back deck and pulled Audrey out, setting her down to close the sliding door just in time. Cameron beat his hands against the door.

It wasn't possible to lock the sliding door from the outside, so it was merely a matter of Cameron figuring out how to open it. If he was the kind of zombie who could figure out doors. Zombies, in every tradition, were kind of dumb.

He took a second to catch his breath. "Audrey?" he said. She stirred, opening her eyes. "Oh, thank God. Audrey?"

"Um, hi," she said. Her smile was large and unconnected to

reality. One of her pupils was larger than the other. That couldn't be good. He had to get her to a hospital. She at least had health insurance. And then maybe they could make it to the old armory in San Francisco, now owned by Kink.com. Or somewhere equally defensible. Despite the bat under his bed, which in hindsight he should have gotten, buried as it was behind old magazines, he'd never expected zombies in his house.

"Michael?" Audrey reached one hand up, and grabbed Michael's jeans. She pulled herself up to sitting. "What's going on?"

Cameron knocked on the sliding glass door. He grinned, then humped the glass. Michael touched Audrey's hair, and she smiled up at him. He had to take care of her, damn all of the zombies. She struggled to stand, and he helped her up. She smelled like peppermint soap and morning-after booze. She leaned on Michael, and he turned her so she couldn't see Cameron. He didn't want her to freak out.

"Audrey, honey, you and I are going to go on a little ride." Michael patted his pocket, and had a moment of panic, trying to remember where his car keys might be. He habitually hung them up on the rack by the front door, where everyone was supposed to leave their keys in case someone needed to move a car. But no, there they were, in his other pocket. He took them out to look at them, just to make sure. Then it was a matter of getting *to* the car. The deck was right off of the street. Michael tried to decide which part of the wall would be easiest to scale. It was made of wood, stained dark. The house's owners had built the wall to allow privacy for the hot tub that used to be on this deck. The hot tub went away, his landlord had told him, when the circuits were repurposed to put in an air conditioning system. Not that Michael minded having AC on some days, but he wouldn't have minded a hot tub. The deck was a small, enclosed space, with a few low-maintenance plants. Normally he used it for storage, but in a cleaning spree before the winter he'd put all of the boxes and crap in the basement, to keep them out of the rain. There was nothing to stand on. Maybe he could knock down one of the walls, so that they could get through, but what if Cameron got out?

They'd have to scale the wall.

"I'll boost you up, and then climb after you," he said. "Can you do that?"

Audrey was having a hard time standing. She leaned against Michael. This might not work. Maybe he should call an ambulance instead. The fire department was only a few blocks away; they had ladders.

Michael took out his phone. There was no signal. Coverage was lousy in the hills.

"Damn," he said.

chapter nine

The Zeppelin had landed with the cabin at a 45-degree angle. The world was sideways. Kate lay on the wall. The zombies were on top of her, their faces close enough to kiss. Blood dripped from Nora's open mouth onto Kate's cheek. Her eyes were so empty. Kate turned away, barely avoiding a bite. Where was her phone? She was really glad that they had tied the zombies' hands, and she was terrified.

The window-side of the Zeppelin was now the floor. Under the window, which was smeary with blood, there was dirt and smashed yellow grass, already dry from the California spring. Land. Even if she broke the window, they couldn't get out that way, unless they dug a hole. That would take too long.

The zombies moaned, and outside the bathroom door, more zombies moaned. The screams had been so loud earlier. Now it was only moans, soft and pervasive, like a choir of tone-deaf monks. It had happened fast, then.

"My whip." Kate said aloud. She managed to stand, planting a foot on each of the zombies. It seemed safe to look away, so she looked to Walter. He was passed out, slumped on the toilet. His weight rested mostly on his head. Kate winced, realizing that he'd taken the brunt of the landing in his spine. He really was going to need to see his chiropractor. "Walter?" she said. Then louder. She reached over and slapped him, gently at first. His nose started bleeding. Kate fought back tears. The zombies moaned and twitched under her feet, threatening her balance. Surely one of them was lying on her phone. It occurred to her that she didn't actually know Michael's phone number. It was programmed into her phone. Kate steadied herself by putting a hand against the wall, which was sort of the ceiling. One of her feet was sinking. She wouldn't look down, didn't want to see her foot squishing into intestines. Blood was soaking into her shoes. It was still warm.

Kate took a breath. Escape was so close. The Zeppelin had finally landed, and they could get away: all they had to do was get out of the bathroom, and then out of the Zeppelin, and they could figure out where they were and hitchhike or call a damn cab—they couldn't have drifted *that* far—and get somewhere safe. And now Walter looked half dead—was he even breathing? Kate put a finger under his nose. She couldn't tell.

"Walter," she whispered. She realized that she actually cared about this guy. He looked so vulnerable. Despite all of their bedroom activities, she'd never seen him sleep. Not that he was asleep now, exactly, but that his face was arranged in something like rest. Except for the blood dripping down his cheek.

Maybe going crazy wasn't a terrible option. That would absolve her of responsibility. And maybe she wouldn't be aware of being disemboweled and eaten, though surely the pain would bring her back. She tried to reason, tried to breathe. Her clothes and hands were smeared with vomit; the room reeked. It was stifling. Her phone, that was first on the list. She looked around the cockeyed bathroom, feeling woozy. There, the phone was in the sink. She grabbed for it, cursing. It was wet. She cursed again. The screen had gone dark. She stabbed at it, trying to turn it back on. She shook it.

Chutzpah, she thought. "*Whapeesh*," she said, gesturing with the phone. Then again, louder. "Hold still," she said loudly.

The zombies grabbed at her jeans, pulling her towards them. Kate panicked. She stepped on Christine's head, trying to bash in her skull with the soft rubber soles of her Chuck Taylors, wishing she wore Doc Martens. She braced herself against the sink—the handrail was on the ground somewhere—and jumped, landing her heels on the zombie's face, then again. Again. Until there were crunching sounds. She didn't want to look, but had to. Christine's face was a bloody mess, her nose broken. Some bone fragments must have lodged themselves into her brain. She lay still. Nora let out a howl. Kate jumped again, holding onto the sink for balance, and brought her weight down on the other zombie's face. Kate's mind was blank, only dimly aware of the task at hand. She could feel teeth and bone through the soles of her shoes. Her feet were wet. She kept going until both zombies were quiet. She dared not believe they were actually down for the count; they might come back. The undead were like that. She and Walter had to get out of there.

"Walter?" She grabbed his hand, pulled at it.

"Wha?" he said, without opening his eyes.

"Walter, wake up," she said. "I'm begging you, wake up. Please."

His eyelids fluttered. Kate saw that his eyelashes were awfully long, and was surprised that she'd never noticed before. Good eyelashes were always wasted on men. She touched his cheek, wiping the blood away. "Walter. Sweetheart. Please. Come back."

His eyes opened. Kate had a rush of fear that his eyes would be white; that the fall had killed him and he was coming back as one of them. But his eyes were blue, like normal, and bloodshot. That wasn't normal, but she could work with that.

"Are you okay?" she said. "Can you sit up?"

"Ugh," Walter said. "Ow." He was at least alive. "Gross," he said, looking at the zombies. "Rough landing."

Kate wiped her hands on her jeans and helped him to sit up. "We have to go," she said. She gestured to the bathroom door, which was now closer to the ceiling. "Can you stand up?" She thought of the Passenger Briefing card—there were two exits on the Zeppelin. One was just across from the bathroom.

Walter made a face. "Ow," he said. Kate pulled him up, and he stumbled a little as his feet landed on a zombie. It made a squishy noise. "Come on, we have to go. Can you walk?" Kate held Walter's hand, trying to steady him.

"You know, I was planning on asking you for a late lunch after our little outing, but I rather would like to go home, I think."

Kate pulled at the door, and a man's body fell inward, knocking them both down. The Zeppelin rocked from the motion. Kate couldn't tell if he was alive or dead, zombie or person. "*Whap-eesh*," she said, gesturing with the phone out of habit. "Hold still." The light came back on, against all odds, and the phone emitted its own *whapeesh*. Kate screamed in triumph. The zombie held still. His eyes were vacant and white. He opened his mouth. Kate struggled out from under him, and tugged on Walter's hand. He acquiesced.

"Let's go, let's get out of here." She pulled herself up out of the bathroom, brandishing her phone. The girl with the pink hair was lying right outside. She smiled and reached towards Kate. "Hold still," Kate shouted, whipping her phone. "Keep still." The zombie obeyed, disappointed. Her eyes tracked Kate. "Hold still," Kate said. She pulled Walter after her.

The cabin was full of zombies. Most of them were still in their seats, with their seatbelts strapped. They moaned and struggled. Maybe they weren't smart enough to free themselves, or maybe they were just waiting for someone to give them permission to undo their seatbelts. "Keep still," she told them. The floor was smeared with blood and offal. The smell was only marginally better than it had been in the bathroom. The exit was just on the other side of the cabin. Kate tried to find purchase to climb up the floor. Her hands slipped. Unable to stop herself, she vomited. The watery puke ran downhill. Tears slipped from her eyes. She wiped her face with her arm and spat. The flight attendant, now a zombie, was moaning. He struggled to his knees. Part of his face was missing. He didn't seem to notice.

"Come on," Kate said. "Walter, come on." She put the phone in her mouth, holding her breath as her stomach rose again. With both hands she reached up and caught hold of the base of an empty chair, and pulled herself towards it.

"Walter?" Kate looked back. He was lying on the slanted floor, covered in muck. The flight attendant was reaching for his face, as if to caress him. Kate put out a hand, and Walter took it. His fingers were slimy; she had to grip him by the wrist. Kate pulled, bracing against the chair. It was a good thing he was slender. The flight attendant climbed after them.

Kate stood on the chair, and reached towards the door. It took a moment to figure out. Finally, she unlatched it and pushed it open. She climbed out and slid down the side of the Zeppelin. Walter slid down after her, and she managed to roll out of the way in time. The door banged shut.

They lay for a while in the dirt and grass, catching their breath. Kate wiped her hands on the ground. Dirt stuck to her skin. Wiping her hands on her grimy clothes wasn't any better. She spat. Her throat hurt, and her mouth tasted of stomach acid and bile. Her water bottle was in her bag, lost to the Zeppelin. She allowed herself a moment to imagine the hotel room at the Claremont. A long shower. Two bathrobes smelling of cotton and bleach. They could throw their mucky clothes out the window. Order room service, enough food for an orgy. Plus a bottle of wine. No, two at least. They could hide out behind that sturdy hotel door until this whole zombie business blew over. Maybe get a room with a hot tub, if the Claremont did that. It was a stupid idea, but she held the image in her mind as if it was safety itself. She wouldn't let herself think about what she'd done to the women in the bathroom. She wouldn't.

She sat up on the grass, and for the first time she saw the view: San Francisco enshrouded in fog, islands and bridges in the distance, a telephone pole. Telephone wires sliced the view of the Bay. They were lucky not to have landed on the wires, which were about as tall as the hill. The blimp's hull was wedged against two tall evergreens at the eastern edge. The hill was flat and just large enough. They were lucky, Kate thought. They must be in the

Oakland/Berkeley hills; further to the east the ground turned to soft valleys for a long time. California's breadbasket, the Central Valley. And beyond that, the Sierras.

The ground gave off a baked-dirt smell. It was patchy with grass that had gone to seed, with waist-high thistle bushes intermixed. A group of gnats moved in a tight circle for reasons only they knew. Birds sang. That seemed weird; they should be quiet, the way they were before an earthquake. The afternoon sun was warm. She stood to get a better look at the land. The hill sloped down towards a snakelike two-lane road not far below. It seemed familiar, but all of the roads up in the hills curved like that. She walked further, avoiding the thistle bushes. There was an empty parking lot below the hill. It looked familiar. Beside it was a small wooden building: a chemical toilet. There was a fence made from wooden posts. There was a sign. It couldn't be. It was. She gave a cheer. "Walter, I know where we are! We're at the start of the Huckleberry trail!"

"Set the damn thing on fire," Walter said. His voice was weak. He lay on the ground, looking rumpled and old. He looked at the Zeppelin with righteous indignation. It had betrayed him. She wondered if he'd demand his money back. If there would be anyone left to demand money back from.

Kate knelt by Walter. "You'll set the hills on fire if you do that. Plus, it's helium, we went over that already. And do you even have a lighter?" He didn't smoke, not that she knew of.

"The door doesn't latch from the outside, now, does it?" he said in a professorial tone. Sometimes he liked to put Kate in her place.

"Maybe they're not smart enough to figure it out?" Kate looked at the door. The flight attendant looked back at her through the windowpane. What remained of him, anyway. The Zeppelin was laid out on the hilltop like a sacrifice to some steampunk god. "What do we do?" she asked, not expecting him to answer.

"You go, and I'll stay here and keep watch." He started humming "Taps," the trumpet solo she used to have to play when the high school marching band did the Memorial Day ceremony. He sounded so melancholy that she shivered.

"Damn you. That's ridiculous, and you know it. I'll call 911." She checked her phone. No service. "Shit. You have any bars?"

He took his phone from his pocket. "No." He tossed it onto the dirt. "Motherfucker, can you hear me now?" he yelled.

Kate picked it up. Walter carried the newest iPhone. She put it in her pocket. He wasn't thinking clearly. "We're less than a mile from my house," she said. "Ten minutes, tops. Can you walk that far, my dear?" Sometimes sweet talk helped with him.

"Zombies," he said. "Zombies." His voice was flat. She was sure he hadn't been bitten. It must be shock.

"Screw them. There's nothing we can do here, and we need to get somewhere to call the cops. We have a magicJack phone, a land-line." She helped him to sit up. She was exhausted. She needed to get back and check on Michael. And maybe she and Walter could both grab a shower, maybe some food; there might be leftover pizza, and there was soup, because when soup was a dollar a can, you bought it. Surely Michael had some clothes that would fit Walter, though it would be loose on him. The mental image of Walter wearing Michael's sweatshirt and jeans didn't sit right in Kate's mind. Too close for comfort. Never mind the zombies that were at the house. She'd never taken Walter home before, and it occurred to her that she'd had reasons. She had different reasons now, not just her messy room and her messy housemates, all the details of her messy life.

"I could go get my car real quick and come pick you up, and then we could go straight to the fire station on Skyline and let them know what's going on."

"Your car."

"Shit, you're right." Her car was at the damn Holiday Inn by the airport. That seemed so long ago. "Someone else will have a car I can borrow."

"And they'll be there with the keys?"

"Probably." She knew he heard the doubt in her voice. Jamie's van would be there, surely. And Jamie's keys would be in Kate's bedroom. Somewhere.

"Couldn't we just flag down a car, or stop at one of the houses and ask to use the phone?"

Kate pushed her hair away from her face. "We look like we just murdered someone," she said, her voice cracking. Walter hadn't been awake when she'd done what she'd had to do. She didn't want to tell him. "Would *you* let us into your house?" Her cheeks grew hot, and she curled her toes in her wet shoes. He always noticed, when he was going down on her, whether she curled her toes. He seemed to take it personally if she didn't.

He sighed. "You're right. I'd better walk with you." He didn't move.

The Zeppelin rocked slightly from something moving inside it.

"Contents may unsettle during shipment," he said, looking up at the Zeppelin.

Kate pulled Walter to his feet, ignoring his pain noises. "Get a fucking move on already," she said. "They're going to get out, and I can't lose you, too, damn you."

"You're next," Walter said thoughtfully. Kate willed herself not to slap him. Just a little slap, to try and knock some sense into him. She squeezed his wrist, harder than she had to, and wrapped his arm around her shoulder. She started walking, and he managed to come along. He leaned against her, and his weight on her shoulders made her feel strong. Capable. She could get through this. *They* would get through this.

"Just think, every step is getting you closer to your chiropractor," she said. "Sort of."

"My chiropractor would tell me to walk it off, anyway. That's the best way to jostle things back into place. Best for me, anyway, now that my knees are shot and I can't run anymore. No, I'm ready to go home. Chalk it up to a nightmare."

She led him down the hill. He fell, and she helped him up. She walked into a thistle bush. Her shins prickled. Thistles were the worst. First they itched, and then they hurt. She remembered, too late, that there was a path that would have taken them down the long way, around the hill. It was paved. She led them through the break in the wooden fence to the street.

"The fire station is on the way," she said. "Five minutes. We have to tell someone about the Zeppelin, at least."

"Five minutes," he said. "I can do that."

They didn't talk for a while. Kate was aware of the sight they would make, their clothes covered in blood and vomit. Yet only a few cars drove by, and they didn't slow. That was disconcerting. Why hadn't anyone noticed the Zeppelin?

The familiar scenery was calming, though Kate glanced over her shoulder every minute or so, just to make sure they weren't being followed. It warm in the sun, though the shade was comfortable. The wind blew inland from the ocean but lost its sea smell by the time it came this far, bearing instead the smells of warm dirt and sage. They walked along the edge of the road; the streets up in the hills had been paved long before there were laws about leaving room for sidewalks and drainage channels. She noticed the lettering on a drainage grate: *EMPIRE FOUNDRY*, on the top. *OAKLAND, CALIF*, on the bottom. Must have been back before the country adopted the two-letter system for states.

The trees held onto green despite the drought. The valley to the right of the road was steep, held together by tree roots and engineering. Expensive-looking houses were built into that hill, supported by stilts and concrete; they'd be the first to slide during the next big earthquake. *For Sale* signs littered front yards; one signpost had lost its sign, and looked for all the world like a little cross for crucifying a one-armed midget. There was a house still under construction, its skeletal wood beams and bare cement a pronouncement of hope against the economic downturn. You had to walk two flights down just to get to the front door, though the driveway was at street level. The front yards on these places were barely large enough to park a car. The nicer yards were finished with smooth, oyster-sized stones. Most of them, though, were dirt.

On the opposite side of the road, the hill rose too high to build into, at least not until more people wanted to buy more houses. That hill was held up by a brick wall, grown over with moss but still recognizable as human work. They walked past it. The road sloped downhill. She tried to keep Walter from stumbling. He was her responsibility. He needed her.

She looked to her right, downhill. They'd seen that view earlier, in better form. The buildings of downtown Oakland, and beyond that, the fog of Carl Sandburg's cat feet. The Bay Bridge, and San Francisco. Alcatraz. It seemed like a dream. Everyone liked dreaming, at least, everyone who had good dreams did. A metal rail separated the road from the steep drop, to keep drivers from plummeting. Underneath it, into the hill, black steel girders were bolted together with wood, holding a berm of dirt to keep the hill in place. A long, black plastic drainage pipe descended down the hill into trees, valley, and nothingness. She paid attention to the scenery, not allowing herself to think about what she'd done.

Kate had walked this road several times a week since she'd moved here, to hike at the Huckleberry trail. Walking always gave her a chance to think, to gather up all of her thoughts and put them somewhere. Walking now, grateful for a moment of quiet, she thought again of Jamie. The way she kissed. It started to make sense, and Kate felt cold, though the sun was shining. If zombieism could come from a bite, surely it could come from a kiss. Maybe that's how Jamie and the pink-haired girl had each gotten it. If that were true, Kate suspected it was just a matter of time before she had it. There had to be an incubation period. She did some calculations. If she'd kissed Jamie around ten last night, after sunset, and it was past two now, it had already been sixteen hours. Maybe it went faster if you were kissed by someone who'd already turned. And Jamie had lupus; maybe her immune system was too busy attacking her body. Maybe Kate still had some time, or maybe she was resistant somehow. She hoped so. And she hadn't kissed Walter, or Michael, not on the lips at least. Maybe that mattered. She ought to have someone tie her up, just in case, but she didn't want to ask Walter. He didn't even have a belt anymore. Where was Michael when she needed him?

Walter spoke. "I hate to bring this up, but what are we going to tell them, exactly? At the fire station?"

Kate gestured with the hand that wasn't supporting him. "That there's a big mess? Someone has to deal with it. People with ladders and weapons and uniforms." Her shins itched from the thistle bush. She couldn't lean down to scratch them without dislodging Walter. "You know why women like men in uniforms? Because we know they've got a job."

He ignored the joke. "You think they'll believe us?" He was recovering. That was good.

Kate looked at her shoes. She had been trying to ignore the squish that accompanied each step. "You think... oh, shit. You're right." She felt a rush of panic. She could be tried for murder. "We don't have to tell them *exactly* what happened. For all anyone knows, the zombies killed each other. Or the crash landing did it. Not me." She wouldn't allow herself to grieve. Grief was a luxury. Kate knew that once you were turned into a zombie, you didn't get to come back.

"But they'll want to know how we survived. They'll surely take us into custody. I mean, look at us. *Smell* us. We're a mess, and it's all evidence. We will have some *'splainin* to do."

Kate considered. He had a point. Damn him. She'd be the one who could be tried for murder, even if it was self-defense. She had to operate as if she were going to live beyond the next few hours, or however long it might take before she turned into one of them. *If* she turned. "We'd be safe for the meantime, though, even if they did lock us up. And you must have a good lawyer."

"I'll forgive you the reasoning behind that last remark." He took his arm away. "I can walk on my own now."

"What? I just meant you were well connected. I thought you were." He'd probably been joking, but the implications of his remark still stung. As if she'd just *assumed* that he regularly got himself into legal trouble, despite the fact that he was thinking like a criminal. Her head hurt. Kate reminded herself that she didn't know Walter very well. He'd never told her, for example, what he did for a living. That information would have been too personal.

They came to the end of the block, to the three-way intersection. When Kate glanced back to check they weren't being followed, she saw a sign: "Fire Warning Today: Extreme. Be Fire Safe!" The "Extreme" was written in yellow letters on a black background.

"I didn't realize the warning went above High," Kate said. "Is it fire season already?"

"Either that, or the fire department has hired a marketing executive straight out of fast food." He must be feeling better.

"I could go for a cheeseburger," Kate said.

"You're *hungry*, after all of that? I think I still have vomit in my nose."

Kate found a tissue in her pocket, crumpled but still clean. She handed it to him. They stopped walking while he blew his nose a few times. It sounded lumpy.

"Well, that's fixed my appetite, not that I had one."

He held the tissue away from himself, making a face, and then put it in his pocket. "Littering is a sin," he said.

Kate spat onto the dirt. Her throat was still sore. She hoped she wasn't getting sick. Maybe that was how it started; maybe she'd be a zombie by sunset. You didn't see a lot of zombies during the day, at least not in movies. "Look," she said. "That's the fire station, right there." It was a small building, on the far side of the little road.

"Yes, but they'll take us into custody, you bet your sweet bippy. This joint won't have a holding cell, so they'll take us downtown, and book us. Separate cells. And what happens when some big guy turns into a zombie? *You* can take care of yourself, Katie Kay, but I am old and feeble." He wasn't; he was waiting for her to contradict him. She didn't.

"Well, we have to tell *someone*." She wasn't sure now. If she did only have a few hours to live, she definitely didn't want to spend it in a booking cell, never mind all of the other unfortunate people she'd end up eating. "Plus I'd like to shower one last time before the world ends."

"A shower sounds like heaven. Haloes and harps and wings and Jesus jokes. I suppose you must have some clothes I can borrow. We should burn these clothes. So let's just *call* them instead."

Kate took her phone from her pocket, and then Walter's. "Still no service. We're in the hills." She glanced behind them. "Nobody following us, either, at least."

"No, not from your cell, baby. Call from your house. Block the number so it's anonymous. Tell them we saw the Zep land. The Zeppelin land, whatever. For all anyone knows, we weren't *on* the thing."

"You didn't pay with a credit card?"

"Oh. You're right. Damn. *Your* name isn't on it, though."

They walked past the fire station. The door opened, and a truck pulled out, sirens and lights blazing.

"Maybe they already know. I can't imagine they don't," Kate said. The truck turned left, the same way they were going, in the opposite direction from the Zeppelin.

"Let's go to my place," she said. She was sweating from the sun. The thing about California was that the sun was warm, but the air wasn't. There just wasn't enough shade to go around.

He sang, "Let's go to my place!" then stopped. "Sorry, *On the Town*. Before you were born. Yes. Your place. That's one of my rules, when a pretty girl invites you up, you go." His singing voice wasn't that bad. Better than her first boyfriend, and she'd fallen in love with him because he sang and played the guitar; he smelled of leather and tobacco smoke, and he was gentle and knowledgeable where it counted, though he'd broken her heart. Several times. They'd called one another Mulder and Scully. That was back when love was all-consuming, for her friends, too; they talked about it often. The entire day was structured around seeing one's boyfriend. The guys she'd dated since Mulder had been much less pathological, but ever since him she'd been trying to understand why she was attracted to some guys—or some people—and not to others, even if they might like her. A guy liking her didn't necessarily make her like him. It was some combination of charm, conversation, and looks. And smell.

They crossed the street. A house on the downhill side of the street had a deck that was at a dangerous angle. The railing was broken. The edge of the deck couldn't hold weight, though no one had roped it off. The occupants must know to avoid it. Kate and Walter walked downhill, in the sun. They were within a block of her house, too late to change her mind. She hoped it was safe. Maybe Michael had gotten his shit together and taken the zombies to the hospital already. Or maybe the zombies would keep quiet long enough for her and Walter to shower and scrounge up some clothes and get out of there before he noticed that something was wrong. If they were quick, it might work.

chapter ten

Michael boosted Audrey over the wall, then climbed over. Cameron howled on the other side of the glass door, his palms against the glass. Audrey sat in a pile on the ground, giggling.

"Come on, Audrey," Michael said. "Please. We have to get you to the hospital." He spoke slowly, hoping that helped.

"Why?" she said.

"Honey, you fell. Don't tell me you don't remember."

"Remember what?" She smiled, and reached her arms up. "Will you smoke me out? I've got a headache."

Michael pulled her to her feet. "I don't have any," he lied. He put her arm over his shoulder, and she kissed his cheek.

"You need a shave," she said.

"Don't worry about that." He walked her to his car and bundled her into the passenger seat. He brushed her thigh accidentally, buckling her in. She didn't seem to notice. Once she was safe, he glanced back at the deck. He could just see the top of the sliding glass door. It was closed. Still, if Kate's friend could light a cigarette, Cameron could figure out a door if he really put his mind to it.

He turned back to Audrey. He didn't expect that she'd been bitten, but didn't want to find out after the car was moving. There were no bites or scratches on her arms or her neck, which was a relief. She did have blood under her fingernails, but he hoped that didn't matter. Blood didn't seem to transmit the infection, if it was an infection. He and Kate both had gotten a little blood on themselves, and blood washes off. No, the infection must come only from being bitten, he reasoned, not from being exposed to blood. There had to be an entry point, or maybe the bug was in saliva. Cameron had gotten it from a bite; because he'd been bitten on the face, near the major arteries, he'd gotten sick fast. Kate's friend must have been bitten at some point, too, just not as badly. He didn't remember seeing any marks, but that also made sense, because if it was small he might not have seen it. Plus it had been dark inside Kate's room. Never mind that the zombie girl had been naked. The memory of her, the way she moved and what she'd wanted to do, and how he'd wanted to do it too, was distracting.

He had to get them help. They were long past the golden hour, during which the human body was supposed to be able to wait for medical attention, so long as you weren't bleeding too much or in shock. That was from a book he'd read as a kid, about a plane crash at night in the backyard of this big country house. In all of the turmoil of triage and getting people into ambulances, there was one kid who'd been put on a couch under a blanket. Head injury, he remembered. She wasn't as bad off as some of the other people, so she had to wait. Of course the kid was forgotten. Michael tried to tell himself that a few more hours wouldn't matter to his friends, if that's how long it took before he could get them medical attention. It wasn't like they were getting any worse. Just as soon as he had cell phone coverage, he'd call for an ambulance to the house. Do what he should have done last night.

Audrey busied herself poking at the radio, though the car wasn't on. Michael closed her door and walked around to his side. He paused to look at the house, as if the cracks in the gray paint, or the arrangement of the pine tree's branches, might spell out his next move. Then he started the car, and put it into gear. The radio came on.

Audrey pushed a button and the radio started playing a song

by Bone Thugs 'N Harmony.

"Wait," Michael said. He turned the radio to NPR. "You'll receive a CD of this entire broadcast, with a donation of $75. You can even pay in low monthly installments, automatically deducted from your credit—" He changed the channel, trying to find the news.

Audrey pushed Michael's hand away, and changed the radio back.

Michael pushed another button. Audrey changed it back. They continued like this until he'd heard all of the preset channels. If there had been a story about zombies, it was over now. He merged onto the freeway. Audrey rolled down her window. They drew even with a car that was playing the same song. There was a surreal moment of surround sound. Audrey nodded at the driver. He nodded back.

"That means you can fall in love, when that happens," she said. "If you're listening to the same song. Two minds but with a single thought. Or maybe it's 'with but,' I forget. Two minds, with butt."

"You're such a romantic."

"No, really. You already know you have one thing in common."

The other car pulled ahead.

"Will you take me home?" she asked. "I'm not feeling great."

"Sure," he lied. "We just have to make one stop. Won't take a Detroit minute."

"*Last* time you said that we had to watch a whole movie at your dealer's house."

He considered how easily she'd corrected him, despite not seeming to know where they were going. Where exactly did her memory leave off? "Audrey, what happened this morning, after I left?"

"Um," she said. "Do you have any pot? I'm dying for a smoke."

He decided to ask easier questions. "Where do we work?"

"Trader Joe's, silly. And two plus two is four."

"Name three kinds of mint."

"Um, spear, pepper, and base."

That was one of her jokes. It was good that she remembered it.

"What day is it?"

"Today." She paused before that one, either because she was trying to remember, or trying to think of a joke. "Today is today, just like every day. Except for that long, embarrassing parade of yesterdays."

Michael kept both hands on the wheel. Her sense of humor was clearly intact. And her long-term memory seemed fine. "Who did I dress up as last night at the party?"

She answered without hesitation. "A really big bug."

"No, tell me for real."

"Some Victorian writer-type. You couldn't do the accent for shit."

That time she'd gotten it right.

"I didn't *try*."

"Well, that explains it."

"And what movies did we watch last night?"

"Fuck if I stayed awake. You know me. I must have been really fucked up; I'm really hung over. My head hurts. I'm not going in to work. You shouldn't either. We can watch movies in bed all day."

Michael considered. If she really did have some kind of concussion-related amnesia, he didn't want to distress her by bringing up the zombies. She remembered coming to the party at least, but it seemed like her memory cut out sometime during it. He wouldn't be surprised if she'd come a bit unhinged. The way she'd lied about the morning, about telling everyone to go home... He didn't dare try to tell her she'd lost her memory. The way she kept repeating herself, he wasn't sure how much she was retaining even now.

Inspiration struck. "Audrey, when did you get back together with Cameron?"

"Who are you kidding?" She changed the radio to some new hip-hop song that Michael already hated. "Not on your life. I've given that boy his chances. He'll break my heart if I let him, and he knows it. I can joke about it, but you know how you can tell sometimes? When someone's so wrapped up in the power they have over you, they kinda just want to see how far they can go? Flirting with other girls in front of me, that sort of thing. I'm just glad I broke up with him when I did."

So she didn't remember the morning. Which meant she wouldn't be able to tell him why their friends were fine when he left the house and zombies when he came back. Maybe she'd recover her memory. Or she was lying. He wasn't sure what to do about it, if anything. Everyone knew zombies weren't very articulate, so it wasn't as if *they* were going to tell him what had happened. That would be a real bummer, if he never knew. Not that he could go back and fix it. But he wanted some kind of explanation.

She leaned her head against the window, cradling her cheek in her hand, her elbow propped on the armrest. Her eyes closed.

Michael remembered that people with concussions weren't supposed to be allowed to sleep. He couldn't remember why, or if it was even true. "Hey," he said, nudging her. "Stay with me, Audrey."

"Where you at?"

"Open your eyes."

She did. Her pupils were the same size.

Michael fumbled his phone from his pocket. Finally, he had service. He dialed 911. It rang a long time before a woman answered: "Highway Patrol, what's your emergency?"

"I need 911," Michael said. He was reminded of that old joke, *What's the number for 911?* "Accident in the Oakland hills, at a house."

"Cell phones connect automatically to Highway Patrol," the operator said in a clipped voice. Too professional to be grumpy. "Putting you through to police and fire." The phone rang again. Michael checked his rearview mirror, just to make sure that he wasn't being followed by a squad car that would pull him over and give him a ticket for talking on the phone without a hands-free device.

"911, what's your emergency?" A male voice this time.

"Um, hi," Michael said. "I need a car, or maybe a couple of cars, to go to—" he almost said *my* house "—this house in the hills. There are a few really dangerous people inside. I think they're contained for now, but they need medical attention." He held his breath, waiting for the operator to hang up.

"Address?"

He recited it, giving the cross street since it was easy to get lost in the hills.

"You say they're contained?"

"Well, they're inside. Doors and windows shut. Can they get out? I mean, are they smart enough? Do you know what I'm talking about?"

"Just stay indoors, sir, and lock your doors and windows. Do you live nearby?"

"Yes," Michael said. He hadn't intended to lie, but he didn't want to get into trouble for leaving the scene of a crime, if it was a crime. He felt like a criminal.

The voice cut off without saying goodbye. Operators weren't supposed to do that.

The car ahead of them braked, and Michael dropped his phone while he remembered to drive. He slowed just in time, then turned onto the off ramp. There was a man holding a sign that read "Need Help" at the end of the ramp, dressed in a brown coat despite the sun. He didn't seem to be concerned about zombies. Michael looked away from the man. He gripped the steering wheel to keep his hands from shaking. Maybe he shouldn't have called the cops. What if they went in and just shot everyone? He thought about getting back on the freeway, the other direction; going back home and loading everyone into a car somehow, and taking them to the hospital. He should have done that in the first place, instead of watching movies and getting blueballed under the blanket. Why would Kate let him get that far and then just stop? He'd enjoyed what they'd done, and knew he should just let it be what it was.

But none of it should have happened. She should have talked him into getting their friends to a hospital. As it slipped further into impossibility, the idea sounded better and better. None of them had been thinking straight, he told himself.

His wallet jabbed him; he took it out of his pocket and put it in the car's console. There wasn't much in it, anyway. He put his phone in the same place.

"You all right over there, kiddo?" He made his voice sound gentle.

Audrey put a hand into her hair, then brought her fingers up to look at them. It wasn't a lot of blood.

Michael concentrated on driving. The street was clogged with traffic. People cluttered the sidewalk, going in and out of boutique shops and restaurants. No one was screaming. No one looked particularly worried. Perhaps they didn't pay attention to the news. He didn't make a habit of listening to NPR or reading the newspaper himself, so he couldn't fault them.

He saw the parking structure off of MacArthur, and drove towards it. This was where he'd come once his health insurance kicked in from work, and he'd decided to get a physical. It had been five years or so since the last one, which seemed about right. He'd gotten lost in the building. It was a huge medical center, two wings and four floors, with all of the major specialty doctors, several pharmacies, and lots and lots of sick people. He wondered at how many doors inside actually locked. He thought that the doors that did lock had big windows.

"'Mergency center entrance is around the block, I think," Audrey said.

Michael obeyed, driving past the structure. Her voice had sounded clearer than before. Maybe she was getting better. He parked in the 20-minute zone, came around to help Audrey out, and locked the car. He held her arm as they entered the sliding doors. A security guard in a black windbreaker nodded at them, arms crossed over his chest. How could the sun be shining, and people be going about their normal business?

He approached the desk. "My friend here needs to see a doctor," he said to the woman. "I think she has a concussion. She fell. It was an accident," he added, conscious that he might sound like an abusive boyfriend.

"Does she have an appointment?"

"No. Why would she have an appointment?" Michael said, trying to stay calm and not make any comments about pre-approved emergencies.

"Kaiser card?" the woman said.

"Audrey, do you have your insurance card?"

Audrey fumbled with her pockets. She pulled out ChapStick, money, and receipts. "I thought we were going to see your dealer," she said.

"That was a joke," Michael said to the woman behind the desk. She didn't smile. "I know she's insured here. I mean, look at her. She needs medical attention. She's bleeding."

The woman sighed. She typed something. Surely other people did this, Michael thought. "Can't you look up her information from her name?"

The woman clicked something with the mouse. She used her computer like an old person, wrinkling her eyebrows.

Audrey swayed, moving like a flag in the breeze. She sat down on the floor, and started laughing. She was a smart girl. She knew how to get attention. It wouldn't be beyond her to fake it a little bit. He'd only dated her briefly before she declared they were just friends; only took her to bed a few times, and he was pretty sure she'd faked it then, too.

"Please," he said to the woman.

Her smile was businesslike. "Just a second. I need to talk to my supervisor." She picked up a phone and cradled it between her neck and shoulder. Michael sat next to Audrey, who'd stopped laughing. "Head injury, no card," the woman said. "Well, with security—"

Michael was readying his argument. That you couldn't re-fuse service in an emergency room, he'd say that first. Then the woman's words filtered through. He understood what she'd meant. Whatever was going on with security had happened *recently*. Which meant there were already zombies here. There had to be; people would bring their friends and families to the hospital. People in their right minds, anyway. But the hospital had to avoid panic, because a huge building full of panicking people would be worse than a zombie attack.

Maybe it was the same thing with the news; that they were keeping it quiet to avoid a panic. Fights over gas and food and supplies that would turn into riots. Freeways clogged as people tried to get out of the cities. Cars stalled out on the side of the road. People hitchhiking. Neighbors shooting each other over the car keys. Cellular phone networks overwhelmed by traffic, and everyone trying to find their families and friends. It'd be like a Max Brooks novel. Michael took a breath, and let it out slowly. Life wasn't really like that.

He stood, and looked past the reception desk. About half of the chairs in the waiting room were filled; the place looked like an airport lounge. Of course, any zombies would be hustled inside, to keep them quiet. At a minimum, they'd be contained, and studied. Maybe it was some kind of mutation on the swine flu. Passed along by something in saliva, delivered into the bloodstream. A virus that caused psychotic behavior and changes in appearance. Because they weren't dead, he knew that much. Cameron's blood had been the normal color. Something had happened to him, for sure, and to Kate's friend, and everyone else.

"Miss? Sir?" The woman called down. "You can wait over there. My computer system is down, so when they call for a Jane Doe, that's you." She smiled and gestured towards the waiting room.

Michael took Audrey's arm and found them seats. His proximity to Audrey, her arm small in his hand, reminded him of Kate.

Someone coughed wetly. Michael's heart beat faster. He leaned over and whispered, "Audrey, are you faking? You can tell me, it's OK. You don't even have to tell me why. But this place isn't safe. I'd rather not stay here if we don't need to."

A young man sitting in eavesdropping distance looked up, and then pretended not to be watching. His cheeks were scarred with acne. He didn't seem to have anyone with him, no mother or girlfriend standing by.

Audrey smiled, and put a hand to the goose egg on the back of her head. Michael leaned over but didn't touch. It looked painful. Blood was drying, dark in her strawberry hair.

He didn't let doubt enter his voice. "Honey, you're a good actor. You've had me, several times already. But you're *not* concussed," he said. He wondered whether her pupils had really been different sizes, or if it had been his imagination. A tricky sunbeam; an angle of light. Still, even if she had been concussed, she was better now. "I know you're in pain, and the past few days, or what feels like a few days at least, has been really rough. I don't expect that you're doing any better than me, and I feel like I might be losing it. Sometimes I hope I am, because it would make things easier."

She didn't say anything. They sat for some time. Michael tensed from every cough or rustle, from every time a nurse came out from the swinging doors and called a name. He put his arm around Audrey. She pulled away.

"Cameron got loose," Audrey said, her voice small but clear. "This morning, just as we were getting up. I didn't want to tell you. I was embarrassed. They subdued him, and tied him back up, but they got bitten. Natalie and Henry. I ran and hid in the bathroom, but I heard it all. I heard them talking about what to do. They called for us to do something—they thought you and Kate were home still. They shut themselves up in Lena's room. Before they turned. They knew what was going to happen. They called for us to stay away. And then they just moaned."

"Audrey?" Michael was startled. It was plausible. He pulled her to her feet. "Audrey, don't fuck with me."

There was fear in her expression, but it felt honest. He craved honesty. Was capable of violence to get it. He let go of her. She stood without swaying.

"Henry let Cameron loose," she said. "I think it was Henry. Or he got loose on his own, I don't know. I thought about calling the cops, and I didn't. I should have. There was no way to go back and save them, and now they're dead and it's my fault." She started crying.

"They're not dead. Cameron's blood—"

"Who are you kidding?" Audrey said. "You're the one who put on the Romero movies. This isn't going to end well." Her voice was getting louder. People were watching. "It's my fault. I stayed in that bathroom in the hallway, and I found your copy of the Wade Davis book, and looked up the whip business. I thought I'd dreamed what happened last night, when Cameron obeyed the whip, but it was in the book. And maybe I shouldn't have let Cameron loose after all that, but I wasn't thinking straight."

Michael realized that they had failed to bring a whip from the house. "There's more to zombies than movies," he said, aware of how lame that sounded.

"Miss?" The woman from the desk called. "We'll call you in just a moment. Please keep your voice down." It was clear from her tone that this was not a request.

The people in the waiting room each pretended not to be watching when Michael tried to make eye contact.

Michael walked towards the exit, holding tight to Audrey. The double sliding doors opened and closed behind them. They were headed towards his car when someone screamed. Michael turned. He could just see the waiting room. He blinked, hard. People were getting to their feet. A zombie had come into the room, moaning. He wore a paper gown, the kind you had to wear when you were getting examined. His legs and arms were covered with dark hair. His eyes gave it away. He licked his lips. The woman behind the desk went towards him, hands out, attempting reason.

"No," Michael said, stepping forward. Maybe the "security" measures hadn't involved telling the staff what the real dangers were. "Don't touch him!" he called.

The security guy stepped into Michael's path, blocking the sliding glass door. "Excuse me, sir, but you'll have to clear the premises. Now." He locked the door from the outside. He would not make eye contact.

Michael felt a chill. He took a step back. There was a scream from inside the hospital. Then another. People beat their fists against the glass door. Michael looked at the lock.

"Beat it," the security guard said, lifting his jacket. He wore a gun.

Michael nodded, grabbing Audrey's sleeve and backing away. He was shaking with adrenaline. The security guard got into an ambulance. Michael expected the guy was going to take off, but he drove it to the door, and parked it sideways. The vehicle covered the glass door. The guard got out, and took off at a run.

Michael looked at Audrey. It was all a matter of information. Maybe the security guard knew more than the staff or the doctors. This couldn't be standard hospital operating procedure. Either way, containment was the bottom line.

"We gotta go," he said. They turned. He looked for his car. There was a little green Volvo in the spot where he'd parked.

"Dude," Audrey said. "Um, where's your—"

"Fucking kidding me. Someone stole my car!" He looked at the sign. Twenty minute parking. There was a phone number for towed cars. "I don't believe it." He cursed. "We can't have been here for that long."

An elderly woman approached. She held out a copy of *Street Spirit*, the homeless newspaper.

"Donation?" she asked. The newspaper had a suggested cover price of a dollar.

Michael checked his hip pocket. His wallet was in the car. So was his cell phone. He felt the loss like he'd been hit. "Sorry," he said. "You should go somewhere safe, ma'am," he added. "Somewhere indoors. With rope. The zombies are coming. You need whips. Tell people!" There was no time to explain.

She shook her head and went to find someone else to solicit.

"Audrey, we gotta hoof it. Can you handle that?" He started walking towards MacArthur, mapping his friends' residences one by one and discarding each. They were all too far. They were at least five miles from his own house, most of it up a steep hill; Audrey lived in Berkeley, which was further yet.

"I guess. You don't want to call for your car?" Audrey was stepping over all of the cracks in the sidewalk. Normally she wasn't neurotic. Perhaps she thought she was being cute. Michael worried that she *did* have a head injury, but there was nothing to do about it now.

"There's no time. You saw what I saw. What happens when those guys start breaking the windows?"

"We only saw one."

"Where there's one, there's more. Who knows how many more?" The building was full of doors and locks, but anyone could get out through a fire exit. He kept an eye out as they walked, watching other people on the street. He kept Audrey close. He wished they'd brought a whip.

chapter eleven

Kate smelled smoke. A lot of the houses in the hills had chimneys, though usually people waited until after sunset, especially in the summer. But it didn't smell like woodsmoke. She walked as quickly as Walter would go. Her house was tucked away on a narrow lane. Maybe six houses, lousy parking, but it was quiet, and the neighbors didn't complain if they made a bit of noise on the weekend, which was the main advantage of a house over an apartment.

"Honey, once I'm decent, I might call a cab to get me back to my car," Walter said.

"All right," she said. "If you want." She tried to keep the disappointment out of her voice. Walter had an entire life that she didn't know about. She wasn't part of that life; was never meant to be. She was a tissue to him. What hurt was that she'd been honest about her friends, her family, her thoughts, about nearly everything that mattered. "Yeah, you should totally do that," she said.

He didn't offer to take her along. She tried to understand why she felt so rejected. Now was hardly the time to stand on ceremony, but she wanted him to ask her to come with him. She'd probably turn him down, on principle. They'd always had clear boundaries; that was part of their arrangement. And maybe he thought she'd rather be with her friends, and that it would be awkward for him to tag along, but still.

They turned the corner. A fire truck blocked the lane. Kate screamed. Her house, where her friends were, was on fire. Flames rose from the flat roof. The house was built down into the hill, so it was impossible to see from the street how bad the fire was. From the front only the carport and the fenced deck off of Michael's bedroom were visible.

She pulled away from Walter and dodged around the fire engine. "Michael—" she shouted. "Audrey! Natalie!" Kate ran down the stairs to the front door. A fireman stepped into her path, and she bounced off of him, falling to the deck. She left a smear of blood on his raincoat.

"Can't be here, miss," he said through his faceguard. He held an axe in his hand: he was an image from a nightmare. No wonder kids were afraid of fire.

Her hands went to her pockets. Her keys were gone.

"The door's probably open," she said. Her hip stung where she'd landed, and she'd skinned her palm.

The fireman opened the door, and closed it behind him. Kate waited a second before she poked her head in. "Audrey?" she called. "Michael?" Because it was right in front of her, she saw the key rack. She pocketed everything, three sets, not sure what was whose.

Standing in the hallway, the fireman said something. Kate realized he was talking into his walkie talkie. What a stupid term that was. Trust the military to give technology a clever name. Kate forced herself to focus. She took a step into the house. The air was thick with smoke. She coughed, and dropped to her hands and knees. "Michael?" she said. Probably they were already dead from smoke inhalation. She'd thought they were dead earlier, but now she really felt the loss. Kate put her head down to the floor, where the air was supposed to be cleanest. She tried to breathe the least amount possible. She crawled through the foyer. It was irrational, and though she knew it was irrational, she couldn't stop herself. She started coughing. She deserved whatever would happen.

The front door opened, a shot of light and air. She felt hands shoved under her arms. Kate was dragged out into the clear air, over the rough texture of the welcome mat.

"You're a mess," a muffled voice said. She started crying, ready to forgive Walter for wanting to leave her. He'd charged into a burning building after her; how else could he prove he cared? He laid her down on the walkway.

"Can you walk?" he said. "You need to get away from the house. Do you have any pets, miss?"

She looked up and stopped crying. It was a fireman. Of course. She shouldn't have expected anything else. She should have known better from the beginning.

"Fuck pets. My *friends* are inside," she said. "And some of them arc zombies. You have to watch out."

The fireman gave her a concerned look, and went inside. Either he thought she was high, or he knew what she meant.

Kate dragged herself to her feet. The neighbors were standing on the street, arms crossed, watching the firefighters. Walter was gone. Probably he'd called a cab already.

She saw him seated on a brick half-wall that bermed a neighbor's front yard. She went and sat by him, coughing into her arm.

He put a hand on her back, and the simple touch was disarming. It meant that he understood, and that he was sorry.

"No one was home when it started, I hope?"

Kate shrugged. She wiped at her face. "I don't know. Maybe they're all dead, I don't know. I don't know if the fire is under control. I don't know that the hills won't burn down entirely." She felt her pockets until she found his phone. She handed it to him. "You can call a cab, if you want."

"Oh, kiddo. I'm so sorry. You were going to call your friend Michael, right?" he asked gently. "He's the one you talk about the most."

She didn't trust herself to talk. She thought she'd said, clearly, that Michael might be dead. She considered her safe place. Lake Merritt wouldn't be a smart place to go now. It was too open, and even if she got a boat and went to the middle of it, who knew if zombies could swim? Kate had a mental image of herself out on the lake. In a paddleboat, weighed down on her side and going in circles. She wasn't afraid of being alone, not while she had friends. Against her will, she leaned towards Walter. He rubbed her back. With his other hand, he dialed his phone. "What's the address here?"

She gave it to him, with the cross street.

"I'll give you a ride to anywhere you want to go, sweetie," he said. "Michael's house, or whatever." Somehow he'd gotten the idea that Michael lived elsewhere. She didn't correct him. "Hello?" he said into the phone. He recited the address.

"Kate?" a voice called. She looked for its owner. It stood in the doorway of the house whose wall they were sitting on. A neighbor kid, maybe five feet tall; he was named Kevin or Devon or something like that. She was a little embarrassed that he knew her name, and she couldn't remember his. The boy came outside. "That was your house, wasn't it?" he asked.

"*Was* being the operative term. We *was* renting, at least." She wasn't ready to talk about her dead friends. Wasn't ready to see them carried out on stretchers.

"You guys want a towel or something?" the kid asked. "You don't look so good."

Kate stood. "I would do unspeakable things for the use of a towel. And a shower, if you were so inclined, and some clean clothes?"

The kid shrugged. "My brother left some clothes here when he moved out. Should have something that'll fit you guys."

Walter finished his call and stood, smiling his meeting-new-people smile.

The kid opened the front door and gestured for them to come in. He smelled like laundry detergent—the smell of a kid who still lived with his parents. Though she was friendly with the neighbors, Kate had never seen the inside of this place. They'd had some work done recently, building a sunroom on the front. The floors were blond wood; the walls and trim were earth tones, red ochre and orange. The house felt large and comfortable. Much more defensible than her own house, if it came down to that. Fewer windows.

"You home by yourself?" she asked. "Devon?"

"Trevin," he said. "Yeah."

"You've been watching TV?"

He shrugged. "I was playing *Halo*. Bathroom's down there, and there's another one through the bedroom. And, um, maybe you should take off your shoes?"

Kate did, feeling self-conscious. "Can you do me a favor, Trevin, my savior and my only friend?"

"What?" The kid looked like he might be wondering whether it had been a good idea to invite them in. He seemed awfully young, but he wasn't that far off from screwing and college. She had to trust him.

"Lock your doors and windows. You ever play *Left 4 Dead*?"

"Yeah, I like running through and mowing down all of the zombies in the tunnels. I mean, it's all right."

He would probably spell it *alright*, too.

"You have to trust me," she said. "They're real. That's why we're all fucked up. I'll tell you all about it after I de-muck myself a bit." She stood on the welcome mat, conscious of her dripping clothes. She decided that modesty was a quaint notion, and shrugged off her shirt and jeans and socks, leaving only the wet bra and panties. She knew how little they left to the imagination.

There was an intake of breath in the room. Trevin blinked a few times, then ran off and came back with two bath towels. He handed them to Kate, and she gave one to Walter.

"Lock the doors and windows," Kate said, and found her way to one of the bathrooms. It took a minute to figure out the faucet, and the water pressure wasn't great. But it was the best shower Kate had ever had. For a moment, it didn't matter that the hills were burning down; that her friends were dead and that she would soon join them. She would be clean and warm, for at least a little while. She cried. Pink water dripped over her feet and down the drain. Her palm stung from where she'd skinned it. Her legs itched from the thistles. She coughed as the room filled with steam. She found a sliver of Dove soap and lathered. She shampooed her hair, twice. The water sluicing down the drain was brown, and then soapy, and then it was clear.

She dried herself, squeezing the water from her hair. She didn't bother combing it. In the bathroom cabinet she found a bottle of Tylenol. She put three in her mouth, turned on the tap, and drank from her palm. Tylenol was the one that was bad for your liver, and she was sure her liver was still recovering from last night. But it was what was here, and her headache hadn't gone away. Maybe she'd die with a headache.

There were some clothes in a pile on the floor just outside the bathroom. She brought them inside. There was a pair of what was clearly Trevin's mother's underwear, way too large and pink, but it was sweet that he'd tried. There was a pair of jeans, which she put on. They were close enough, though she'd ask for a belt. Just on principle, she should have a belt. She put on a black T-shirt that read *D.A.R.E. to Resist Drugs and Violence* in faded red ink. She remembered the DARE program from school; it was dorky to wear the shirt back then, but once she'd graduated it took on an ironic coolness. She picked up her wet underwear and padded out to the living room where Trevin and Walter were watching TV. Walter wore a Bank of the West T-shirt and drawstring sweatpants. His feet were bare, and his wet hair stuck up. He looked smaller and softer without his own clothes.

"Hey, thanks, Trevin. I feel so much better now." She tossed her wet underwear onto the pile of her clothes in the foyer, where she'd dropped her shirt and jeans. Walter had put his ruined suit in the same spot. She would be happy never to see her clothes again. She thought about taking them out. Putting them on the house, into the fire. Burn it all down, like Walter had said. She felt dizzy, and went to sit on the couch. There was a box of Ritz crackers and a block of yellow cheddar on a plate. Walter, who she'd imagined wouldn't be caught dead with such pedestrian fare, was eating.

"Did you lock up?" Kate asked Trevin.

"Yeah," he said. He was flipping through channels. "But there's nothing on the news about zombies."

Kate cut a hunk of cheese and put it in her mouth. Then a few crackers. It tasted wonderful. A last meal of sorts. She got up and went to the kitchen, found a can of Coke in the refrigerator. She drank from the can. Bubbles and sugar were supposed to be good after you puked, to calm the stomach, plus the caffeine couldn't hurt. She felt a burp rising.

Walter's phone rang then. "Hello?" he said. Then, "Be right out." He disconnected the call, and wiped his mouth with the back of his hand. "Son, thank you for your hospitality," he said to Trevin. He put a soggy twenty-dollar bill on the table, then stood and approached Kate. She turned her cheek when he tried to kiss her. She could feel the prickle of an afternoon shadow where his cheek brushed hers. She held her breath so she wouldn't burp on him. He put his hands on her shoulders and smiled. It was an apology. "Will you come with me?" he asked. "Won't you come with me?"

It occurred to Kate that she hadn't asked Walter to stay, or to come back. Her reasons for being upset at him seemed obtuse now.

"Or I can give you a ride to wherever you want," he added.

She burped, and took a step back. "No, I'll be fine," she said. It would be shitty to just leave Trevin. There were keys in the pockets of her sodden jeans. She could take someone's car, if she and Trevin wanted to leave. She didn't need Walter.

"C'mon, I'll walk you out." She put an eye to the peephole, checking the street. No zombies, just a yellow cab. Kate unlocked the deadbolt. She opened the door. The fire engine was still parked in the lane. Kate could smell smoke, wet now. Firemen were standing around talking. They were probably waiting for the ambulance that would come and take away the bodies. If anyone was still there. She wouldn't let herself think about it.

She went out as far as the porch. Kate squeezed Walter's elbow, just as much to touch him again as to forestall any hugs and kisses that would make things difficult. She'd never see him again, she knew. Even if she survived the day, things would be different between them. They worked well together in a crisis; you couldn't say that about a lot of couples. Not that they had ever been *together*, exactly. On their first date, he'd said something she was sure he'd cribbed from an old movie: "If we are to have an affair, there will be no 'I love you.'" She'd agreed to it, a little weirded out by the suggestion that she might really come to care for him, and half-thinking it was a joke. She'd thought she'd been the one in control in their relationship because he wanted her more than she wanted him. Now she knew. He didn't need her; never had. She didn't dare tell him that she needed him. She found herself holding onto his sleeve. She let go.

He raised his eyebrows. She nodded, thinking he was asking whether she was OK. She wanted to reassure him. He nodded, then walked away barefoot.

Walter waved from the cab. Kate waved back. When it was gone, she went inside, and locked the door. She called Michael. It went to voicemail, and she hung up without leaving a message. She called her absent housemate Lena. She had to warn her about the zombies, and tell her about the fire. It went to voicemail. Kate's mind went blank. "It's Kate, from the house, give me a call when you get this. It's really important."

She felt terrible. To distract herself, she gave Trevin an account of the Zeppelin ride, while she ate the rest of the cheese and crackers. The zombies. The whip noise. Their close escape. His expressions cycled through surprise, disbelief, fear, and amusement.

"I keep waiting for somebody to jump out with a camera, and then you start laughing," he said. His face grew serious. "You're not shitting me." It was not a question.

She regarded Trevin with respect. "You saw our clothes, man. I mean, maybe I'm crazy. That's possible. Nothing on the news, but that makes sense in a way. Waiting until after something is endemic before telling us about it. Just like the economic meltdown.

Zombies with lipstick, they call the banks. We're all operating on borrowed capital."

She went into the kitchen and opened the refrigerator, looking for beer. There wasn't any. She found some vanilla ice cream in the freezer, and got a spoon from the drying rack by the sink. On second thought, she decided to use a bowl. Her throat hurt, and her head still ached, and if she was catching something, she didn't want to pass it to anyone else. Even the apocalypse was no excuse for bad manners. The ice cream was half-eaten and freezer-burned, which made her feel better about taking it. Not like it was going to be missed.

"Isn't it dangerous for that guy to be outside, then?" Trevin asked. "I mean, if there are zombies out there?"

Kate was pleased that the kid didn't refer to Walter as "your father." Neither did he call Walter "your friend." She sat on the couch with her bowl of ice cream, and considered. It was a valid question. "They don't move very fast," she said. She couldn't bring herself to talk about last night, about Jamie and about Cameron. It was too personal, and too painful, and not this kid's business, anyway. "He was going home. I think he'll be fine," she said.

"Unless the driver turns into a zombie. Or zombies attack the car." The kid was getting into it. His eyes grew wide, expounding on all of the bad things that would happen.

Mostly to shut him up, but also in the interest of full disclosure, Kate gave Trevin her theory about how zombieism had several vectors. The bite, obviously, but a kiss would also do it, if the person was infected. She felt guilty. "Do you have any Internets?" she asked.

Trevin pointed to a desktop computer at a desk in the corner. "Internets like what."

"Your parents, where are they?"

"My mom's gone for the weekend at a conference in L.A. She goes once a month."

"Your dad?"

He shook his head. "Sperm donor. Same guy for me and my

brother both."

"Oh." Kate sucked at her teeth, trying to dislodge the feeling that she had put her foot in her mouth. "And where's your brother?"

"Fuck if I know. He moved out. Work, maybe." Trevin started to look scared, which made him seem younger.

The computer was on. She opened a browser and went to Boing-Boing out of habit. There was a post labeled "Oakland McDonald's: Baby Zombie (Disturbing)". She hit play on the video.

It had obviously been filmed on a handheld, probably a phone, and could have been subtitled "Vertigo" for the camera work. Kids were playing in the ball pit at a McDonald's, screaming and laughing, swimming in brightly colored plastic balls. A toddler, maybe three years old, started wailing. The video quality was low, but the kid's hand looked bloody. He might have been missing a few knuckles. There was a moan, higher than Kate had heard before. Little vocal cords. Kate felt cold.

"This is it," she said. "Can you see?"

Trevin leaned closer. "Shit," he said.

The crying kid was pulled under the surface. The video ended.

"I'm telling you, this is it," Kate said. "And it's not on the mainstream news. Probably they don't want people to panic. Or they don't think it's real. This is the apocalypse that will only be covered by gonzo journalism. Forget the reporters in rain gear during Katrina, or Tom Brokaw embedded in Iraq—this'll be about blogs and Twitter." She'd put off getting a Twitter account, and now it was too late.

"What's Gonzo got to do with it?"

The only Gonzo he knew was a muppet, she realized. It made her feel old. She was less than ten years ahead of him, but it made a difference when one of you was maybe still in middle school. "Gonzo journalism, like Hunter S. Thompson? *Fear and Loathing in Las Vegas*? It's a little before my time, let alone yours."

"So *that's* who the muppet's named after? The blue one with a nose like a hangy downy dick?"

She laughed. "You're all right, kiddo."

He was unconvinced. "So what do we do?"

She put a hand over her mouth while she thought through all of the wrong things to say. "*Do*? I haven't done anything yet," she wanted to tell him. Maybe that had been the problem all along. She had to be proactive. Get out while there was still time. Boarding up the windows only led to hiding in the basement.

She went and got her phone and the car keys from her jeans pockets. She found her lipstick as well, and the cash she'd taken from Walter. She counted it. Nearly three hundred, in twenties. She thought it'd be a bit more. She pocketed them. Walter had left his wet clothes, but taken his wallet. The tissue he'd blown his nose into was a wet lump in his pocket. She touched it before she figured out what it was. Kate wiped her hand on her jeans.

"Well, you've seen zombie movies," she said, shaking her car keys so Trevin would see them. "We can either hole up here, or try to go somewhere safer, if we can think of something. I don't know." She felt guilty. The house *did* feel safe. There was food and water. "I don't have anywhere to go. I mean, not anywhere I *need* to go." She blushed, realizing she hadn't asked permission to stay. She'd assumed he would want her to. The social protocols of the zombie uprising were still new. "This place doesn't have a basement, does it?" she asked, to change the subject. Unlike hers, this house was on relatively flat land. She wasn't surprised when Trevin shook his head. Basements were rare in California.

"Zombies, no shit," he said. He glanced at Kate's tits, covered now by the T-shirt, but braless.

Kate wondered if she was wearing Trevin's brother's shirt, or Trevin's. He was getting a kick out of it, either way. She decided to take it as a compliment. "We should figure out the safest place in the house, away from windows, behind a door that locks, if possible. Like during a tornado?"

He gave her a blank look.

"Right, you don't know what that is. I'm from the Midwest, where the sky turns purple and green and houses are pulverized by wind."

"I *do* know, we just don't have them out here. Sort of expected that they were made up."

Kate kept going. "Maybe the master bedroom? And we need to stockpile some food and water, a flashlight, radio, that sort of thing. You have an emergency kit, with first aid supplies and shit, right?"

"I think my mom does, in her car. She drove it to L.A. She could fly, but it takes almost as long to go to the airport, and all that."

"That's good for her. You should call her, and your brother." Kate thought she might have sounded bossy. "Don't you think?" she added.

Trevin went for the cordless phone, which was buried in the couch cushions. Kate sat in the computer chair. She typed a comment to the video on BoingBoing. *Zombies respond to whips. I don't know why, they just do. Or the Indiana Jones iPhone application, which makes a whip noise.* That done, she had the urge to check her email, for the last time, just in case anyone had said anything life-changing. It felt like everything she did was for the last time.

"Hi, Mom?" Trevin said. He went into the hallway, probably going to his bedroom.

She had no new email. She thought about composing a few notes, just to let people know what they'd meant to her. It felt too maudlin. A waste of time. She re-read the last email from Walter. She'd sent him an email full of jokes, describing a Giants game she'd gone to with Michael. He'd won tickets from a newsletter he subscribed to, from a science fiction bookstore in the Mission. They'd sat in the unseasonably hot sun for close to four hours, and Michael had explained about baseball while they sweated and drank iced lemonade. "So this is the seventh-inning stretch?" she'd asked. "When they make you stand up and sing about how great America is, and 'Take Me Out To the Ballgame?'" Root, toot, toot for the Giants, and all that. They had screamed insults at the Mets outfielder, the closest player: "Sheffield, get your glove out of your mouth! This isn't T-ball!" She'd asked Michael what was happening on the sidelines: "Are they warming up the catcher, or what?" Relaying all of this to Walter, Kate had thought she'd been reasonably entertaining. Walter had written back with a report on a book he'd read, and a Puccini opera he'd seen in San Francisco. Walter hadn't said who he'd brought to the show with him. She hadn't asked. It was always easier to talk about things than it was to talk about feelings. She missed Walter, despite herself.

She logged out, then went to Facebook. She updated her "What are you doing now?" headline to "Fighting the zombie apocalypse with whips & gags. Seriously. They obey whips. Also the iPhone Indiana Jones app. Worth a dollar." Her friends had status updates that involved studying, trying to find jobs, breaking their sunglasses, making pasta. She felt jealous of their tiny problems. She had an invite to join the group "Real friends kill friends who become zombies." She accepted. Then she closed the browser.

The ice cream spoon sat in a bowl of melted white soup. Ice cream wasn't as good as beer, not in her book. She took the bowl to the kitchen and rinsed it out. Outside the kitchen window, the fire engine loomed. Just to have something to do, Kate found the dish sponge and washed her bowl and spoon, placing them in the drying rack next to the sink. She directed water over the cereal and the less-identifiable crust coating bowls and plates, setting them aside to soak while she washed glasses and spoons. Water could wash anything, given time.

Her mind went to the thing she was most worried about, like a tongue to a sore tooth. She should really not be here. What would happen when she turned into a zombie? Not *if*, but when. Would this kid be able to take care of himself? Were there any guns here?

Trevin came into the kitchen. "My mom says we do have an emergency kit in the house. Under the sink. But she thinks I'm joking. She asked me if I was high. She wasn't joking. I'm lucky she's miles away."

Kate dried her hands. The kid trusted her, she realized. "Sometimes it's easier to lie and tell people what they'll believe," she said. "When you try to tell the truth, sometimes they just think you're making it up."

Trevin watched the BoingBoing video again. Kate left him to it. In the cupboard under the kitchen sink was a plastic tub labeled *Emergency Kit*. She pulled it out and examined the contents. There was a box of cereal which had expired two years ago. Same with the rest of the food, PowerBars; cans of soup and what looked like dolmas. Also an expired bottle of Tylenol. She set those on the floor. Latex gloves, face masks, medical tape, gauze, a hand-crank flashlight. Duct tape. Toothpaste, and four toothbrushes. Why *four*? Maybe his mom used to have a live-in boyfriend, or girlfriend. There was also a kitchen sponge. The apocalypse is no excuse for a mess, she reasoned. She found fifty bucks in cash, which she pocketed. No weapons. No whips. No bottle of booze, which is what you really need for the apocalypse. She had a quart of Jim Beam in her emergency kit for herself and all of the friends she would make. But her kit was inside her house, melted, and in terms of food and first aid kit, not much better than this one.

Kate had once written a poem about the apocalypse, for school. The point of it was that she fully expected to die in the first wave of whatever it was. Bioterrorism. A dirty bomb. An earthquake, or a fire. Those were real crises, something you could get behind. And localized; you could get away. Being outside of an urban area was probably a really smart idea. She and Trevin could take a car and drive inland, away from the heavily populated Bay Area. Maybe find a cheap hotel off of interstate five, or maybe just keep driving. She could give Trevin the keys. Warn him that when the power goes out, the pumps at gas stations won't work. Give him the cash, on the assumption that even during the apocalypse, cash would be worth something. Maybe she could just walk away when the kid wasn't paying attention, like an old cave dude sneaking off into the woods when winter grew too long and there wasn't enough food to go around. Kill herself quickly; there would be a hill or a deck she could jump from. The question would be how she would know when she was turning. What that might feel like, and whether she would have any control over it. She doubted her ability to resist.

Kate's phone rang. She wondered for an instant which of her friends were calling, and felt the loss all over again.

chapter twelve

There was a crowd pounding on the sliding glass door of the hospital. Michael waved to get their attention. He saw the guy who'd been by himself in the emergency room. Michael gestured, as if he was holding a whip.

The guy repeated the gesture, a puzzled look on his face.

Michael mimed a zombie walk, his arms out and his face blank. Then gestured with the whip. He switched back to the zombie character, and lowered his arms.

The guy pointed towards the door, his face twisted in anger. *Enough charades*, his expression said. *Let us out.*

Michael didn't have keys for the ambulance parked in front of the door. He didn't have keys for the door. There were no bricks on the ground to throw through the glass. He stood rooted, unable to help and unable to run. "Find a fire exit," he called.

Something touched his hand. He jumped, snatching his hand away before he saw that it was Audrey.

"Time to cut and runny, honey," she said. "We can take a bus, but it won't go all the way up to the house." She pronounced "house" as "huss."

"We're not going there," Michael said. He let her pull him away from the door. Away from the look that guy was giving him.

"But my purse is. I mean, not that it's going there. Like it had little wings! It's there already. That's the last place I saw it. Unless it's in your car."

"So's my wallet. And my phone. Fuck. I can't believe this is happening. You got any change to make a call? If there are any payphones left, that is?" Kate would have to come get them. He slapped his pockets. Nothing there.

"It has no pocketses," she said. "It is a black man who has asked the country for change, and yet it has no pocketses." Now she was being careful to step on *all* of the cracks in the sidewalk.

"You're getting Obama mixed up with Gollum," Michael said. He tried to believe that this meant she did *not* have a head injury. A hospital full of people who were about to be turned into zombies, and his car gets towed. He supposed it was a matter of information. Of course the tow trucks would be in service, since those guys didn't know what was happening. Still, that meant there weren't many zombies running around. If there were, people would be reacting. Wouldn't they?

He looked for the woman who'd tried to sell them the street newspaper. Surely *she'd* have some change. He wished he smoked, so that he would have something to barter. Cigarettes, chocolate, lipstick, and nylons, that's what soldiers had in their parachute packs during World War II. Regardless of the actual currency of where they landed, they could make some friends. Now he had nothing but his personality. Plus the homeless woman was gone.

Michael had come to a conclusion that he didn't like. The closest place where he could find friends and supplies was Trader Joe's. He wanted to reject it out of hand; who'd go to a grocery store during the zombie uprising? That was way too *Dawn of the Dead*. Still, it was less than two miles away. And Kate was there. He had to get to her. Together, they could figure out what to do. She was the only one who would understand.

He turned on MacArthur. It went underneath the freeway, to the bad side. Audrey stayed quiet, which he was thankful for. Michael wondered if he could look like a pimp. An off-duty pimp, out on a date with one of his bitches. He wished he still had his hoody.

He didn't want to be approached.

Dudes walked by, and women. Even a few moms with strollers. They avoided eye contact, or they gave him the friendly upward chin-bob that meant "What up?" He wanted to warn them, but kept his mouth closed. Better not to draw attention. He kept Audrey close, scanning the landscape for places they could run and hide, if they had to. Doorways to apartment buildings. Alleys. Cars that they could climb on top of. He looked for weapons. He'd expected there would be sticks, cinderblocks, something, but the street was remarkably clean. He sweated in the afternoon sun. Approaching Lake Merritt, he turned left on Grand. The Trader Joe's was on Lakeshore, a few blocks away. They arrived.

Jake stood in the entryway, wearing his black security uniform.

"Sup?" Michael said. Audrey smiled.

Jake nodded. He was a big guy. He always reminded Michael of the guy at Walmart that had been trodden to death a few Christmases ago. The guy had been sent up front to hold the doors against the crowd eager for early-bird sales. The crowd had broken down the door before the store was scheduled to open. Surely no one had intended to hurt the dude, but they knocked him down and trampled him to death.

Michael entered the store. There were two sets of sliding glass doors in the vestibule. If they had to, they could lock the doors and roll down the metal wall over one of them. But it wasn't the most defensible place. The store was full of people with shopping carts and baskets.

It felt normal. Cashiers working away, occasionally ringing the bells that sent employees running up front for price checks or to help a customer outside. He nodded and waved at a few people. Kate wasn't working up front. He headed for the wine aisle; if she wasn't cashiering, that was where she usually was. But she wasn't there. He had a sinking feeling. Maybe Audrey was right, and Kate had lied to him. He went to the employee area, which was full of head-tall stacks of plastic yellow interlocking shelves on wheels, loaded with bread and produce and boxes.

"And I was going to call in sick today," Audrey said, trailing him. "You're not even on the schedule."

Michael didn't answer her implicit question. They were there to get help. In the employee area, someone had opened a bottle of lemonade and left it on the free food table with paper cups and an open bag of house brand chips. Usually there was more food than this: manufacturer's samples, unopened returns that they couldn't sell, or merchandise that had been damaged but wasn't worth throwing out. Sometimes the free food was all he ate on a given day at work. The best was Odwalla Day, when the Odwalla driver came in with new product and took all of the soon-to-expire juice and smoothies off the shelf. Michael poured two cups of the lemonade and handed one to Audrey. It wasn't very cold, but it was at least wet. He helped himself to a handful of chips. He was aware that he hadn't yet eaten that day.

He went into the office, expecting Kate would be there. The only person in the room was their captain, TJ's parlance for manager. Darren sat with his feet on the desk, talking into the phone. The employee schedule usually hung above the aging copy machine, inside the office life preserver, but it wasn't there. Michael hadn't noticed, until he'd started work there, that TJ's had a nautical theme: captains, first mates, bells, life preservers and oars on the walls, even the Hawaiian shirts. Michael lifted the lid on the copy machine, and found the schedule, face down.

Kate wasn't scheduled, just as Audrey had said. She had lied. Or maybe she'd been mistaken. Where was she, then? Cameron was supposed to work this afternoon, too; Audrey was right. Michael ducked out before Darren could notice him. Privately, the crew called him Fearless Leader. Michael had come up with the name, a *Rocky & Bullwinkle* reference. He'd grown up watching the show on videocassette. Some of his coworkers were old enough that they'd seen it the first time around.

Michael drank from his cup and then refilled it, realizing he was thirsty. He itched to get somewhere safe. Somewhere defensible.

If only someone he knew owned guns. With the waiting period in California, you couldn't buy one the same day. He supposed he could go to a shooting range and steal one. He suspected that the guys who ran a shooting range would be armed, and that would therefore be a bad idea. The closest range he knew of was in Marin. It would take an hour or more to get there, even if he could get a car. He felt defenseless. Shopping carts wouldn't be much of a weapon once the zombies came.

People bustled in and out of the swinging doors, moving stuff around just like a normal day. He ought to tell them. But tell them what? Michael looked for someone to approach. Jordan was pricing supplements on a flat-top cart. He was a cool guy, well muscled. Audrey was already flirting with Jordan, one hand on her hip.

"Baby, what it do?" Jordan said. "Aren't you early?"

"NGNCNF, what up?" Audrey said. "At least *someone* around here keeps track of my comings and goings. New Guy, Not Cool, Not Funny, you are my friend."

"I'm not the new guy anymore, hon," he said. He saw Michael. "Mike-O, you all right? You look hella bad." Jordan clicked the pricing gun, applying the labels with a practiced gesture. Fish oil, multivitamins, and the gummy bears that served as kids' vitamins. The company was supposed to be coming out with an adult version.

"I have had better days, to be honest," Michael said. He wanted to say something like, "Kettle, this is pot," just to be mean, but he thought better of it.

"What are you doing here, then?" Jordan said.

Interrupted, Audrey wandered off, probably to sit in the break room with whoever was there. Even though she claimed not to like their other coworkers, she enjoyed getting the gossip from them. She took pleasure in hearing who had hooked up with whom, and who had broken up with whom. It felt like high school to Michael, and he tried to avoid it.

Michael leaned on Jordan's cart. "Jordan, man, you know what a zombie is, right? You've seen movies." When Jordan nodded, Michael gave him a short version of the previous night's events. He emphasized how heroic Kate had been. After a moment, Jordan stopped working. He held the price gun as if it were a weapon.

"Sexy zombies are, like, done already. It's past April Fool's," Jordan said. Michael gripped the cart. Several of them had tried to convince Jordan, on April Fool's Day, that the Price Fairy had declared a ten percent discount on store-brand pills. Jordan had to redo at least an hour's work. They'd had to buy him a few beers at Cato's, just to make it up to him. It had been funny at the time.

"OK." Jordan said. "If I believe you, and I'm not pretending that I do, what do you want to do about it?"

"See, the thing is," Michael told him about the hospital, and the security guard, and how his wallet and phone were in his car, towed to a lot somewhere.

"Why don't you call the number and get it back?"

"There's no *time*. Car's nothing to be proud of. And it's not like I have a lot of money stashed away. Cash is what it'll come down to, cash and moveable goods. That's why I came here. We gotta go somewhere safe. Somewhere defensible. Like an armory, somewhere inaccessible, with weapons and food and not too many people. I mean, we have food here. We could use that as barter to get to safety. Like to an island or something."

"You're crazy, first." Jordan said. He priced a few bottles of gummy bears. "Why not stay here? Not that I adore work, but where better to weather an apocalypse than a grocery store?"

Michael gave him some reasons. Sure, there was food, but the building's doors weren't secure. And the place was full of people, customers and crew who might turn into zombies at any moment from some hidden bite. Everyone who looked healthy was a potential time bomb. There were at least three factors in finding a safe place, he decided as he talked. Defensibility from the outside threat, minimal crowds, and resources.

Jordan nodded, as if he believed. "What about IKEA, then?" he said. "Think about it. Two entrances, one at the front, one at the back. Barricade both of them." He was talking about the IKEA in Emeryville, the next town north. "Everything important is up-stairs. Lots of furniture that can be used as secondary blockades. Some food. Lots of things that can be used as weapons. Little house structures where we can set up camps."

Michael considered, then shook his head. "You've seen *Dawn of the Dead*. Zombies can go up an escalator."

"Not if we shut it down."

Perhaps Jordan had a point. Or he was just making fun of Michael.

"And all of the people who are already there, how do we know that they might not themselves be zombies?" Michael said. "That's the real problem. They don't necessarily turn right away. It has to do with how bad the bite is. Plus I think that women can hold out longer. Maybe it's chemical. Hormones or something."

Jordan tucked his long hair behind his ears. He was an attractive guy, which was surely why Audrey liked him. "You wanna know how to make a whore moan? Don't pay her."

Michael smiled, to be polite.

"Sorry. Cheap but topical."

"Nothing wrong with cheap and topical. Some of the smoothest things in my life fit that description."

Fearless Leader emerged from the office. "Cameron's a no-show," he said. "Tried calling him, but it went to voicemail. Mike, what are you doing here? Feeling shiftless? Want to pick up some hours?"

"No, just stopped by to say hi." He didn't like when people called him Mike. That was a kid's name.

"Don't waste Jordan's time, then, son." He went back into the office. A chair sighed from his weight.

"You're not going to tell Fearless Leader?" Jordan asked.

"Tell him what, exactly?"

"I guess you're right. Besides, he already *is* a zombie. He does everything exactly the way corporate wants it, and you know that the more money he can save by not giving us raises, the more money he gets. We're slaving away here, and he's on vacation and shit."

"You're exactly right." It was a conversation that happened regularly, and probably Jordan's attempt to return to safe ground.

"Bet you that if that door locked, he'd be watching porn on the computer, the scurvy wench," Jordan said.

"He's not smart enough to find it." Michael didn't correct Jordan on his gender slurs; if you could call a guy a bitch, surely you could call him a wench.

"Not smart enough to find porn on the Internet?" Jordan laughed. "That's what the Internet was *invented* for. He probably couldn't find his nose on his own face."

"You call that a face?" Michael said. He stopped. It was too easy to play along. "So what it do?" he said. "Are you up for this?"

"What about everyone here? Are we going to leave them in the dark?" Jordan shook his head.

"If there's anyone you trust, you can tell them. Bring them along. You have a car, right?"

"Yeah, but it's a two-seater. Glorified grocery shelf in the back, though a person will fit if they're reasonably bendy. It was a prezzie from my mom when I graduated with my liberal arts BA from Cal last year. My do-you-want-fries-with-that degree. Instead of MacDoodle's, I come running up front when the bell tolls because Candy can't remember what the cat cookies cost. So are we going back to your place, or what?"

"No, my place is no good. Too many windows." He was a little jealous that Jordan had a degree and was wasting his time working the stock room. If *he* had a degree, he'd be working in an office somewhere, making decent money, thirty grand a year with weekends off, even if it was the Michael Scott Doodad Company and he fell miserably in love with the receptionist. "So it's you, and me, and Audrey." He knew that Audrey was a point in his favor. Everyone liked her.

"IKEA?" Jordan asked.

"Too many people." He was about to ask Jordan what his own place was like. Then he thought about how he'd felt trapped in the bathroom that morning, with zombies in the bedrooms and Audrey and Cameron in the kitchen. The ceiling vent. The prisoners at Alcatraz who'd tunneled out. "Say zombies are real," he said. "They probably can't swim, at least not past the riptide. What about an island? What about Alcatraz? Not a lot of resources, but it's defensible as hell. And it'll be empty after the last ferry comes back to the mainland."

"I like it. That ferry costs like forty bucks or something, though." He clicked his price gun.

"We're not going to take the ferry. Too crowded. We'll have to hijack a boat or something." He said it as if he did it regularly, just for fun. He knew about ropes and knots; that had to be worth something. He should be able to figure it out. Hotwiring might not even be necessary, not that he knew how. Probably someone would have left their keys under the seat.

"Got a buddy who has a boat off Treasure Island, come to think of it," Jordan said. "Only fits four, I think. It's little, has to stick close to the shore, but I think we can take it to the island."

Michael nodded. "That's cool. I was thinking we could steal a boat if we had to, but it'd be better if we could do it honest." Jordan seemed like he was up for it, and since Jordan might be his last chance, that was a good thing. "I'll be right back," he said.

"You not going to tell anyone, then?" Jordan priced his index finger.

Michael shrugged. He should tell Barry-with-the-eyebrows, and Cindy, the older woman who always made extra food for crew when she did product demos, and Michelle, the OSHA-says-don't-do-this poster child who was so tiny that she had to climb onto the edge of the hip-height freezer of tamales and enchiladas in order to restock the chocolate on the shelf above it, and a dozen other people. He should tell all of the crew, regardless of whether he liked them. He should tell the customers, even if they started panicking. Or laughing. It might be the difference between life and death.

"So you're in, then?" Michael said to break the silence.

"I'm off at six. And I gotta finish this, or the Price Fairy's going to kick my ass."

He understood that Jordan was telling him to get lost so that he could bust through his work. Michael looked at the clock. It was after five. He could gather some supplies, and they could get out of there before any of the ticking time bombs went off. Maybe.

"OK. I'm going to assemble a few things. Then we should go." He was trusting Jordan, and he didn't like it.

Michael wanted to collect some supplies, but he couldn't take anything off the floor, where the customers were, because that might get him in trouble. He needed food and maybe some booze. Both would be necessary in the long run, for trade as well as for their own use. He went through the backstock, eyeing the labels. He'd have to sneak out the back; after some suspicion of thefts, the captains were supposed to look through everyone's bags before they left. Most shift captains would just wave employees through, or glance at their things, but if Fearless Leader was there, he insisted on doing it himself. He was meticulous about checking all of the pockets of people's bags. Kate had bragged about putting her tampons near the top of her bag, trying to embarrass him. She hadn't even been trying to steal anything; said she'd wanted to make a point about privacy. Michael admired her for that. According to her, he'd let her through with a cursory look. Michael missed Kate, missed how ballsy she was. Wherever she was, whatever reasons she'd had to lie to him, maybe it didn't matter. If he could forgive Audrey, he could forgive Kate.

Michael decided that since he wasn't working that day, the regular rules wouldn't apply. He'd leave through the receiving door. If he got himself fired, he could get another job. Sure, TJ's was pretty cushy, as retail went, thirty-five hours a week, starting at ten dollars an hour with regular raises, plus health insurance after 90 days, but he could work at Walmart with the toothless, tattooed, heavily made-up white trash if he had to.

He found an empty box. Wine was too heavy, not enough return on investment. He settled for a few bottles of hooch. He didn't take the store-branded 18-year-old Macallan single malt, though he could have, but a few bottles of bottom-shelf stuff in plastic bottles. Less likely to break than glass, and after the third drink, you didn't taste it anyway. He looked for shelf-stable food, something that would transport well. He disregarded tuna, though it was compact and a good source of protein, because he didn't have a can opener. He considered pasta and rice, but those had to be boiled. Then he found a case of Indian food in the silver envelopes. That would work. He assembled a box of his favorites, Matter Paneer, and chickpeas with tomato sauce. Worse came to worst, you didn't even have to heat this stuff up. You didn't need a can opener, or a plate. You could tear the foil packages open and squeeze it into your mouth. It was a fair combination of calories and water, without being too heavy. He filled a cardboard box, adding a few bottles of water, though he was pretty sure that Alcatraz had water fountains, and threw in a package of crackers. He left enough space to close the box. It didn't seem like enough stuff, but it was what he could carry, especially if Jordan had a two-seater. He left the box on the floor by the receiving door, which was open. That seemed like a bad idea, to leave open a door so large that you could drive a truck through it. Michael felt guilty about his coworkers working away, unaware. He couldn't be responsible for everyone, he told himself.

Michael went to the break room to get Audrey. She wasn't there. That wasn't good. He shouldn't have let her out of his sight. On instinct, he checked the punch clock. Her card had been punched in. She must have borrowed a uniform. Someone would have an extra Hawaiian shirt in their locker, and would be happy to loan it to her in exchange for some unnamed favor later. He walked through the store, dodging shopping carts and customers. He helped himself to a little paper cup of coffee from the silver urn, and a sample of pad thai and a plastic fork from the demo counter. Cindy looked up from plating food into the paper cups. She was friendly, and for some reason she liked serving food and talking with customers.

"Hiya doing, Mike? Shopping today?"

"Sort of, yeah." He swallowed the pad thai, which stuck in his throat. The coffee was too hot. "Today's a really weird day," he said. They were surrounded by customers, which made him nervous.

Cindy gave him a sympathetic look, and proffered more of the pad thai. "You look like you've seen a ghost, hon," she said.

He spotted Audrey in the meat section, shelving chicken. "'Scuse me," he managed to say. He made his way over to Audrey. She wore a Hawaiian shirt that was way too large, and a nametag that said "Jorge." That guy hadn't worked there for months. She smiled. Her pupils were the same size, but her smile was larger than the situation called for. She thought she was being funny by going to work. This was all a joke, for his benefit.

"Honey, what are you doing?" he asked. He grabbed her wrist, and she dropped the chicken she was holding. It fell into the beef section.

"What does it look like, dairy?" she asked. She was trying to hold onto her smile. As if to remind him that this is just another normal day at work, making jokes and moving products. "I swear, you're a weird dude."

"How did you get here?" he whispered. He held onto her wrist. She looked pained. He loosened his grip. "I mean, to Trader Joe's. Do you remember this morning? Do you remember last night?" He realized that he was trying to break her. Force her to understand what was going on. She wasn't smiling any more. He might have pushed her too far. She'd be useless if she went back to being psychotic, and if she started crying it would be worse. They'd never get out of there. "Never mind, honey, just, please," he said, trying to sound soothing. "Don't think about it. Don't worry about it. Look, there was a mistake in the schedule, and you're not supposed to work today. So, to celebrate, we're going to go on a little trip. Come with me."

She stood. Perhaps she was humoring him, but she let him lead her into the back of the store. He found Jordan pricing.

"You're an ass, Mike, you know?" Jordan, in his work shirt,

smelled like he'd been working all day. He held his price gun with
the righteous wrath of the Price Fairy.

Michael nodded in agreement. He had his box of stuff by the
door. He had Audrey. It wasn't nearly enough. He needed to call
Kate. At least find out where she was. He wished he could touch
her. "I just have to make a quick call before we boogie. Hang out
with Aud while I do it?" He held out Audrey's arm, and Jordan
took it from him.

"You have to make an announcement," Jordan said. "Tell everyone what's happening. Or we're going without you. I mean it."

Michael went into the office, which was at least empty. Fearless
Leader had gone elsewhere. He picked up the phone, conscious of
Jordan and Audrey watching him. He felt like a hostage. The worst
part was that Jordan was right. He hit the nine key, and then the
speakerphone button. He was going to lose his job for this. He'd
fantasized about making so many inappropriate announcements
during his time at TJ's. None of them, oddly enough, concerned
zombies.

"Attention, Trader Joe's customers and crew. Attention everyone,
please." He cleared his throat. He had no idea what to say. "This
is not a joke. It has come to my attention that the walking dead
are among us. I mean, they're not exactly dead, and they do other
things than just walking. They will bite you, for example. Whether
or not you want them to. And you *don't* want them to. There will
be blood. You will turn into one of them, and bite your friends
and family, and also people you don't like. You won't necessarily
turn into one of them immediately. It might take hours. Anyone
here might have been bitten. I highly suggest you proceed home,
in an orderly fashion, board up your windows, lock your doors,
and check the news for further instructions. Keep in mind that
zombies obey whips. If you encounter any, the best thing to do
is to tie them up. Gags are probably good, too. Lock them in a
room, and don't let them out. There's no reason to kill them. I
have faith that they can recover. This is not a joke. I really wish
it were. My jokes are normally better than this." He hung up. His

hand was shaking. He looked at Jordan.

"I guess that's all right. I'd have done it, but I really don't like public speaking. Plus, it's your responsibility. Your zombies, man."

"Speaking of, I just have to make a quick phone call." Michael pointed at the door. "Do you mind?"

Jordan shook his head. "Not at all." He sat in one of the chairs, and Audrey sat in the other.

Michael would get no privacy. He picked up the phone, then realized that he couldn't remember Kate's cell number. He hadn't memorized a number since he'd gotten his first cell phone. He found the crew directory, a coffee-stained printout in a drawer underneath a hardened starfish. He dialed.

chapter thirteen

Kate answered her phone, even though she usually screened
calls from work. Probably they wanted her to pick up a
shift because someone had called in sick. She'd arranged
her schedule that week so she'd have the day after the party to recover. But she was ready to talk with anyone who cared to call.

"Kate, it's me." Michael's voice. It gave her the chills. She sat
down on the floor, hard.

"Where are you?" she said, then realized that that was a dumb
question. "You didn't answer your phone. I thought you were
dead!"

"What? No, I'm at work, and you're not." He sounded irri-
tated.

Shit, she had told him that she'd be at work. "The house is on
fire," she said. She was close to crying. He *wasn't* dead. "I mean,
was on fire. It's out now. The firemen are standing around talking about the size of their penises." She probably shouldn't have
said that last bit. It wasn't going to make him believe her. She
couldn't help herself from making jokes. It was the only way to
hold off tears.

"You're shitting me," he said.

She tried to think. "There's a long story explaining where I
was and why I'm not there, and the main point is that—" There
was so much to say. He'd never believe about the Zeppelin. She

wished she'd told him about Walter. Maybe then he'd believe her. "I mean, I think the fire is out. The fire department is there. That's the truth. I'm at a neighbor's house."

"Look, I don't have much time. Audrey and I are here at TJ's, with Jordan, and we're about to bug out and go to Alcatraz. You want a ride?"

She was touched that he asked. "I'm *not* shitting you. I went out, before, and it's a long story that you won't believe anyway, and I'm sorry that I lied about it, but there were zombies. We barely got out alive. And the house was really on fire, when we got back. I went in all Rambo-style, trying to get you out. I thought you were still in there."

"Who's *we*?"

"Um, this guy I know." She stood, feeling shaky, and turned on the cold water tap in the kitchen sink. She didn't want Trevin to overhear. "Seriously, I was on a date. No one you know. He's a dick. I'm done. I'm never going to see him again. I mean, he's nice enough, but—" This might be her last chance to talk with Michael. There was so much to say.

"Well, I went back to the house after dropping you off, and Audrey and I barely got away. They're all zombies, Kate. Oh, God. It was terrible." His voice dropped to a whisper. "It's my fault for leaving," he said.

By which he meant it was her fault for making him go. For not staying with him and fixing things. "Oh, no." She tried to process what he was saying. "Alcatraz? The Rock?"

"It's defensible. Especially if you're telling me that the house is burned down."

"It's not burned down, not exactly."

There was a pause. "Oh, fuck. Shit, shit. I thought I'd put out that fire your belly dancer friend started, before Audrey and I had to run."

"I thought you said they'd all been zombified? *What* fire?"

"That doesn't mean they're actually *dead*. She was smoking a cigarette, and she dropped it on the carpet. I thought I'd put it out. Fuck."

"Yes, they *are*. Shit, Michael, you have to come to terms with that. They're dead. You wouldn't believe what I've seen. What I've done." Her voice broke. He must be wrong. There was no way the zombies were still alive. No one could recover from that. "It's my fault. I should never have left."

"Yeah, well. They're *not* dead. Why would they be drinking and smoking and dancing and shit if they were dead? It's like they return to what they know. Never mind. Believe this. Audrey was acting all concussed, so I took her to the hospital, and this zombie comes into the waiting room. From *inside* the hospital. Audrey and I get out, but when I try to go back and, like, tell someone about the whip thing, because it worked with Cameron, you re-member, the security guard drives an ambulance in front of the door. Total Gestapo shit."

"And the whole waiting room full of people was just shut up with everyone inside?" Kate tried to understand. "And that wasn't the Gestapo, that was something Roman. About a church burn-ing down full of people, with locked doors. For all we know, the fire department *started* the fire, like some *Fahrenheit 451* shit. A neighbor could have called because they saw zombies inside."

He was quiet for a second. "Was anyone still there, when you went in?"

"I told you, I don't know. I got pulled out by a fireman because I was about to pass out from smoke inhalation. That's how much I care about you." She realized what she'd just said. "And our friends. This is real, isn't it? If they're at the hospital, this has to be real."

"So where are you, exactly?"

"At a neighbor's house. This kid, Trevin, he's cool. He gets it. We might be safe here, even. You could come here if you wanted. Or come get us. Or I could come get you. I—" She didn't want to tell him she needed him. But she didn't trust anyone else enough to tell them she was infected. Michael would be able to handle it. He'd be able to tie her up. "And why didn't you answer your cell?"

"Long story. I'm a dumbass. Don't have my phone right now.

Or my car."

"I have keys—"

"Shit, I gotta go," he said. He hung up.

Kate was rattled. She started to call back, then stopped. There was no new information she could give them; no way she could help. She called anyway. They should at least figure out if he would come and get her and Trevin, or if they should meet somewhere else. The phone rang. No one answered. She called again. No one answered.

She turned off the tap. The crud on the dishes was softening. She picked up a bowl that had probably contained pasta. She threw it down on the floor, and the shattering noise was a balm. She did it again, with another bowl. It was hard enough losing her friends the first time around. Michael and Audrey were still alive. Who knew what was going to happen to them now?

"You OK?" Trevin called from the living room.

She was embarrassed to be caught in her tantrum. She wiped her eyes and went into the living room. Trevin was sitting on the couch. The TV was on, and he was changing channels. "I'm a klutz," she apologized. "Was trying to be helpful, doing dishes."

"Who was on the phone, your mom?"

"Friend of mine," she said. "He knows about zombies. He's freaked out."

"Someone else from the Zeppelin?"

"Not exactly. No. But I should call my mom, you're right. Excuse me." She left the room, then came back. "Do you have any guns here, by the way?"

"Um, no. My mom says that the whole Second Amendment thing is misinterpreted. A free militia was about the states having armies, in case they had to fight the gizmet, for taxes or whatever."

"Kismet?" She struggled to pay attention. She wouldn't think about Michael.

"Government. Gizmet for short. Family slang." He looked so scrawny, sitting on the couch. He'd turned the TV to CNN, which was showing an excerpt from a football game.

Kate nodded. She was thinking about kismet and karma. Whatever that meant. They had to do with one's own deeds, and how they were punished or rewarded. Maybe she'd come back in another life as an animal, after this. Or a bug. A really ugly one that had no friends and was always hungry. She dialed her parents' house, a number she knew by heart.

"Hello?" Her mother's voice was so familiar. This was the woman who'd taken care of her since before her memory began. It was two hours later there; early evening already, and her folks would be home.

"Mom? It's me."

"Hi, honey. I recognized the 510 area code, and figured it was you. How's California?"

"Not great," she said. Nickel dime, that was what the deejays on the hip hop stations called Oakland. She went into the kitchen, conscious of Trevin in earshot. She sat at the kitchen table, then stood and looked through the cupboards. "You won't believe me, and that's OK, but you have to know that I'm not high, and I'm not drunk, or crazy. OK?"

"Honey? Hold on a sec, your dad's home." Her parents would each pick up a phone when she called, which always made her suspect that neither of them wanted to face her alone. It was a silly thing to think; they were raised back when long distance still cost something greater than minutes on a cell phone plan. It'd take less time if she explained everything once, anyway.

"Hi, kitten," Dad said. He sounded tired, as he always did.

"Mom. Dad. It's good to hear your voices. I miss you." She found a dusty bottle of Jack behind the good china. There was an inch left. She drank from the bottle.

"We miss you too," Dad said. He often spoke for both of them.

Kate took a breath. It wasn't going to get any easier to say if she put it off. "OK, so, you have to listen to me and believe me here. You're going to think I'm crazy, but I'm not. I swear. Zombies are real. I've personally been in contact with several of them. I won't tell you what happened; there's not enough time. But I'm safe, at least for now. They're not movie zombies, not really, but they're definitely dead, and they're out for brains. Or just flesh. They're ravenous. It started last night."

"Kate?" Dad said.

She tried to explain. Nothing she could say would come close to making someone else understand what she'd been through. She couldn't tell her parents about the sex, so she skipped over it. She talked about Jamie, and the Zeppelin, and the women, skating around her relationship with Walter. Her parents were in the Midwest. For all they knew, Zeppelins were common in California.

They were quiet, after she'd finished.

"Are you OK?" Kate asked. "Um, how's things there?"

"Fair to midland, as per normal," Dad said. "Your brother's got a new puppy. I raised hell, but he threatened to move out and quit school. So, now we have a new puppy."

"No zombies?" She was disturbed at their reaction, as if they could just talk around whatever Kate said. Pretend it wasn't happening. That was so Midwestern. Probably it wasn't a coincidence that it was the Chicago news bureau that made famous that quote about "If your mother says she loves you, check it out!"

"The news hasn't covered it at all," she said, "though there's something on BoingBoing, online. If you Google it, you'll find it." Her parents, though reasonably hip for being middle-aged, weren't up on blogs. "I just wanted to warn you. Tell you I love you."

"Love you too, hon. The puppy's name is Shazam," Mom said, not skipping a beat. "It's a black retriever. Really cute. You should hear your brother, like a new mom, talking about putting down the puppy for a nap. Giving him soft food."

"It's like training for having a baby," Dad said.

"Or a girlfriend," Mom added.

"Except you don't really have to put them down for naps."

"That just happens naturally."

They were at it again. There was nothing worse than hearing your parents flirting. Except for when they were doing it while they weren't listening to something important you were telling them.

"That was part of the deal for him getting a dog—that he would take care of it, and clean up after it," Dad said. "We haven't had a dog in years. It reminds me of Jonah, back when you were little, remember? Anyway, they're going to a training class starting next week. Mostly, I think, to teach your brother how to train him."

"Dad. Mom. I want you to stay inside. Maybe this is contained to the Bay Area, whatever's causing it, but I'm worried about you."

"Katie," Dad said. She could tell he was trying to be careful. Dad was a little more likely to believe her. "Maybe you should take some time off of work, or something. I could send you some money."

"No, that's not what I want. If I did, I'd just ask. I want you and Mom and Jake to be safe. Stay inside. Maybe it's just a Bay Area thing, but you know how fast the swine flu traveled. Is he home?"

"No, he's at the gym. The puppy's here. Want to say hi?"

She didn't have time to protest. Kate listened to silence. "Shit-breath, listen," she said into what was presumably the dog's ear. She didn't care if her mom, on the other phone, heard her swear. "Bark a lot, and bite the zombies." Then she imagined a zombie dog. Maybe the infection would go the other way, if a zombie were bitten. "Strike that," she said. "Just bark a lot. Look big."

"He's a cutie," Dad said. "You should see his paws."

"Humor me and stay inside for a few days," she said. "And check out the website. BoingBoing. I have my phone with me. Call if anything happens. And I love you. I gotta go." She listened to their love yous and goodbyes, then hung up. She felt lost. It was hopeless. Maybe she should have told them about the fire. They'd believe that, but it would press buttons that she didn't want to press; the fire in the trailer where they'd lived a decade before she was born. Stuff was replaceable, but trauma lasted.

She turned off the kitchen tap. "You OK in there?" she called.

"As rain." Trevin was looking out the window. "Kate?"

"Is it raining? I can't hear it." She went to look. She closed her eyes, counted to three, and looked again. A dude was walking past the house. Slowly. He raised his head, as if scenting the air. Could zombies smell? He paused, looking at the house. At that distance, she couldn't tell whether his eyes were white. But his movements were awkward. He had to be one of them. Or else he was drunk, and you didn't tend to get wandering drunks in this neighborhood, so far uphill. She closed the curtain. "It's starting already," she said. She wasn't sure she was up for it again. At least it wasn't one of her friends. "Stay away from the window. Don't worry, they don't move fast. I don't think it's a big deal if there's only one of them. Just give me a few minutes. I gotta make another phone call," she said. "Life or death, you know? My brother. Then we can go."

"Go? Where?"

"Or we can stay," she said. "I don't know how much you know about zombies. I don't even know that what I know is accurate." She talked through her logic about how hiding in the house only led to hiding in the basement, and there wasn't one. Out there, they might stand a chance.

Trevin shrugged. Teenagers could be so expressive. "How do you know Alcatraz is safe?" he asked.

"Because my friend Michael and I did the tour there not long ago, and it's totally defensible."

"OK. I'm in."

"Cool. Would you pack some stuff?" she said. "A change of clothes for both of us. Money. Maybe a few sleeping bags, if you have them, or blankets. We need to be able to carry everything on our backs."

"All right." He left the room.

"A belt for both of us," she called after him. "I mean, for each of us. I'll sort through this emergency kit." She hoped she wasn't making a mistake in taking him away. Packing would at least give him something to do. She didn't want him to feel useless.

Boredom was the worst, especially during an emergency. They were just waiting. Sitting ducky. Waddling around the house. Still, they were safe, for now.

She scrolled through her recent calls until she found Jacob's number. She dialed it on the house phone. Even if his skinny ass was pumping iron at the gym, maybe he'd answer.

"Hullo?" Her brother's voice was unmistakable. He always sounded like he was just about to smile. She was relieved that he'd answered. People were talking in the background, but he could have been at a bar or a really loud library for all that meant.

"Hi. It's me."

"Hi, dork-face," he said. "I'm at the gym with Erik. He says hi." One thing their parents didn't know about Jacob was that he had a boyfriend. Jake was still in the closet, despite her encouragement; he thought that as long as he was in school and living at home, he had to keep it secret so the parental units wouldn't kick him out. She'd known since they were kids, and he'd finally come out to her a year ago. Erik wasn't out either, and she got the sense that the boys were one another's life rafts. She didn't know if other siblings talked about this stuff; she and Jake never discussed sex, but they talked about their relationships. She had to tell him she'd broken it off with Walter, but there were more important things to say.

"Hi back. Listen—" She gave him a quick account of the Zeppelin ride. Every time she told it, it got shorter. She was skipping over important details. For the first time, she included the part about the two women in the bathroom hooking up before one started eating the other. When she'd told the story to Trevin and her parents, she only told the part about them turning into zombies. She hadn't told anyone about what she'd had to do, after. Phone cradled between her neck and shoulder while she talked, she sat at the computer and Googled Alcatraz. The first link that wasn't an ad was the site that booked tickets for the ferry. She and Michael had gone just after Christmas, when they'd both had some extra money. The ferry was the only way to get there. The last boat left at 3:55. She looked at the clock in the computer's system tray. It was way past then already. There were no night tours tonight. She wondered how exactly Michael was planning on getting to the island.

"Wow," Jacob said when she stopped. "No shit?"

"No shit." She was starting to feel the shot of Jack. She wanted another already. But she needed to drive. She told Jacob about the previous evening. Without going into detail, she allowed that she had hooked up with Jamie, and had fooled around with Michael. And Walter, the next day. While she talked, she went back into the kitchen, still holding the phone against her shoulder. She put the mess of the emergency kit back into the box, careful of the broken dishes on the floor. She'd sweep later. Or never. If there were zombies wandering around, it wouldn't matter if there was a little mess. She took the box to the table. She sat, sorting through the stuff while she talked.

"That's really wacky," Jacob said when she'd finished. "Doesn't sound like you at all. I mean, the hooking up. Not passing judgment on hooking up; you just don't seem to do it that much. I know you'd be able to handle zombies. But those women in the bathroom? The pink-haired zombie going after the flight attendant? Something weird is happening."

"I know, right? *Thank* you." She was glad he thought so. Finally someone believed her, and more than that, understood her. "That's not what this is about. I mean, Jamie's *hot*. Anyone would be lucky to hook up with her. It's not that I wouldn't have done it, under other circumstances. Maybe."

"You've never talked about women before." His voice was gentle, chiding.

"I don't know what came over me. I just, I couldn't help myself. You know when you're really attracted to someone, and you know it's a bad idea, but you can't help yourself? When they're so funny and clever and sexy that you just want to lean in and see what it feels like to kiss them? Or they make a move, and you're so startled, even though you suspected it might happen and maybe even wanted it to happen, that you don't say no?" She found a package of hand-warmers in the mess. They were still bendy: still good. She set them aside. "It was kind of like that."

"I know exactly. Your IQ drops like forty points when you're around them. And then you come across them again, weeks or months after things went bad, and you have no idea what you saw in them in the first place. Except that they'd had good timing. I can't tell you how many times I've started to fall for some dumb closeted twink, just because of the way he looked at me. You can smell how desperately horny they are, and sometimes, just being wanted is enough."

"Touché, my sweet closeted bro." She worried about Jacob being safe. Getting his heart broken, or, worse, getting some sexually transmitted infection from an ill-advised tumble. Everything snapped into place then. Jacob had explained why she was being so stupid. Hooking up with Jamie, and Michael. Leaving the next day to see Walter. He'd explained the women fucking in the bathroom. Jamie kissing her last night. If she really was infected, that meant she wasn't entirely responsible for her bad decisions. It was the zombie bug spreading itself. It didn't make her feel much better.

"You've heard of Cupid's Disease?" he asked. "It sounds just like that."

"Um, no."

"There's this article by A.R. Luria, or maybe it's Oliver Sacks, I get them confused. Anyway, this old woman comes into the doc's office saying that she's suddenly gotten really flirty and jokey. Like, her friends are complaining about it. And she thinks it's syphilis because she worked in a brothel when she was a teenager and had it, and it went away and now decades later it's coming back. The doc thinks about it and agrees and says he'll treat it, and it turns out she's right and it *is* syphilis. But see, the thing is that the woman *likes* who she is now. She doesn't want to go back to who she was before. But fortunately for her the damage is done. The part of her brain that controlled her inhibitions was gone. So she gets treated and goes home. My point is that—"

"This is what's happening," Kate said. "But it's not syphilis. I think it's transmitted by saliva. Did I say that part?"

"Oh, no." He was a smart cookie. He understood. "Are you sure?"

"I haven't kissed anyone. Not since Jamie. And, um, I think I would have noticed if she'd been bitten. She did get kissed by this homeless-looking guy, that must have been how this all started. I don't know how long it takes, if I am infected. Jamie took a few hours, and it's already been almost a day."

He burst into tears. She knew that sound.

"Jacob—" She felt terrible. "Jake. Hey, here's a dumb question. Any zombies there? Anything weird on the news? You'd have said something already, I'm sure, and not just let me flap on about it."

"No."

"Hey, suck it up, baby brother. Listen, I don't have much time." She hated being short with him.

He sniffed, reining himself in. Having a good cry was one of his hobbies.

"I tried telling Mom and Dad, at least some of it. They aren't very good at listening. Promise me you'll be safe. Get yourself a whip. Or anything that can make a whip noise. An iPhone or whatever. There's whip apps. I'm serious. Take Erik with you, and go home. Be ready to go to the basement. If you can get a gun, that's probably not a bad idea. I'm guessing you'll hear about this on the news soon. Then you'll know what to do."

"I guess so," he said. He blew his nose. Trust Jacob to have a tissue, even at the gym. Or maybe just a towel.

"I'm not trying to out you, but you know that now might be a good time to tell them. There's lots of other stuff to talk about. And you could just Netflix some movies for a few days, until all of this blows over. For all I know, it's localized to the Bay Area."

"It won't *stay* there. What about Erik's family? What about all our friends? I can't just *not* tell them."

Jacob was a better person than she was. "If I were you, I'd tell them to come over. To bring food and drink and blankets and whips. Tell them you're having an End of the World party, or something. And keep an eye on them. But take my advice with some salt. *My* friends are all zombies already. Except for Michael and Audrey, and this kid I met, Trevin. I gotta go, hon. Be ready to board up the windows. We're headed to the Rock. Love you."

He squeaked. She hung up the phone. She cried then, not caring if Trevin heard.

chapter fourteen

Michael found himself being lectured by Fearless Leader. Darren had stormed into the back room, mustard on the front of his Hawaiian shirt. Michael surmised that he'd been across the street having a sandwich at the café, which was the only reason why he hadn't been on top of Michael before the announcement was over. Someone must have called him. He was angrier than Michael had ever seen him. He was actually dripping sweat. Jordan and Audrey slunk out of the office.

"—can't believe you would do something like that. People are freaking out. I'm losing customers. It's pandemonium out there."

"Weapons-grade pandemonium, I bet," Michael said. "Other people are probably buying more stuff, at least." He thought about just walking out, but he hadn't been fired yet. That meant he had to stay there and listen. Usually he liked his job. Now he was losing faith that things would ever go back to normal. He understood that the bridge was burning. He might as well cross it.

"I quit, sorry," he said. He walked past his ex-boss.

Darren grabbed Michael's collar.

Michael prepared himself to be struck. When it didn't happen, he shrugged off the other man's grip. Without a word, he left. His box was still by the back door. His friends weren't.

"Mike!" Jordan came running up. He was out of breath.

"Something's wrong, dude. Come check it out."

"Fuck." Michael hurried after Jordan, slipping his belt off as he ran. He wanted to have something weapon-like in his hands. He wished he had a whip. A whip worked by moving so fast through the air that it created a little sonic boom. Belts didn't do that. Then he remembered that he could double the belt, and pull both ends together, to make a cracking sound.

Jordan led him to the demo counter. Behind it, Cindy was bracing herself on the counter, her head down and her hair hanging over her face. Sandra, a dark-haired girl, had a hand on her shoulder. "You all right, Cee Cee?" she was saying.

"Get away from her!" Michael said. "Sandra!" A crowd was gathering, customers and crewmembers. Michael fought his way to the front.

He was too late. Cindy embraced Sandra. Sandra patted Cindy's back, the way you do when you want someone to let go. Cindy put her mouth on Sandra's neck. Sandra screamed. She fainted.

Cindy watched her fall. Her eyes were white. Blood dripped onto her Hawaiian shirt. Cindy knelt.

Customers and crew were screaming. The crowd backed up, holding their shopping carts. Several people ran away, clutching kids or groceries. There was the clatter of coffee cans falling to the floor. Shouts echoed throughout the building.

Michael grabbed a shopping cart from an old man. There was no time to apologize. He shoved the cart against the double swinging door that separated the demo kitchen from the rest of the store. He got a second cart, took the toddler out of the kid seat and handed it to the woman who held out her arms. The kid was crying. Everyone was yelling and pointing, as if you might miss the zombie if you weren't paying attention. Michael rammed the second cart against the first, barricading the walkway to the demo area.

Michael cracked his belt. "Hold still," he called. "Cindy. Stand up. Let go. Let go."

She looked at him, angry. Or maybe just hungry. She obeyed, but licked her lips. He was relieved that the whip sound had worked.

So it wasn't the motion of holding it above your head. It had to be the wavelength of the sound.

"Get out, everyone," he said, looking at the crowd. "Go home. Get yourself a whip, or a belt. The zombies obey simple verbal instructions, if you can make a whip noise like I did. Board up your windows. Watch out." Some people ran. Others seemed frozen.

"Jordan, listen," Michael said. "She's totally safe as long as I've got this. You gotta climb over the barricade and secure her hands."

"Dude, this is so not cool," Jordan said. He turned to look at the mobs that were throwing canned goods into their carts. The front door, open beyond it. As of yet, the only zombie was behind the counter. "Why can't *you* do this?" he asked. "You're the one with experience." His expression said, "I'm sorry for not believing you before, but I might not forgive you for making me do this, if I manage to live."

"I have to do what I'm doing. You're doing great. Just take her hands, hold them behind her back. We have to secure her. Put her in a bathroom. Something with a door that locks."

Jordan looked at the front door again. Then he climbed over the carts into the demo area. He moved slowly towards Cindy, holding his hands up, as if showing her that he wasn't armed.

Cindy sized him up, but stayed still. Sandra was lying on the floor mat, bleeding, eyes closed. She didn't move. Michael was pretty sure she was breathing.

"Take Cindy's hands, behind her back." Michael held his belt, ready to snap it.

Jordan held Cindy's hands behind her back. He touched her as if she would explode at any minute.

"Grab her tight. Don't be a sissy," Michael said. He ignored the comments and questions of the remaining crew and customers.

Jordan followed instructions almost as well as the zombie.

Michael went to the door on the other side of the demo area, and gripped the handle. This was where it was going to be dangerous. He tried to think. The bathrooms had locks, but like everything else they locked from the inside. That would still be an improvement over the demo area. Then it occurred to him.

"We're going to the Box," he said. He opened the door. Jordan emerged with Cindy, walking her like a convict through the store. Customers and crew followed as they went through the double doors to the employee area.

"What are you people still doing here?" Michael called. "Fucking go *home* already. Leave. You'll be next." A few peeled off, looking embarrassed. There was a thudding sound. The woman with the toddler had grabbed a wine bottle and was trying to break it on the demo counter to make a weapon.

"Next," Cindy said. She was looking at the toddler. Maybe kids tasted better. Fewer toxins. Softer flesh. Just like lamb.

"No," Michael said. He looked around. Audrey was nowhere to be seen. Jordan looked ready to piss himself. Time was burning away. The roads would soon be a post-apocalyptic mess. They weren't going to make it to Alcatraz if they didn't get a move on. Michael opened the door to the walk-in cooler.

Jordan pushed Cindy inside. Cindy stumbled and fell to her knees among the stacked groceries.

"Sorry!" Jordan called.

They closed the door. The trucks came early in the morning; thankfully, the crew had had time to unload enough stock to make space for a person inside the Box. A few people.

"Now we get Sandra," Michael said.

"Sandra didn't *do* anything," Jordan said. "You put her in there, and Cindy will eat her. We saw it. We need to get her to the hospital. Both of them."

"You remember what I said about the hospital," Michael said.

"It's one thing to put a zombie in the Box," Jordan said. "But not Sandra. Not with the zombie."

"I'll do it." Michael handed the belt to Jordan. "Here, just snap it if anything happens. I don't know if the person who holds the whip has to be the one giving instructions, but you might have to say something. Just like I did. You can do it." He went into the demo area through the door. Jordan followed.

"Shouldn't we call the police or something?" a man said. It was the old dude whose cart Michael had taken.

"Be my guest," Michael said. "Didn't do a hell of a lot of good when I tried. Personally, I think you should get out of here and go somewhere safe."

Sandra was lying on the floor. Girls could hold out longer, Michael knew. Who knew how long Cindy had held out? Still, he was afraid. Sandra could turn at any moment. Cindy had been on shift for at least a few hours, probably. And he'd liked Sandra. She seemed cool, was in art college. She did the hand-lettered signs and cashiered. Everyone had to work the register.

He dragged Sandra, his hands under her armpits. She opened her eyes. She fought against him. Blood ran down her neck.

"Mike?" she said. "Help me."

"Sorry I have to do this," he said. "I'm really sorry." He felt awful. He reminded himself of all of the people that would be affected if another zombie were allowed to run loose. How much more quickly it would spread. All of the people, out there, who might be bitten. Mothers and old dudes and cute girls; customers and crew and even people who'd never be caught dead shopping at Trader Joe's.

"Sandra! You OK? Let her up. What are you guys doing?" Audrey hadn't been there a moment ago. Her work shirt hung almost to her knees, covering the skirt of her vinyl dress. She was chewing something. It crunched. She dropped shards of it onto the floor and brushed her hand on her shirt, leaving a smear of salt and oil.

Michael stopped pulling Sandra along the floor. He didn't let her go. "Audrey, you know what I'm doing. I'm cleaning up the mess." Sandra felt so real in his arms. Just heavy enough to be a person. He dragged her through the swinging doors into the employee area. Crew and customers followed.

"I'm not anyone's mess," Sandra said. "Is Cindy OK?" She touched the bite on her neck, then looked at her fingers. "I'm bleeding. Oh, God."

"I mean it, you have to go," Michael said, trying to look each one of the customers and crewmembers in the eye. "Get the fuck out already! This could happen to any one of you. You have to be ready. This place isn't safe." A few crewmembers were still watching. Others were going to their lockers, extracting car keys and sweatshirts, exclaiming to one another. Jordan was looking at one girl, Gracie, as if he had something to say.

"Man, I need you," Michael said. "Stay with me. Pay attention. Talk to her when we've got this done."

"Fucker," Audrey said. She hit Michael, hard. "I remember perfectly well, and this is *not* the right thing to do."

Startled, he let go of Sandra. Her head made a sound like a ripe melon when it hit the floor. Not that they carried ripe melons. She hadn't fallen very far. Her face crumpled.

"Sorry," he called. He looked around, embarrassed. The remaining crewmembers were starting to back away. People he knew and liked, and ought to have warned earlier. Finally they were starting to get that something was really wrong. No one believed until they'd seen the zombies, and maybe not even then. Yet people believed so much stuff that they'd never see. History, for example.

Audrey knelt. "Oh, honey," she said. She touched Sandra's cheek.

Michael bit his lip. He had to keep going. Put Sandra in the Box. He knew what would happen otherwise. But for now she was still a person. Still someone he knew and liked. She deserved to be treated as such.

"Oh," Sandra said. She stiffened. "*Oh*." She sat up and touched Audrey's cheek. Audrey held her hand there. Sandra moved towards Audrey. They embraced, sitting on the floor. They both smelled amazingly good. Michael knew he ought to stop them. But if girls could hold out longer, maybe they weren't in much danger yet.

"Honey, it'll be OK," Audrey said, stroking the other girl's hair. "We'll take care of you." There was such tenderness between them. He'd always wanted to see two girls together. In person, not just in porn. They would be so tender. He thought of Kate and the girl who'd turned into a zombie. It had been so much funnier when he'd thought it was a joke. Makeup. Everyone knew zombies weren't real. He wished Kate were there. She wouldn't let him get maudlin.

Sandra moaned in pain. "Something's. Ow."

Michael knelt. "Audrey, we gotta go." He grabbed for her hand.

Audrey screamed.

Sandra's mouth was on her neck. It had happened fast. In what felt like an instant, Audrey was on the floor. Sandra was on top of her.

Michael grabbed Sandra, yanking her away. Audrey's neck was bloody. It was too late. Everything he did would always be too late. And now he was going to lose Audrey. The one person he'd saved so far.

Michael held Sandra's hands in his own, trying to keep her out of biting range. He looked around for Jordan; found him talking to Gracie.

"Jordan, fucking. Snap the belt. I mean, whip." He didn't know how much the zombies understood.

Jordan fumbled the belt into position and snapped it. "Stop," he mumbled. "Stop," he said clearly.

Sandra held still. She looked peeved.

Audrey was crying. Michael wished she would faint. It would make things easier. Jordan opened the door to the Box. Michael threw Sandra in. He heard her fall. He shut the door. The latch clicked. He would get very drunk, he promised himself. Vomiting ugly drunk. If he managed to live. He would forget all of this.

He went to Audrey. "I'm so sorry," he said. He kissed Audrey's hand, avoiding the blood. "I'm so sorry," he said. There was nothing else to say. He wiped his face on his sleeve.

She didn't fight him. It would have been better if she had. "I'm sorry, too," she said. "It's all my fault. I let Cameron out. This morning. Our friends. My fault. I just thought—I don't know what I was thinking. All of it. I don't know why I lied. I didn't want you to think I was stupid. I didn't want to admit it was my fault."

Michael helped Audrey stand. He hugged her. The logical part of his brain screamed for him to get away. She felt so good. Beautiful. Damaged. He didn't want to let go. He picked her up. She wrapped her legs around him. She kissed his earlobe. He wanted to push her against a wall. Fuck her. He loved it when girls wrapped their legs around him. He felt wanted. Needed. He imagined what it might be like, when she bit him. It would hurt, for a moment, and then there would be nothingness. Simple hunger. Desire. Release.

"Dude," Jordan said. "What are you doing?"

Michael was tired of people asking him that. Audrey stuck her tongue in his ear. He was vaguely embarrassed, not sure of the last time he'd cleaned out the wax. But she didn't seem to mind. His knees grew weak. He braced Audrey against the wall. He was hard. He pushed against her. She giggled. He did it again. She moaned. It was a nice moan. Just for him. They had been good together, for the short time they had been together. He'd heard a song like that, on the radio. Something like, "Not that the thrill is gone / but that another thrill came along." He thought of Kate. He thought of nipples. Taut, hard nipples. The sounds that girls made.

"Dude. Come on already," Jordan said.

Michael wasn't listening. He didn't feel it, the first time. Jordan hit him, on his back. Then again. Michael let go of Audrey. She landed with a thump, on her ass. Now he'd dropped two girls in the space of something like ten minutes. That had to be a new Trader Joe's record.

"Dammit, man," he said. He turned back to Audrey.

"Aaah," she said. She closed her eyes. "Just give me a minute," she said. She made her pain noise a few more times, then stopped and opened her eyes. "That one's going to fester. Imagine turning me over, taking down my pants, and seeing this fat bruise on my ass. It'll purple up. I'd still want you. I don't care if it hurts. I like it like that. I learned that from you, Michael." She knew what she was doing to him. That only made it better. They'd experimented, back in the day, with talking dirty. She'd been giggling then.

"Fuck me. Right here. Let them watch. No condom. What have we got to lose?"

Michael held out a hand to her. She took it. He understood something. Attraction was in a direct relationship with guilt. Everyone felt a little sheepish, after. He kissed Audrey's hand. Her collar was dark with blood. He would come in a few thrusts. And then, after. She'd get hers. And he'd be free.

He could hear people yelling, but he paid it no mind. He pulled Audrey to her feet. He could almost taste her lipstick. It wouldn't matter that she wasn't Kate.

"Come on, man," Jordan said. He pulled at Michael's elbow. "Let her go, or I'm leaving you now."

Audrey touched Michael's cheek. He leaned into her hand. They stood like that for a while. Then Audrey took a step back.

"He's right," she said in a small voice. "I gotta go." She turned away, stopping only to grab the bar they used for moving around cases of milk. It was a few feet long, made of metal, and the hook on the end wasn't sharp but you could do some damage to someone if you really tried.

Jordan stood by the door to the Box. "I'm so sorry, Audrey," he said.

She smiled at him, but didn't say anything.

"You ready?"

Audrey took a breath, then nodded. He opened the door, and she went inside. Jordan shut the door. The cooler locked from the outside. It was relatively soundproof.

Michael fell to his knees. Now he'd have bruises, too. That felt right. People were saying things, asking if he was OK, but he didn't have an answer. He was torn. Audrey was still alive. Maybe they could save her. Maybe she could save herself. He buried his face in his hands, waiting for his feelings to ebb. They always did, in time. He stayed like that for a while, not caring who was watching.

"C'mon, Mike," Jordan said. "She's TOS." He held out a hand. Then he wiped it on his jeans, and held it out again.

"She's not Temporarily Out of Stock, dude," Michael said. "Not yet." Michael wiped his own hand on his shirt. He took Jordan's hand. He stood.

"She's gone, dude," Jordan said.

"Let's just go."

There was nothing else to do. There were still people alive. Maybe Kate was among them.

Without talking, they left through the receiving door. Michael walked as if in a dream. He barely remembered his box of food. Gracie came with them. She held hands with Jordan. Other people followed.

"Drive yourselves," Jordan called. "I don't have room, sorry. Go somewhere safe. We're going to Alcatraz. Get some supplies and come along, or go home and board up the windows. Lay in some supplies. Be careful. Don't get sentimental."

Jordan unlocked his car. He looked agitated. He took Michael's box and put it in the trunk. "Can't save everyone," Jordan said.

Without being asked, Michael climbed into the back of the car. The upholstery and air were warm and dusty from sitting in the sun. He settled as best he could in the tiny space. Jordan hadn't been kidding about the grocery shelf. Jordan closed the trunk. For all Michael knew, both of them could turn into zombies at any minute. He couldn't bring himself to be concerned. Everyone he cared about was going to be ripped away from him. One by one. The universe was testing how strong he was. Or how stupid. He felt as wrung out as if he'd just taken a long sauna. He'd done that with Kate and a few of their friends recently, at a place down the street from Cato's that rented sauna rooms by the hour. At first they'd been talking and making jokes, like always, but as the heat set in, they grew quiet. In the shower, after, he was too exhausted to stand. It was nearly a spiritual experience.

Jordan got into the car. He started the engine, and rolled down the windows. There was a welcome whiff of breeze. Gracie got in, and shut the door.

"You OK?" Jordan was asking.

"Um." Gracie was trembling. "You know." She screamed then, covering her mouth with her hand. "I mean, what the fuck?"

"Exactly my sentiment," Jordan said. He looked in the rearview mirror, catching Michael's eye. "I didn't believe you, you know." He repeated to Gracie what Michael had said about zombies. She asked questions.

After a while, they fell silent.

"I'd better call some people," Jordan said.

Michael found his voice. "Sure, just don't get pulled over for driving while talking. It's like a twenty-dollar ticket, but we don't have the time to waste. We're already heading towards sunset."

"I know a dude, on Treasure Island. With a boat. We'll be cool." He put a hand on Gracie's thigh. "All cool, I promise."

Michael looked out the window while Jordan drove. Promising was dangerous. Jordan spoke on the phone, describing the zombies at TJ's. In Jordan's version, Jordan was the brave one. Michael didn't care. He focused on not listening. Gracie was busily texting with someone, or several someones. Life was all about the transmission of information. Whether or not anyone understood you. That was why zombies didn't talk much.

Michael knew he ought to call his own family. His dad had left when he was a baby; his mom he called on her birthday, his birthday, and Christmas. She'd moved recently, and he hadn't memorized her new phone number. He had no siblings. He felt old, as if everyone he cared about was long gone.

The car smelled of plastic and sweat, but the air had at least started to cool. They got on the freeway, and then onto the bridge. Jordan drove in the right lane. Michael looked out at the beginnings of the second Bay Bridge, which had been under construction for longer than anyone could remember. The Bay Bridge itself was constantly under repair; hardly big enough for the amount of traffic it saw every day. The only reason the bridge had two levels was because the bottom one used to be for trains. He didn't know when it had been changed over for cars. But it made sense; people going to San Francisco got the top view of clouds and ocean. People going to Oakland, on the bottom, got the hemmed-in Morlock view. The bridge toll was four dollars, not that he had any money. He hoped Jordan did, or Gracie. You had to pay to get into San Francisco. It was free to come back.

He looked out the window while they waited in line. Cars sat, bumper to bumper, easing forward inch by inch. They finally reached the window. Jordan paid the toll, still talking on his phone. He drove forward, slowly, while they waited for the meter. One car per green light, per lane. Michael looked out at the other cars. There weren't any zombies, not yet. This had to be normal traffic. The lights turned, and turned. Red, green, red, green. After a while, it was green for them. Jordan drove.

"Hello?" Jordan said. He looked at his phone. "Must be between towers. Damn." He pocketed it, and put on the radio. He flicked between drive-time deejay blather and rock music. Rock was a dying art. Hip hop had already taken over as popular music. Aside from country, which nobody liked, it was the only narrative form of music left.

Looking out the window, Michael's head cleared. They'd left without Kate. She might be expecting them to come get her. "Guys, we gotta go back. We gotta get Kate," he said.

"I can't turn around now," Jordan said. "I'm on the bridge."

Michael knew Jordan was right. "Fuck."

"Sorry, dude."

"It's not you that I'm mad at," he lied. Mostly he was angry with himself, though. Maybe she'd meet them there.

Bridge traffic was sluggish. Windows open, moving at walking speed, they'd be a perfect target. Stuck in the backseat, Michael knew he wouldn't be able to get out. He was a little surprised to find that he still cared.

They passed a parked car. The driver wasn't inside. Whenever a car stopped on the bridge, flat tire or out of gas, they'd bring a big truck, like a snowplow, and push you to the other end of the bridge. Only then could you get a tow truck. There was an equation there, stalled traffic and lots of people delayed versus one car getting fucked up. Being humiliated as everyone saw you being pushed off the bridge. The one person always lost. It had happened to a school friend; his car died and he couldn't get it started. He'd sat on the hood, smoking a cigarette and waiting while people honked and made faces.

"Fuck, guys. Empty car over there," Michael said.

"Maybe it broke down," Gracie said.

"But where's the driver?"

"Maybe he got a ride with someone else? Or she," Gracie said. She didn't sound like she was convinced.

"We're going to see the shamblers soon."

"Coming back from the dead?" Gracie asked.

"No, corpses would have the decency to lie still. It's the zombies I'm worried about."

Then he heard the scream. There was a stopped car ahead. The driver's window was rolled down. A heavy woman leaned in, as if she were a prostitute giving a john a taste of the goods. There were sirens, far away.

"Roll up the windows," Michael said. "Now."

Jordan did. The car grew warm. Michael's shirt was damp. Jordan tuned the radio to NPR. The traffic report mentioned stalled cars on the bridge. The announcer warned that people should stay in their cars; callers had been describing a violent woman. Maybe psychotic. The announcer mentioned other instances of people becoming violent. In the Oakland hills. At the Kaiser hospital. Somewhere in Berkeley.

"Jesus, it's hot," Jordan said.

"Shut up." Michael wanted to hit him. "*Listen.*" He'd missed something. The announcer was telling people to go home and stay there.

It had never occurred to Michael to call NPR. The media still hadn't figured out that everything was connected. As if zombie-ism was merely a few psychotic episodes. Something to do with the water, or people's meds, or the moon. People wouldn't believe that zombies were real, so it made sense that the news wouldn't cover it for fear of being taken as a joke. Or if the media knew, maybe they were sitting on it, lest people started rioting. Someone needed to tell them it was real.

"Jordan, man, lemme use your phone."

"No service."

"Radio just said that people are calling in from the bridge." He was starting to feel panicky. "Give me the damn phone. I have to try."

"Oh, I *do* have service," Jordan exclaimed, looking at the phone. "Shit, I didn't a second ago. I need to call—"

"Give me the damn phone." Michael grabbed it from Jordan's hand.

"Dude, give it back!"

"Not on your life."

"Gracie, give me your phone. I need it." Jordan groped for Gracie's phone.

She held it away from him. "*I* need my phone," she said. They wrestled for it while Jordan drove. The car swerved. Someone honked. Jordan let go of Gracie's phone.

Michael unlocked the keypad. He tried to think of who might have his mom's number. He didn't know any of their numbers, either. He thought of calling Kate. Instead, he dialed information and got the number for the local NPR station. The needs of the many outweighed the needs of the few. Spock had been right. Michael described the bridge situation to the woman who answered the phone. He explained about whips, and sound, and how it worked. He was rushing, afraid that the signal would cut out at any minute. "You need to tell your listeners," he said. "Zombies, whatever you want to call them, they're real. They obey whips. Snap a belt if you don't have a whip. I think they respond to the sound."

The other end of the phone was quiet. "Hello? *Hello?* Oh, fuck." He looked at the phone. It had dropped the call. He pressed the end call button and held it down, restarting the phone. No service. He wanted to hurl it through the window. He could hardly breathe, it was so hot.

"Doesn't this thing have AC?" he asked.

"Don't normally need it," Jordan said. "It died a few years ago."

Gracie was texting. Her phone kept vibrating with new messages.

"Give me your phone, Gracie," Michael said. "I need it."

"Not on your fracking life," she said. "I Twittered the zombie uprising, and then I told my whole address book what's up. I need to keep responding. I've got just enough signal to keep texting. You can't call from my phone because there's not enough service to call, but there's enough to text." She was scared, holding her phone with both hands. Maybe she was lying. Or maybe she was telling the truth.

Michael forced himself to sit back. He'd grown up in the Bay Area. Nearly everyone he knew was still around. How were Gracie's friends and family more important than his?

"We'll have service in a minute," Jordan said. "Once we get to the island. I'm sure there's a tower there."

They passed the stalled cars. Traffic picked up. Jordan rolled down the windows without asking. Michael's skin and lungs felt ready to burst. The cool, moving air was a balm. He counted his breaths. His shirt was soaked.

Jordan pulled off at Treasure Island. The exit was a hairpin turn. He seemed like he knew where he was going.

"It's around here somewhere," Jordan said. The island was devoid of traffic. It was beautiful out here. Quiet.

He was a good guy, Michael thought. He'd already saved Michael's life once today, and was trying to keep the three of them in the black. Michael thought of how close he'd been, with Audrey. He belonged with Audrey and Cindy and Sandra, cooling their heels in the walk-in, and it was only because of Jordan that he wasn't there.

"Here we go." Jordan pulled up at the marina. He parked the car. Gracie got out, and moved the seat up to make room for Michael.

"Thanks," he said. He handed Jordan his phone. It still didn't have service. He was embarrassed at their argument. He barely knew Gracie, for one thing. She was relatively new; he hadn't spent much time with her. It would make sense that she and Jordan, as the new kids, would have had something in common. Not that he'd been at TJ's very long. A few years. What had he been doing with his life?

Michael retrieved his box from the trunk. It didn't seem like enough food, and certainly not enough water. He decided to think about Treasure Island instead. It was small, only a mile or so, built out of dirt and rocks left over from when they dug a tunnel through Yerba Buena island to put in the Bay Bridge. The island was riddled with suburbs now. You had to get on the bridge to go anywhere. Or a boat. The BART train, which ran through a cement tube on the ocean floor, did not stop at the island.

The dock itself was small, only a few rows of boats. Any of them would do. Jordan kept walking past them. The whole place was eerily quiet.

"Is your friend going to meet us here?" Michael asked. Alcatraz wasn't far, at least. What would have been better, it occurred to him while he looked out at the boats, would be to get themselves a yacht, load it up with food and water, pilot it out to the middle of the ocean, and just wait out the storm. Your only enemy would be boredom, and if you brought some interesting friends and some books and games, you'd be OK. He wished he'd had the idea sooner, and that he had any way of making it happen. Surely other people would think to do that. After a while, when the supplies were dwindling, there would be pirate-style battles and raids. Rich people fighting rich people. Some of them might even have guns. There'd be ships where someone turned into a zombie, and their friends had to deal with it. Toss their friend overboard. Or they all end up being bitten, and then you'd have zombie ships. Drifting. Being raided by *nouveau* pirates that had 401(k)s and stock options and golf injuries.

"He said to go ahead," Jordan said. "He'll get a ride with someone else. I just worry about how he'll find the island."

"Dude, it's a *light*house," Michael said. "Brightest thing in the bay, all night long."

"Well, when you put it like that. Ah, here we are." He leaned down and started undoing a hitching knot.

"You're kidding," Michael said. He closed his eyes, then opened them. Jordan had picked the only paddleboat on the island. It was made of white plastic, and had two seats with bicycle pedals in the front, and a bench seat in the back. Michael had only seen paddleboats on lakes. Ponds. They might not work in more than three feet of water. "I should have just let Audrey bite me. I thought you said you had a *boat*."

"What's this, then, a turkey sandwich?" Jordan said. "Alcatraz is only like a mile away. We'll be there in no time. Lickety-split. Go ahead, it won't bite. Gracie, maybe you should sit up front with me."

"All right," she said. She was typing with both thumbs. "All those spin classes are about to pay off. We'll be going in circles with you trying to keep up with me."

Michael looked around at the other boats. The turkey sandwich thing had made him remember that he hadn't eaten that day, aside from a few mouthfuls. He didn't relish the thought of cold vegetables and cheese in curry sauce. He should have grabbed trail mix. The rest of his life was starting off on a bad note.

"We should just steal one of these other boats," he said. "Somebody's got to have left their keys in the ignition." He climbed into a few of them, checking under the seats. Nothing.

"And you can drive one of those?"

"How hard can it be? Mechanics do it."

Jordan climbed aboard the paddleboat. He held out a hand for Gracie. The boat bobbed from their weight. They sat. "Come on, then. Or not. Just untie us."

Michael stowed his box on the back of the paddleboat. He undid the knot, then climbed aboard and sat on the plastic bench. The boat sank on his side. He didn't want to be left alone. Moving forward was the only option. There was nothing left to go back to. He hoped that Kate would meet them at the island.

"Clear to go," he said. He held onto the grab bar. Jordan and Gracie started pedaling. What the hell were they thinking? This was ludicrous. They were all going to die. The bay was a murky greenish blue. He put his hand in. The water was cold. How deep was it? Too deep. They weren't wearing life jackets. He couldn't swim a mile, not in water this cold. He'd drown.

The breeze smelled of clean, salty air and dead fish. In the distance he could see the Oakland/Berkeley hills. His house was there somewhere. Burned down, according to Kate.

A man stood on the dock, his arms out. He wasn't waving.

"Jordan, is that him?" Michael asked. "Your friend?"

Jordan looked back. "My buddy's still at work."

The figure was joined by a few others. They walked strangely, as if their limbs weren't entirely under their control. Maybe on Treasure Island the zombies already ruled. That would explain why they hadn't seen any people, or even any traffic.

The zombies stepped into the water. Zombies couldn't swim, Michael surmised. But they could walk. He imagined zombies sinking to the ocean floor. Struggling against the current. The zombies would be nibbled at by fish, like those insane pedicures he'd heard about. The flesh-eating fish that would clean up rich people's feet, eating all of the dead skin. It was like applying maggots to a wound; they'd eat the dead and rotting parts, leaving the living. He was starting to think of zombies as being dead, as Kate had insisted. It made everything easier. And sadder. There would be no redemption.

"Where is he, then?" Michael asked.

"He can't answer his phone while he's at work. He knows people; if he wants to get a ride out, he can."

"Oh, OK." For all he knew, Jordan was lying about having a friend with a boat. It didn't matter. He looked to the shore. The figures had disappeared into the water. "It's just that I think we're being followed. No worries. They don't move fast."

"What do you mean?" Gracie asked.

"I mean, the walking dead." It sounded right, when he said it. "I think there's a few of them following us. Just to let you know. Not that I think they can catch us. Or that they know where we're going. Maybe they can swim, but we can move faster."

"We're headed to the prison island, yes?" Gracie said. "Jordan told me you knew people there. Ah, shit. Lost service." She pocketed her phone.

"Sort of. I think it's the right place to go. Defensible." He felt perversely glad that they were all without service now, and then felt guilty about it. He should be pedaling, not getting a free ride. As if that even mattered. He had greater things to feel bad about. He'd abandoned Kate, and Audrey had to be dead by now. She'd trusted him, too.

"If we're not careful, we'll be swept out to sea," he said. The tide felt like it was going out. "We have to go towards the right. The lighthouse tower. There's a dock on one side. I think it'll be the near side. The rest of it is steep rocks and cliff." He remembered that from the Alcatraz tour. The reason why the famous escapees didn't head for San Francisco, but towards Angel Island. Not only because they didn't want to be caught, but because the current between Alcatraz and San Francisco was so powerful. If this little boat was caught in it and pulled past the Golden Gate Bridge, they'd be lost. Sunburned, dying of thirst.

"So when is the last tour over on Alcatraz?" Jordan asked.

Michael felt a jolt of fear. He hadn't checked. "Sunset, I think," he said.

"You *think*?"

"You have a better idea, at this point?"

The sun was descending behind clouds and fog. Already the heat of the day was fading. It would be cold soon.

It started raining then. Cold, fat drops at first, and then the sky opened. Thunder sounded. Thunderstorms were rare in California. They were drenched within a few minutes.

chapter fifteen

Kate heard thunder. She wiped her face and blew her nose into a paper towel. She went to the window. It had started raining. The fire truck was gone, the street empty and dark.

Trevin came into the kitchen. He held two backpacks. "I didn't bring any of my school stuff, just some books and video games and batteries for my DS. And clothes, like you said."

Kate thought about arguing. They needed to bring essentials for survival, not comfort. "You can carry whatever you like," she said finally. He looked so young.

Trevin set the backpacks on the table. They were both little Jansports; she'd had one in high school. When the zipper broke, or the fabric started to tear, you could send it away to backpack camp, and it would come back repaired. She'd kept the same backpack for four years that way. Kate opened them both, and started shoving in first aid supplies, the flashlight, rope, handwarmers; things that looked useable from the emergency kit. Trevin sat across from her at the table.

"You doing all right?" Kate asked.

"I'm worried about my mom, and my brother. I called some of my friends, too, when I was packing. They didn't believe me." Trevin bit his lip. He was too manly to cry.

"OK, listen," Kate said. "So Jesus is walking through Nazareth, and he comes upon this big crowd. They're clustered around this chick crouched in the dirt, and they're going to stone her for a whore. 'Hold up,' Jesus says. They stop. 'Let the one among you who is without sin cast the first stone.' The people all look at one another. They think about it. Jeez has a point. They set down the rocks they're holding. Everyone's feeling spiritual and brotherly, asking Jesus and one another to forgive their sins. And then this huge rock comes from behind the crowd. Beans the chick, and she falls over, stone dead, so to speak. Jesus looks at where it had come from. 'I swear, mother, you can be so self-righteous some-times,' he says."

Trevin nodded soberly. Maybe she should have picked a different joke. "It was the Virgin Mary," she said. Jokes were no good once you had to explain them. At least he didn't look like he was going to cry. "You OK?" she asked. "Seriously? I was just trying to cheer you up."

"Yeah, I guess." He was working to sound brave.

"We don't have to go anywhere. We can stay here. Honestly, you can tell me to go away. You don't have to believe me." She stood and got the bottle of Jack from the cupboard. She took a swig. Then she offered it to Trevin. He took a healthy sip, then ran and spat it out in the sink.

"So I guess we should go," he said.

Kate patted the sets of keys in her pocket. "I'll go get the car, and bring it to the door."

"Who are you kidding? I saw the dude wandering around earlier. I'm going with you. Where is it?"

"In front of my house."

"It's raining," he said. "Lemme get some ponchos or something." He went into the living room and opened a closet.

"And water bottles?" she called after him.

"In the fridge."

When Trevin was out of sight, Kate drank the last sip of Jack from the bottle. She knew better, but it would be her last chance. Might take the edge off. She opened the refrigerator and found the water bottles. They were the little tiny ones, eight ounces. More of a fashion accessory than a storage device. Still, better than nothing. She stuffed a few of them into each bag. Then she drank from the kitchen tap, filling her belly.

"We should both pee," she said, walking past him to the bath-room. She washed her hands and face, after, and looked at herself in the mirror. Her skin was its normal color. No signs of zombie-ism. Mostly she just looked scared. She heard a toilet flush from inside the house, and took that as a signal. She put on a raincoat from the closet, and picked up the heavier backpack. She felt the whiskey taking effect. It helped.

"Trev, I gotta tell you something." They stood in the entryway; he wore his own raincoat and backpack. The keys were in her hand. She fought with herself. She had to say *something* now. Then she remembered Trevin drinking from the bottle, right after she had. She'd been so stupid. Maybe alcohol would kill the germs. Now she *couldn't* tell Trevin she thought she was infected without implying that she'd infected him. If saliva was really the vector.

"Remember that anyone can turn into a zombie, at any mo-ment," she said. "If it happens to me, you need to be able to deal with it. Brain me, or tie me up. You don't have any whips here? Take my phone; it'll do. The *Indiana Jones* app." She demonstrated, then made him show her he could do it.

"I have my learner's permit," he said. "How about I drive?"

"I could hug you." She clasped her arms around herself. Her raincoat made plastic noises when she moved. "I mean, are you OK to drive?" California had a zero tolerance policy towards mi-nors driving with a BAC of more that .01%. Friends of hers had gotten in serious trouble for drinking during high school. But surely the cops would be busy. She didn't want Trevin to change his mind about driving, mostly because she didn't want to turn into a zombie behind the wheel.

He took the keys. "You know where we're going, right?"

"Yeah, sort of. Get in car, go to water, find boat. The official ferry's done already, but it can't be that hard. My friend Michael's going to meet us there."

Trevin went to the computer and called up a map. He pointed. "Emeryville Marina, that looks like our best shot straight across to Alcatraz. Maybe we can rent a boat there."

"I have some cash," she said. "We can bribe someone to take us. Like the Native Americans who occupied Alcatraz after the prison was closed in the '60s and before it got turned into a national park. They'd arranged for a boat, but it didn't show, and so they bribed a fisherman."

"I got forty-eight bucks, counting that wet Jackson that guy left on the table."

"Ew. A wet Jackson sounds like a made-up sex act. Like a dirty Sanchez or something. 'Baby, come on over and I'll give you a wet Jackson. The shoes have been in the refrigerator since last night, and I got unsalted butter this time. Give me another chance!'"

Trevin laughed companionably. "How do you know Mr. Wet Jackson?"

"Long story," she said. If she'd had another shot or two, she'd be tempted to tell it. "He's kind of a trip." Walter's idea of kink was limited to oral sex; he was so vanilla that he didn't even like ass-play. He had always made sure she came first, though.

The street was quiet when they went outside, except for the rain. She led Trevin to Jamie's van. He unlocked the driver's side door and climbed in. She tried the handle on her side. It was still locked. The locks clicked. She glanced behind herself. The street was still empty. She pulled the handle again. It worked. She got into the car.

"This yours?" he asked.

In the daylight, Kate saw that there were photos taped to the dashboard. Women in coin bras and low-hipped skirts, their arms around one another. The coin bras, Jamie had explained once at class, dated back to some tribe in North Africa which had required the young women to go to the city and earn their dowries before they could come back home and marry. The women wore the money that they made, sewing it into their clothes, and the more coins a woman wore, the more talented and desirable she was. The women danced for money, of course, but they were also prostitutes. Knowing this did not stop modern women from wearing coin bras.

"A friend's," Kate said. "Mine's at the airport. Sort of. Long story, again." It was hard being in the car again, confronted with Jamie's personality. Her effects. There was a photo of Jamie with her arms around a Golden Retriever mix. It occurred to Kate that no one was going to take care of Jamie's dog.

She looked out of the window. "Thanks for driving," she said. The booze cushioned her headache, but didn't make her stomach feel any better.

"We might have nothing but time." He started the engine and took off the parking brake.

"Speak for yourself." She didn't mean to sound snappish. "Sorry. You just have to forgive me for being bitchy. I'm normally loads of fun."

"I bet."

"Hey, if we get through all of this, we'll hang. I'll get you drunk on some nice easy stuff. Peach brandy."

"We can invent the Wet Jackson," he said. "Maybe it's a drink."

"Yeah, scotch and olive juice. With cinnamon for garnish."

"Or a shoelace." He drove them down the hill with the ease of a resident. Things were quiet. Nobody was out. The traffic light on the corner was blinking red in every direction.

He drove onto the freeway. That was when it got bad. They passed stalled-out cars. People wandering around on the road, mindless. They saw a man embracing another man, *Dracula*-style. Half a mile later, a kid lay on the side of the freeway like roadkill. They heard screams. Other drivers looked horrified, but didn't roll down their windows or stop.

"Shit," Trevin said. "It's happening. It's really real."

"It's not too late to go back."

"Back to what, though? No basement." He drove. He knew where he was going. They reached the marina. He pulled in and parked the car. "You ready?"

"As rain." It was coming down hard. "This is really late in the season for rain."

"Weird," he agreed. "Oh, check it out." There was a woman crouched over a stroller. The child was shrieking. "Gross," Trevin said.

"It's what they do. Maybe it won't notice us. We'll have to move fast. See the gate?"

"The closed gate? With the barbed wire on top? Yeah."

"That's where we're going. We just need to wait for someone else to open it."

After a while, the gate opened, and a woman came out. She was moving fast, car keys in hand. Kate and Trevin opened their doors and ran. Kate's hair was soaked within a few steps, as were her borrowed shoes and jeans. She caught the door just before it closed, smashing her fingers. "Be careful out there," Kate called to the woman. She pointed to the zombie, who'd turned from its baby carriage at the commotion.

The woman who'd opened the gate turned around. "Fucking looters," she said. She turned away and started jogging.

Kate was stunned. "I'm not—"

Trevin grabbed Kate's arm. He pointed.

The zombie had gotten to her feet. She walked towards them, trying to decide which of them to eat first. She was still wearing most of a tracksuit. She grinned.

Kate opened the door. Pulled Trevin inside. Closed it. Pulled on the doorknob until she heard the latch snap into place.

The zombie stood on the other side of the gate, both hands reaching in through the metal bars next to the door. Her wrists and forearms were thin. A bone stuck out from one forearm, impeding her progress. She pushed the other arm in past the elbow. She was close enough that Kate could see her eye makeup. It must be the waterproof kind. Her chin and teeth were dark with blood. The child had stopped sobbing.

"Mama?" the zombie said. Her voice was like a truck on gravel.

Kate and Trevin backed away. She found herself holding Trevin's hand.

A car started. An engine revved, and tires crunched over pavement.

"We should have asked that woman for a ride," Trevin said.

Kate sneezed, turning her head so that she wouldn't spray over Trevin. The muscles in her left shoulder tensed, and stayed knotted. She was stunned by the pain. "Oh, ow," she said. She couldn't relax the muscle. Her shoulder wanted to hang out by her ear. She blinked at tears. Maybe this was what Walter had meant about wanting his chiropractor. She was too young for this.

"You all right? What happened?"

"Muscle spasm, I think. Gotta walk it off. Pick a boat." She couldn't see through the pain.

"How about that one?" Trevin stopped. He knocked at what looked like a door.

"We don't want any," a male voice called.

"You have to let us in," Trevin called. "Oh, shit." He held tight to Kate's hand. "Down there."

She wiped at tears and rain. A bearded figure in a raincoat was staggering towards them on the dock. His arm hung at an odd angle.

"The woman who let us in must have been running from him," Trevin said.

"Please," Kate called. She pounded on the door, then decided that might not be the right way to convince the occupant that they weren't dangerous. "We're just kids that need help," she said. "I swear. There's a crazy guy out here, and he's going to rape me." The lie came easily enough.

The door stayed closed. This is what it must have felt like to the people in the Zeppelin, on the other side of the bathroom door.

"I have cash," she said, lowering her voice. "About three hundred. It's yours if you let us in."

The door opened. The guy was younger than she'd expected, maybe early thirties. He wore a week's worth of beard. She preferred scruff to a clean shave; liked the way it tickled her cheek. He held a crowbar. He eyed both of them, then moved aside to let them in. He shut the door behind them.

"Thank you so much," Kate said. "You don't even know how freaked out we are. We're trying to get to Alcatraz." She stood, dripping on the floor. Rain thrummed on the ceiling, a metallic sound that reminded her of being a kid, falling asleep in the family car on long drives. They were in a houseboat, a single room with a fold-down bed. In the corner was a bathroom, its door open. It was smaller even than the one on the Zeppelin. There was a rack of presumably clean dishes sitting on the covered toilet; a shower head above it, and a drain built into the floor. The room smelled like unwashed hair.

"You just saved our lives," Kate added. The throbbing had moved from her shoulder to encompass her neck and upper back. She was afraid to stretch. It might make the pain worse.

"And the dude outside, that you said was after you?"

"Um, this is going to sound crazy."

"Zombies?"

"Yeah." It was a relief not to have to explain it all. "So that's why we need to go to Alcatraz. And, um, my name's Kate, and this is Trevin."

The guy looked them up and down. He dropped his crowbar. It clattered, and Kate tensed. Pain shot through her shoulder.

"Paul," he said. "And you are on the *Mary Celeste Big Pimpin'*. After my mother."

Kate understood that he was referring to the boat. And that he was trying to be friendly. "Ladies is pimps, too."

He smiled. "Thank you, Jay Z. Go on, take your rain gear off. Sit a minute while I make us some Model-T coffee and we can discuss the money. You have the choice of anything you want, so long as it's black." He folded down a table from the wall.

Kate did what he said. Trevin elbowed her when Paul's back

was turned. Thankfully, he hit her good side. She had a good side, now.

"I have it under control," she whispered, hoping that she did. "Let me do the talking." She resisted the urge to apologize. She'd put the kid into danger. They were lucky to be alive. "Just you on this ship?" she called.

"Too small for more than one. Don't you think?" He sat. "Coffee's a brewing."

"And time's a wasting," she wanted to say. "Thanks," she said instead. "It'll be good to warm up a bit." She was wet and cold. Her hair was dripping down her neck. Paul didn't offer them towels.

"About that money," he said. "Can I see it?"

Trevin started to move his hand. Kate nudged him with her knee, and he stopped. "I've got it," she said. "Just a second." She pulled the cash from her pocket and put it on the table. A pile of wet Jacksons. What Walter had given her, and what she'd taken from the emergency kit, was all she had. She might have had a five in her wallet but she didn't take it out. Five bucks wouldn't change anything. She felt the loss as Paul counted the cash, facing the bills as he went as if he'd been a cashier, too. Maybe money was useless already, or would be soon, but it was a bargaining chip she'd no longer have. Which was fine if it got them to safety.

"Cool," he said. "And you want to go to Alcatraz? Because of the zombies." He made it sound silly.

"Yeah," she said. In the movie of her life, this scene would be shot in black and white. She'd be the noir detective-type, off to the Rock to fix shit and kick ass. Not running for her life. Not in pain, or if she was, she'd be hurt from a real wound. Knives or bullets. Not a muscle spasm.

"You're lucky I have an engine. Just installed it, in my copious free time."

She understood that he was unemployed.

"That's the only reason I'll accept your generous offer." He pocketed the money. "So what do you kids like to do for fun?"

The coffee machine beeped. Kate was grateful. They were one

step closer to getting away. Paul made her nervous. He was a cipher. He was taking her money. But he had a sense of humor. They might have been friends, if she'd met him under different circumstances. She could imagine what it would be like to rub her face against his. She knew better, but knowing and feeling were different.

"I like to watch TV," she lied. "Especially reality shows. Also anything with food."

Paul smiled. He must know she was joking.

So she told the truth. "I like to go on hikes, and run. Novels. Movies. I take literature classes. I have parties from time to time." Trevin's leg was still tangible next to hers, like an anchor to the world. "I have a boyfriend," she added, not sure whether she meant Michael or Walter.

"You're in good shape." His gaze flicked from her eyes to her mouth to her tits. He stood, finally, and went to pour the coffee. "I used to date a girl looked like you. Best girl ever."

"My kid brother here, he plays video games," she said, pretending she hadn't heard. Maybe if Paul thought they were related, he wouldn't try anything.

He served coffee in three mugs. It was lousy, but it was hot. Kate warmed her hands on the mug. She vamped while they sat, talking about movies and TV. Paul seemed to expect it, and he chimed in a few times, agreeing or disagreeing. He didn't offer liquor, and she didn't ask.

She finished her coffee. She could feel the caffeine coursing through her. She wanted to stand, wanted to be moving. The tension in her shoulder grew tighter. Her eyes watered from the pain.

"So, Alcatraz?" she asked.

Paul didn't move. He touched Kate's hand. She pulled away after a moment.

"Dude," Trevin said. "We gotta go. I mean, thanks for the coffee and the rescue and stuff, but how about it?"

Paul laughed. "Kid's got some spunk." He patted Trevin's hand.

"He's good for you." Paul stood, and put on a raincoat. "Gotta untie. Just a second." He opened the door.

"Be careful," Kate said. "They're out there. I'm serious. Not funny."

He gave her the thumbs-up sign, then picked up the crowbar and showed it to her. The door shut behind him.

"I hope he dies out there," Trevin said. "He gives me the heebie jeebies."

"Shh. He won't die out there. He'll come back in here first, and then we'll die too."

"We could kick him out."

"Who's going to pilot the boat then, us?"

"We just stay here."

"And when they break the windows? What then?"

"I don't like him," Trevin said.

Paul came back in and closed the door. There was blood on the crowbar.

"OK, so, that rope's done for. Had to cut it with my knife. *Always* carry a knife," he said, gesturing with the crowbar towards the door.

Kate didn't know if that was advice or a threat. Not that a man holding a bloody crowbar needed to make a veiled threat.

"What happened out there?"

"Never you mind."

Maybe it had been the pirate-looking guy. "Were you bit?" she said. She knew she had to ask. She knew also that he might lie, if he knew anything about zombie stories.

"Hell, no. I'm too fast. Except for where it counts, sugar."

She looked away. She could see Alcatraz through a gap in the curtains. So close. She concentrated on looking unattractive. Maybe she could fart. Unless he was into that, somehow.

"Well, after I've gone through all that trouble," he said. "I guess we'd best go, then." The engine turned over with a rumble of diesel. He backed the boat out of the dock, through the rain. "You're lucky I'm as nice as I am," he said. He was shaking. He'd turned his back because he didn't want them to see it.

"I am, indeed." Kate took a breath. "Do you want to come with us? My friend says Alcatraz will be safe. Defensible." She had to shout over the motor.

Trevin elbowed her. Maybe she was making a mistake. "I mean, it's got no resources. Have to truck in water and food. It'll probably be cold and miserable."

"Yeah, no. You young people go for it. Not me. Ol' *Mary* and I are in it together. I've had her five years. She's stuck by me longer than any other girl ever has. That's not a comment about my mom."

Kate was relieved he'd said no. Mostly for Trevin's sake. Paul would probably be finc on his own. Not that he was her problem. "You might just want to stay in the water for a while," she ventured.

"What?"

"Nothing."

Paul put on some music. Early stuff, sounded like Run-DMC. He bobbed his head. The noise of the engine made conversation difficult, which was fine. She patted Trevin's knee, under the table. She looked out the window. The sky was dark. The light from the lighthouse was coming closer. Paul lit a cigarette. The smoke drifted through the cabin, calling up memories. Kate wrapped her hands around her empty coffee cup. It was cold. If she could just hold still, be calm, they'd be all right. Her shoulder hurt, way worse than her head. She started to feel seasick. She focused on breathing. *This will pass*, she told herself. Everything did, eventually. It would be worth it. She and Trevin would be at Alcatraz within a few minutes. They could set up camp in one of the buildings. Michael would be there already.

Paul pulled up to the dock. He got out, then came back in. "I'm not going to tie off. We're close enough. You can jump."

Kate retrieved her backpack and raincoat from the floor. She put them on. Trevin did the same. "Thanks, Paul," she said. "Much obliged."

Paul stood by the door, holding it open. He leaned in to kiss her. Kate turned her cheek. "I have a cold sore," she lied. "I'll look you up sometime."

He squeezed her ass. "No, you won't. I can tell." He smelled of smoke and yesterday's T-shirt. But the look he gave her made her feel like he understood. He'd been lied to before. This was nothing different.

She touched his cheek. His beard felt like she'd imagined.

"Let's go," Trevin said. Without waiting, he leapt over the black water to the dock. There was, mysteriously, a paddleboat tied to the far side, plus a rowboat. What kind of dumbass would take a paddleboat out on the Bay?

Kate jumped. Her shoulder and back and neck ached from the landing. She looked back and waved. "Thanks!" she called, hoping he could hear her over the engine. Paul closed the door. The *Mary Celeste Big Pimpin'* left in a cloud of diesel fumes.

"Well, that's that," Kate said. "A little lighter, cash-wise, but still intact. Let's go find a building with a roof. You got my phone still?"

He took it out. There was no service. "I'm really glad we're done with that guy. He's a total douche."

"You kids and your language. Do you even know what a douche *is*?"

They walked uphill, discussing it. The rain hadn't slowed down. Barbed wire topped the tall fence. It faced inward, guarding against prisoners. She tried the door of the gift shop at the bottom of the hill. It was locked. The place felt empty, but there were those boats. *Someone* was here. She noticed a staircase behind a building near where the tour started. It was fenced off, but the padlock was unlatched. This might be the staircase from which a girl fell, years ago: the daughter of one of the leaders of the Native American rebels. That would explain why it was fenced off. Kate had bought a book at this gift shop that said that the girl had probably been pushed, because other kids were jealous of the attention her family was getting.

"Let's try going up there," she said. "Get a look around

the island."

"Heya," a male voice called. "How *you* doin'?"

She hadn't heard them approach. If they could construct sentences, chances were that they weren't zombies. She turned at the waist, because it hurt too much to turn her head. Three figures in ponchos were standing on the walkway.

"Hey," she said.

"You looking for a safe place?" the same voice called. He came closer. In the sodium-yellow lighting his face was a swarm of shadows under his hood.

"That's why we're here," Kate said. Probably these guys weren't just being altruistic. "My bro and I, we've got some gear to share, in exchange. Looking for a friend of mine—of ours—guy named Michael? Kinda tall?"

"This is our island," the guy said. "We work here. Got a text from a bitch I know, and my buddies and I slipped the ferry back. Figure it's safer out here. What with the zombies, and all. You're here because of them, right? Is it crazy out there?"

Kate was relieved that she didn't have to explain the whole thing. Still, she didn't like his language. She didn't mind swearing, but that in the context he'd used it, *bitch* was derogatory. "I know, tell me about it," she said. "We saw a mother eating her kid like maybe an hour ago."

"See, I told you," the guy said to his friends.

"Yeah," Trevin said. "They're all over the East Bay."

"Is it safe here?" Kate asked. "I mean, I imagine all of the tourists went home already. My name's Kate, by the way."

"Trevin," Trevin said.

The leader of the boys stepped forward. He took down his hood. He was good-looking, clean shaven, short hair. His face was angular. He seemed like the kind of guy who was concerned with respect from other guys. The kind of guy who couldn't keep a job for long. She'd worked with his type before.

He smiled. "Katie," he said. "That's a nice name. You can call me Rob, and this is Will and Ray." He didn't indicate which was which.

"We've got a nice setup. Hot plate, blankets, out of the elements. We've been expecting the apocalypse for a while."

Kate made herself smile. If they had a safe, warm hangout, what were they doing traipsing around the island? "What kind of apocalypse?"

"What'cha got? Power outage, fire, earthquake, dirty bomb. People act the same, regardless. If there really are zombies, we're ready. And the Rock is the place to be."

"Are there a lot of people here yet?" she asked.

"No. You planning on throwing a party?"

"Oh. No. Just curious. That's cool."

"What about the boats?" Trevin asked.

Kate kicked his shoe. "How about we get out of the rain? Why are we just standing here?"

"What boats?" Ray asked.

"He just meant that, um, don't you normally have some boats docked, to get back and forth? Or do you just take the ferry?"

"Ferry," Ray said. "That's what I said. How did you guys get here?"

"Dropped off," Kate said.

"There anyone else tied up at the dock?" Rob asked.

"I don't remember seeing anyone," Kate said. Probably Michael wasn't even here. Probably he wasn't going to make it at all. He'd be gathering up a group, trying to save everyone, and the group lag would make it impossible to leave. Unless the paddleboat was him. That she could believe. "I'm going to go look for him."

"Why don't you come with us?" Rob said. "Get warm first. If he's here, chances are he's inside the main building anyway. Everything else is locked up snug."

"All right," Kate said. "Lay on, MacDuff."

"Who's that?"

"Sorry, old movie reference. Means 'after you.'" She knew it was Shakespeare, but these guys would think she was being a snob if she'd said so.

Rob led them to the main prison building. The island was

eerie at night. Inside the prison it was barely warmer than the
air outside, but at least it wasn't raining. They went in through
the showers, which were draped in plastic sheeting. Still under
construction, or restoration, or something. Signs in various languages gave information about the tour. They went up the cor-
rugated metal staircase, the steps rubbed smooth from the feet
of prisoners and tourists. Their footsteps echoed. Kate couldn't
help looking around. The place was so empty. She could feel the
presence of hundreds of angry men, locked away without hope.
Rob led them through the prison to the gift shop at the end. It
was a big facility. She remembered there being another gift shop
in the outbuildings; the island was big enough to support two of
them. Rob took a bottle of water from the shelf and drank.

"Dude, seriously," Will said. "The whole zombie thing? It's not
like *we've* seen one. We'll lose our jobs for sure if we trash the
place."

"Don't worry about it." Rob knocked over a display of books.
"This is what I've been waiting for." He took off his poncho.

"Do you have any whips?" Kate asked. "Because that's what you
really need." She took off her raincoat and sat on the carpet. It
was good to sit. The buzz from the coffee was already wearing off.
Trevin sat next to her. They were both dripping wet. She opened
her backpack and drank from one of her bottles of water. She
thought of offering the rest of it to Trevin, but caught herself in
time.

"Whips?" Rob asked.

She explained.

"Bitchin'," Rob said. "Some BDSM shit. That's pretty hot."

"Not at all, actually," Kate said. "In theory, maybe. Not in practice. There's a difference." She wanted to try to rub her aching
shoulder, then decided against it. She didn't want to give anyone
ideas.

Rob sat. "We have access to the gun cabinets. Shotguns, all that.
I'm not worried about protecting myself. And we can protect you,
if you want to stay with us." He flicked his gaze down, and up.

"You couldn't hope for someone better," Trevin said. "She knows everything you need to know. She's already saved my life a few times. You wouldn't believe what it's like out there. Zombies with bones showing, and they don't even care."

Kate looked at him. She'd nearly gotten him killed, several times. Maybe he was counting from the other direction. "I have personally killed," she stopped to count. "Two zombies. And subdued two more, by tying them up. You don't have to kill them."

"Two by two, we go to the Lord," Rob said. He laughed. "Baby, we should talk, just the two of us. Maybe you guys could go check out the island?"

Ray and Will looked at one another. Kate looked at each of them, willing them to say no.

"G'wan. I won't bite her." He laughed at his joke. Then he grew serious. "If there are other people who think like us, or like them, this place will be full by dawn. Probably full of unprepared people with," he dug into Kate's bag. "Handwarmers? You think that's what you needed?" He tossed the package onto the carpet. It did seem rather useless, now.

"We didn't have long to pack—" she said.

Rob talked over her. "Nevermind the resources. People can be cold and hungry and live just fine. What I'm worried about is having a refugee camp full of potential zombies. We don't know who will have been bitten, and how long it'll take for them to turn. I need to know what you know. I need to pick your *brains.*"

"You have a *prison,*" Kate said. "Even *I* can operate the doors on the cells. A ranger showed me, last time I was here. Three levers. You know. State of the art in 1933."

"1934," Will said.

"Whatever. So if you're serious about this, you lock people up in cells, and let them out after a couple of days, if they haven't turned into zombies. If they *do* turn, they're locked up. Nothing can happen."

"That means we'll have to lock you two up," Rob said. He looked boyish when he smiled.

"Go for it," Kate said. That would solve everything. "Seriously. You have no reason to trust anyone. Not us, not even each other."

The guys looked at one another. "We've been here all day."

"OK." Kate shrugged. It was better not to argue too much. "You don't know you're not infected. But still, let us prove that *we're* safe."

Rob stood. "You guys go outside. Bring anyone you find to the main prison and lock them up. Standard cells; don't use the isolation ones. I want to be able to see them."

"All right. Let's go." She shoved her things into her backpack, then stood.

"I need to talk to you first," Rob said. He put a hand on her shoulder.

She made a noise from the pain. "Sorry, muscle spasm. My whole back's on fire." She sat. That was what he wanted her to do.

"Well, that sucks." He turned to the guys. "Bring the kid with you. He can tell you what he knows, and she can tell me what she knows."

Trevin squeezed Kate's hand. "You'll be fine," she whispered to him. She let go. Their footsteps echoed as they left. She wished she were going with them. Rob was a little creepy. Still, she let them leave.

When they were alone, Rob sat back, cross-legged, leaning on his hands. "Tell me everything," he said. "Want some water?"

She accepted a bottle. "Well," she said. "Last night, my friends started turning into them." She told him mostly everything, the way she'd told her parents, skirting around the sex. He was a good listener, asking questions and making sympathetic faces. She grew calmer, sitting with him. She'd much rather have been trying to find Michael, but maybe she was better off staying in one place, so that he could find her.

Rob took her hand. Ran his fingers over the top of it. It felt nice.

She pulled her hand away. "I have a boyfriend," she said.

"I have a girlfriend," Rob said. They don't need to know." He grabbed her hand again. He brought it to his mouth and kissed her fingertips. "I want you," he said. "I like you."

She shook her head. "No," she said. "Let's go down to the prison floor. Put me in a cell. If I'm still cool in a few days, we can try this again." She stood.

Rob stood. "Honey, we can do this the easy way. You'll like it, I promise. Sit down, relax. Where were we?"

She was afraid of him then. Angry with herself for ignoring the signals. "I should go find Trevin. We can set up camp elsewhere. Leave you guys the gift shop. Hell, the whole main building. It's cool."

"Honey, don't play like that. You like me, I know you do. You wanted them to leave as much as I did."

"I'm on my period," she lied. "I have HIV."

He shook his head, smiling. "No, you don't." He pulled her to the floor. Her back sang out in pain. They sat among the displays of books and souvenir mugs. "I'm sorry I'm scaring you off. I don't mean to. Give me two minutes. I have a proposition," he said. "Seriously. There's going to be lots of big dudes here soon. You said as much; people will come here. People who understand about surviving at all costs. We'll protect you. Your brother, too. You'll be safe with us, I promise. I've seen so many movies about the apocalypse. Read every book I could get my hands on. I know how it works. I can handle it."

"I gotta go," she said.

He wouldn't let go of her hand. "Wait," he said. "I didn't want to do it this way; I'm not this kind of guy, but—" He uncovered a shotgun from the mess on the floor. "Up close, this'll blow your mind. Even your brother wouldn't recognize you. How about you take off those wet pants? Get warm? I swear I'm a good guy."

Kate froze. She was too scared to cry.

"Don't run," he said in a voice as gentle as Mister Rogers. "Don't make me do something we'll both regret. I know how the apocalypse works. I've read Max Brooks. You need a dude to take care of you when people resort to cannibalism. You'll like me, I swear. We just have to get to know one another a little bit."

She shook her head. Pain flared up through her shoulder and her neck. She should never have come here. It would have been better to be eaten by a zombie when she had the chance. Trevin was outside with the goons. He may as well be a hostage. Michael probably never made it to the island.

"OK, then," Rob said. "We'll be good for one another. I need you. I need you alive." He took her hand again, kissed it.

Was this what happened when society fell apart? She'd heard about the so-called paper-thin veneer of civilization. This guy was full of his own power, living his favorite movies and books. Convinced that the apocalypse was here, and all bets were off. But bad shit happened in books; it was why you kept reading. You'd get all attached to a character, and then they'd die. Maybe she'd turn into a zombie soon: maybe her pheromones were driving him mad. It made sense, if sexual transmission was really a vector. It was in the interest of the bug to get around. He probably didn't act like this with girls normally. It didn't excuse his behavior.

Maybe the gun wasn't loaded. Clint Eastwood's voice in her mind: "You feeling lucky, punk?"

He went around to sit in front of her. His breath smelled of mint gum.

"Not that," she said, turning her face away. "I swear, no. This thing is transmitted by saliva. I've got it."

His hand fisted up. He would hit her, she knew. Knock out a tooth. That was the difference between a high-price hooker and a common whore, back in the day. High-priced girls had all their teeth. So did zombies, somehow. In the movies, you never saw a zombie with missing teeth, or dentures.

She watched her hands undoing her jeans. It was as if they were someone else's. She'd forgotten to get a belt. Yet another failure, but one that didn't matter anymore. Nothing mattered. The bug inside her was going to get out. She pulled her wet jeans down. She was naked underneath. Pale and frightened. She rolled over, ass in the air, facing away from him to keep him from kissing her. Crying now. Waiting for it to be over. As long as he didn't go down on her, he might be safe. Maybe.

"You need a condom," she said. But why did she care? She rather *wanted* to doom him. They'd both be zombies then, walking around and eating people. He probably didn't have the balls to shoot her anyway. But she was afraid for Trevin.

She heard him unzip. He sighed as he entered her. He pumped. It hurt. There had been no telltale rip from a condom wrapper. She grew wet. She'd read an article once about women's sexuality that said that women were turned on by all sorts of things. Researchers measured women's physical response by sticking some tool inside them, then showing them pictures. The women didn't report being turned on by the images they were shown. Yet they were wet. That made sense to her now. Throughout primate history, females were raped. There would be damage, without lubrication.

Rob gripped Kate's sides. "Yes, baby, yes," he was saying. She rocked back against him, wanting him to come. Her back ached. She tried to pretend that this was OK. That she wanted it. If she waited until after he came, he'd be defenseless.

Rob slowed down. "Can't spurt too fast," he said. "Takes all the fun out of it."

"Fuck," Kate said. "Give it to me hard. You know you want it." Her shoulder and back were on fire. Tears fell onto the carpet. She wanted it over. "Come on, baby."

He sped up, then gasped. His fingers dug into her. When he let go, she moved away. She pulled up her jeans. He was kneeling on the floor, tucking his junk into his pants.

"Baby, this is the start of something beautiful," he said, smiling. "I knew you'd come around. So to speak. You like a little power play, yeah?"

She hit him. Her shoulder flared with pain. He fell back, startled. She kicked him in the ribs. He let out a pained breath, and grabbed for her feet. She kicked him again, as hard as she could.

"Fuck," he said. He got a hand around her ankle.

"Yeah, fuck," she said. She landed her other foot on his nose. She wanted to break it. If she was stupid enough to let this happen—if she'd already murdered two people and brought an innocent kid to a dangerous place—this was nothing. There was no escaping. And it felt good. If the apocalypse was an excuse for rape, it was certainly an excuse for murder. She brought her foot down. He screamed. His face was a satisfying mess. She kicked him in the side of the head. It snapped to one side. She did it again, until he lay still, eyes closed. She stopped. He was still breathing. She couldn't bring herself to kill him. She heard a voice, her voice, echoing through the empty gift shop. "Who needs a chiropractor *now*, motherfucker?"

She dragged his body back through the prison. He was heavy, and she had to do it with one hand because of her wrecked shoulder. It was easier once she got past the carpet and into the cell block. Rob left a smeary trail of blood. She put him on the floor in an open cell, and went to the box at the end of the row. One lever was kind of like the clutch. Another you used to pick which cells. The third lever kachunked the doors open or closed. She shut the door. Rob moaned. He was still alive. She rather wished she'd killed him, and then thought of the agony he'd have in store. Turning into a zombie, his hands reaching through the bars. Wanting, agonizing, over what he wouldn't have. That was its own revenge. As long as he stayed in the cell.

Kate went and found a bathroom. She was sore. She washed as best she could. Goop was dripping from inside her. Her shoulder and back were a solid knot.

The adrenalin ebbed. She went back to the gift shop. She used the phone behind the cash registers to call her cell phone, hoping that Trevin would answer. It went straight to voicemail. Her own voice saying, "Alas, you've missed me. You know what to do." She hung up. She knew what to do. First she called Michael. She didn't bother leaving a message. If he survived, and she didn't, it would only make him sad to have a message from her.

She took the rope from her backpack, leaving the rest of her gear, and went to an empty prison cell. One with a mattress. It smelled of dust. The room was tiny, three paces by two. A bed, a sink, a toilet full of concrete. You could go crazy in here.

She tied one wrist to the bed frame, using the knot Jamie had shown her. She drew it tight. Pity you couldn't close the cells from inside. Everyone was at risk because of her. She didn't care if she might be in danger. Nothing bad could happen. Nothing worse than what had already happened. She would protect all of the people who'd come to the island to be safe.

She lay down to wait.

chapter sixteen

Michael tied up the paddleboat. He scrambled onto the dock. "Pass me the box?"

Jordan handed it over. "See? I got us here," he said.

"Yeah, just barely, dickwipe," Michael said. The three of them were soaked through with rain and ocean. He might have had a better time swimming to the island. They'd barely found the dock.

"Be cool," Gracie said. Her teeth chattered. "Now we're here. Now what?"

"Let's find somewhere dry," Michael said. "Somewhere inside."

"You know for sure that there aren't any zombies here?" Gracie said.

"This is the most defensible place in the bay," he said. He knew he wasn't answering the question.

They walked uphill. He mostly remembered the layout of the island. "How about one of those guard towers? We could climb up. See everything from there."

"What, that?" Gracie pointed. "It's barely got a roof. That does not count as *inside*."

"OK, fine. The main building, then."

"That's the first place anyone will go," Jordan said. "Plus it's creepy."

"You don't want to meet anyone? I tell you, we're not going to survive if we don't talk with people. We're going to want shelter."

"Yeah, but who knows who's here? That rowboat on the dock? *Someone* is here. You think they're retail slaves like us?"

Michael didn't answer. They walked past a sign that said *United States Penitentiary* in black print. Above it was handwritten in red ink, "Indians Welcome." They walked past the officers' club, which had burned down during the Indian occupation. Only walls remained, grown over with moss like some Celtic ruin. The fire had been an accident, depending on who you asked. There were several garage-like structures further in. The doors were padlocked closed.

"We can break in," Michael said.

"Do you know how to pick a lock?" Jordan asked.

"Don't need to." He went to a building, examined the padlock. The hasp was rusted. The only problem with breaking it was that it compromised the security of the door, which they'd care about later if they had to keep zombies out. He walked around the side of the building. The windows were dirty, and thin. The place wouldn't be very secure, but they could always retreat to the main prison.

"I'm guessing that the zombies aren't going to make their way *en masse* out here anyway. We can handle them one at a time. Maybe we just get inside for a little while, warm up. Take stock of the island in the morning." He wished he'd brought a hatchet, or a hammer. Any kind of tool would do. He took a bottle of scotch from his box, glad that he'd thought to get the kind in plastic.

"Why don't you use a rock?" Jordan said.

"Find me one." Michael started hammering at the hasp. It would give. It had to give.

"Hey, what's that?" A voice yelled.

Someone else was here. They must have heard the noise. A guy stood outside of a building further uphill. Michael thought it was a guy, anyway. Gracie and Jordan backed up.

Michael stepped forward. "Hey!" he called. "We're just looking for a place to chill. I mean, to get warm. We have booze."

The guy went back to the doorway, and opened it. There was a light on inside. It looked warm. He went inside, then came back out. "You holding?"

Michael thought about it. The Bay Area wasn't rough on prosecuting, not for personal use, anyway. That would be the least of his worries. This wasn't a cop. "Yeah," he called.

"Well, come on in, then."

Michael looked to Jordan and Gracie. "Shall we?"

Gracie took a step forward.

"I don't know," Jordan said.

"We'll be fine," Michael said. "We were going to have to make some friends, anyway, sooner or later. Maybe they know where Kate is." He picked up his box and walked. They followed. He knocked at the door.

The guy opened the door. He wore a flannel shirt and had long black hair. His eyes were already squinty. The room reeked of pot. "I'm Gabe, come in." Two women sat on the cement floor. They were eating out of cans with their fingers. Pasta, looked like, in the light from a camping lantern on the floor. "Ana and Trish," he gestured. Gardening equipment lurked in the shadows. The three of them were probably in their late twenties, or early thirties.

Michael introduced himself, and his friends. Gabe shut the door. "I thought we'd just smoked our last. That's the one thing we should have brought a bunch more of. If only for making friends. Had to move fast; I only had my personal stash. Not enough by half."

There was nothing else to do. Michael surrendered his to Gabe. "Do the honors? Not much, but it's classy stuff. Still in a bag, so it should be dry."

Gabe opened the bag and put it to his nose. He smiled. "Purple Haze. I know the guy who grows this stuff in Santa Cruz. I'd recognize it anywhere."

Michael nodded. It wasn't Purple Haze, but there was no reason to correct him. "So you guys here by yourselves?"

"Place is ours. No one in sight. Siddown," Gabe said. "I'll roll it."

Michael put down his box and sat on the floor. Gracie and Jordan followed. It was marginally warmer inside. Still, they were shivering. Michael wasn't feeling great, himself. He handed the bottle of scotch to Jordan, who took a swig, and passed it to Gracie. She drank and passed to one of the girls.

"Shouldn't we save some?" one of the girls asked. She took a hit from the bottle. "What about tomorrow?"

"You want to wake and bake? I'll set aside a bit." He looked to Michael. "I'm guessing that you guys are here for a while. You're welcome to stay the night."

"Thanks, but I'm looking for someone. Her name's Kate? Pretty girl, wearing a Hawaiian shirt?"

"Haven't seen her," Gabe said. "You're the first people we've seen since we got here. We were at work when it happened. A customer just, you know, turned into one of them. The whole store was a mess before we figured out what was going on. We're lucky we got out with our lives."

"Where do you work?" Michael was curious.

"Whole Foods." One of the girls; he wasn't sure who was who, lit a cigarette. "Ana and I are in the studio art program at CCA, but our boy here is a lifer."

"Am not. I just don't see the point of a corporate job. What's your guyses' life story?"

Michael considered his words. "We work at TJ's. When the zombies came, we figured Alcatraz was the safest place in the bay."

"Us, too," Gabe said. "We're pacifists. I'd never own a gun. I don't even like box cutters. So we figured, come to the place where the zombies can't get to."

"How'd you get here? The rowboat we saw?"

"Stole it."

Michael noticed that their new friends weren't offering to share their food. "If anyone's hungry, I've got some food." He selected a box of the Indian food. He considered eating it. The cardboard was damp.

"Cold?" Gracie said. She looked doubtful.

"This is the apocalypse," Michael said. "Get used to it."

She rummaged through the box. The bottle came around. They all hit it.

"This isn't the apocalypse. Come the apocalypse, I'd want a shotgun," Gracie said. "I'd walk down the middle of the street with it strapped to my back, because I wouldn't be walking on the sidewalk where any dork could jump out and whack me. When the apocalypse comes—" she trailed off.

"What are you doing *here*, then?" Gabe asked at the same time. "You could stay home and protect yourself, if you felt like that."

"Can I borrow your phone?" Michael asked Jordan. He tried to think of Kate's number. He scrolled down Jordan's contacts, hoping it might be there somehow. It wasn't. He thought of the coffee-stained list of employee phone numbers. A few numbers swam behind his eyes. He dialed. Miraculously, he heard Kate's voice. Or rather, her voicemail. The phone hadn't even rung.

"I don't actually own a gun," Gracie said.

Michael sent a text to Kate. *On the island. You?* Maybe she'd be able to see it.

"See, the thing about owning a gun," the girl that he thought was Trish said, "is that you have to be ready to use it. You don't just get to pull it out and have motherfuckers run away. You have to be ready to kill. Think about it. You pull it out, and either you use it right away, or they'll shoot you."

Kate texted back. *Who this?*

"What about if they don't have a gun?" Gracie asked.

"Well, why'd you need one in the first place, then?"

It's Michael, he texted. *With Gracie and Jordan.* And a couple of potheads, he thought but didn't type. *From TJs.*

"Loan us one of those?" Gabe held out his hand. He wanted a box of Indian food. Michael gave it to him. Gabe removed the pouch of food, set it aside, and flattened the cardboard to make a workspace. He started breaking the green fragrant bud.

Where you?

"I guess so," Gracie said. "I just came here because that's what my friends were doing. The reason why I don't own a gun is because I'm convinced that I'd pull it out, if some meth head was breaking into my apartment or something — self defense, you know — and I'd drop the gun, or forget how to use it, and he'd take it from me. And then I'd be killed. Being robbed is one thing, or even being raped, but I'm a klutz. Plus guns are expensive."

Alabatsay, she texted back. *Rock.* She must have predictive text on. But that meant she was here. His skin grew hot. He needed to see her.

"But since you don't own a gun, you're one of us," Ana said. She licked her fingers. "Gandhi's, like, my hero."

Where? he texted.

"Peace is cool," Gracie said. "I mean, it's not like I want to murder anyone. Hell. Just seeing my friend turn into a zombie today was enough to throw me into a total mental break. I got past it," she added. "But it'll take a while to get *over* it, if you know what I mean. Survival is one thing, and processing is another."

The girls nodded. "You say you guys work at Trader Joe's?" Ana said.

"Yeah. It's all right," Gracie said. "Get to meet guys like these. Maybe saved my life, who knows?"

Outside. Late in prison.

He wasn't texting with Kate, that much was clear. Probably "Late" meant Kate. Michael remembered. Kate had been hanging out with the neighbor kid. *You OK?*

"I gotta go," Michael said. "Kate's here, in the prison."

"So what does Whole Paycheck pay?" Gracie asked.

"Well, I hired in at nine seventy-five, and then I was supposed to get a ninety day raise—" Ana said. "And six months passed, and I asked, and asked, and finally went to the general manager. By then I was training people making more than me."

Gabe lit the joint. He inhaled. He coughed the squeaky cough that people do when they're trying not to exhale. "You'll miss out," he said, holding out the joint.

"Kate from work?" Gracie said. It was her turn with the joint. "Bring her back here."

Michael left, moving fast. The rain was cold. He walked uphill, around the snakelike curves of the pavement. There wasn't much light to go by. Kate wouldn't have given her phone to the kid if everything was copasetic. How much danger was she in? Michael broke into a run, wishing that he bothered to exercise more. Since the stick fighting group had fallen apart, he didn't do much. Kate was always going on hikes and runs. She'd never asked if he'd want to come along. Sure, he'd made fun of her for it, but he'd been gentle. He hoped he'd been gentle. He had to find her.

The door to the prison building was propped open. That wasn't very secure. He went in. "Kate?" he called. "You here?" His voice echoed. He went up the stairs. It was a big building. A big, empty building. He passed the racks of headphones where you could pick up your guided tour. It wasn't that long ago that he and Kate had been here, wearing those headphones. He ran up Broadway, the prison's main drag. He looked from side to side into the cells, calling her name, not caring who else might hear him. Every time she didn't answer, he grew a little more concerned.

"Who goes there?" a voice answered.

Michael ran past the cafeteria, which was fenced off. It still had the outlines of several different kinds of knives on the wall, black paint on white, so that anyone could see if a knife was missing. "Who *goes* there?"

A guy was approaching at a run. Another guy trailed him, holding the arms of a middle-aged couple wearing raincoats and carrying camping backpacks. The couple didn't look like they wanted to be there, but they weren't struggling.

"You seen a pretty girl, my age?" Michael called. "I have to find her."

"Michael?" a voice called. He'd know that voice anywhere.

"*Kate?*"

"Go away. Get out," she called back. She sounded as if she'd been crying.

"We gotta get these folks into a cell," one of the guys said. "Then we'll deal with the new guy."

Michael found Kate, tied to a bed in an unlocked cell. She looked miserable. Her clothes were as wet as his. She'd kicked her shoes off.

"Kate! You're still alive." He ran to her. Sat next to her on the bed.

He saw that someone had tied her to the bed frame.

"I'm going to put them in seven," the voice called. "Dude, lock it up for me."

Michael started to untie the rope. "Who did this to you?" he asked. He was angry. She shook her head, moving away from him.

"Don't you think you should keep them separate?" a voice called.

"Don't untie me," she said. "Please don't." She looked like she was in pain.

He worked on untying her. She pulled the knot away from him. "Don't," she said. "Please don't." There was such need in her. He stopped.

"Kate. What happened?" His hand hovered near her cheek. "Are you OK?" he asked. It was obvious that she wasn't. Whoever it was that tied her had done the knot right, though. It was the same knot Jamie had used last night. "I'm sorry I brought you out here. Something bad has clearly happened to you. I'm so sorry."

"OK, they're in seven and eight, so they can hold hands through the bars," a voice said.

"Softie," the other voice called. "That's good. I suppose we can double them up later, if we have to."

"All right," the first voice called. "Stand back. Clear?"

"Clear."

"I thought you were dead," Kate said. "I'm sorry I left this morning."

The clank of the cell door rang through the building. That was what the prisoners had heard three times a day, plus showers, and a monthly trip to the barber. The bells of hell.

"Shit," Kate said. "Oh, shit."

Michael followed her gaze. They'd been locked in.

"That wasn't it," a voice called.

"Sorry. Can't read the numbers. Trying again."

"We'll just ask them to open it," Michael said. He tucked her rain-soaked hair behind her ears. "There are worse things than being here. At least we're safe, inside. You wouldn't believe what I've seen today. Well, maybe *you* would. You're the only one who would. I feel so bad about what happened to Audrey."

"Kate?" A kid stood at the bars.

"Trev, you all right?" Kate asked, looking at the kid. "I have to tell you something." She turned back to Michael. "What do you mean, what happened to Audrey?"

"Wet, but I'm OK. They're locking people up, like you told them," the kid said. "What happened to *you*, though? Did Rob do this to you? And are you Michael?"

"Did you have Kate's phone? Yes, I'm Michael."

"Trev, do you have my phone still?"

"Yeah."

"Trev, listen. You remember the *Indiana Jones* app. When Rob the zombie comes after you in a few hours, you need to be able to use it. Do it for me now, just so I can hear it."

"There's zombies here?" Trevin asked. He looked up and down the cell row. He had good instincts.

"There will be. Do me a favor and get Michael out," Kate said. "Let them lock you up, but in your own cell. Take some food and water. I'm staying here. I told you. This is it. Real friends kill friends who are zombies." She looked at Michael. "That's why you set the fire, isn't it?"

"*I* didn't set the fire. I didn't even know about it until you told me. I'm not leaving you," Michael said. "Not after as long as it took to find you." He couldn't bring himself to tell Kate about Audrey. The scene was burned in his mind. He understood those religious guys who'd whip themselves into a bloody mess. Penitence, or penance, whatever it was, it couldn't come close to assuaging his guilt. He could have saved Audrey, and he didn't.

"Like this?" Trevin asked. There was a tinny *whapeesh*.

"Dude, check this out," a voice called. "Dude. Open number one the fuck up. Rob's in here. He's messed up."

"What happened?"

"Just *do it*!"

"Yeah." Kate let out a breath. "That's it. As long as the battery lasts, you should be safe. You just have to sack up. Don't let the zombies scare you. Make the whip noise and tell them to back away. Trust me. They're docile as kittens."

There was another tinny *whapeesh*. "Um. OK."

"Can you do it?"

Whapeesh. "Yeah." There was more confidence in his voice this time.

"Well, don't waste the battery, then. Just get Michael out."

"Hey, Kate, did Rob do this to you?" Trevin put a hand through the bars. His skinny arm went in clear to his bicep. It was sweet. This kid cared.

"Don't you dare let that asshole out," Kate called. "He will fuck you up. He's going to be a zombie. Or just wait, and see, and then you'll all be that way. Fuck." She hit the wall with her fist.

The cell doors clanged. They all jumped. The door to Kate's cell stayed closed.

"Rob," a voice called. "Are you all right?"

"Damn," Kate said. "Trevin, get yourself into a cell. It's the only way. Bring food and water." She turned to Michael. "I don't have much time. But I think I understand something. You said our friends were zombies. So you set the house on fire. I get it."

"No," Michael said. "What? No! They were fine when we left. Something happened. I think Audrey let Cameron loose, and things went downhill from there. I don't think she did any of it on purpose. I came back and Cameron nearly took a bite out of me, until Audrey stopped him. She had her whip. That was what made me understand. That was when I called you."

"Get him out of here," Kate said. "Trevin, please. Then get those boys to lock you up. Alone. Michael, you too. Take some water and food from the gift shop. It'll suck for a while, but it might save your lives."

"And I thought those guys were cool," Trevin said. "We walked around, and I told them about the zombies we saw. And your story about the Zeppelin. They believed me. Then we found this couple at the dock, and we're putting them in the lockup to make sure that they're safe. Like you said. We explained it to them."

"What's he talking about? A Zeppelin?" Michael asked. No wonder the kid was worried about whether people believed him. "Tell me, honey, who did this to you."

Kate wouldn't make eye contact. "That's not important. What's important is that I am going to turn into one of them. Believe me, if you've ever believed anything. I swear on my mother's life. Zombieism is transmitted by sexual contact. By saliva, and I'm sure by other fluids." She lowered her voice. "And I've got it. I can feel it already. I can feel it happening. I got it from Jamie, last night. You don't know what it was like. And now that asshole Rob's got it. Trevin knows who I mean."

"What?" Trevin said. "Know what?"

"What?" Michael held her hand. She was cold. "What do you mean?"

"Rob? Oh, God. Did *she* do this to you?" one of the guys said.

"All's fair in love and war," another voice said. He sounded like he was in pain.

"This isn't love, it's war," Kate said. Her voice was deep. Maybe she was catching a cold. He didn't care; a cold didn't last long. Future Michael could deal with it. Present Michael was here, and now. The here and now always took precedence.

"We can't win this war. They're slower, and stupider. But their recruiting methods are unbeatable," Kate said.

"Of course we'll win it," Michael said. She'd set him up for a punch line from Brother Dave; she'd want him to follow through.

"We're going to win it, and save it, and put it somewhere, and forget about it. Go off playing with a tennis ball."

She didn't register the joke. "No. Get lost. I mean it. Go. I had to kill two of them, earlier today. I mean, they were already dead, but I had to take them out. It was terrible. You won't believe me, and you don't have to. I beat that dude within an inch of his life, and I wanted to kill him. I'm not sure why I didn't." She held his hand to her cheek with her free hand. She was beautiful.

"I believe you," he said.

"Then get the fuck out of here. But do me a favor?" She offered the other end of the rope to him. Michael took it. She trusted him. It unhinged him, that gesture.

He took her wrist. Her skin was soft. He tied her to the bed as tenderly as he could. She lay on her back. Her shirt rode up, showing naked belly. He wanted her. Nothing else could matter.

"Trevin, get him out of here. Now!" she called.

"OK, OK."

Michael heard footsteps.

"Guys, we have to let the dude out," Trevin called. "Oh, wow. Is *he* going to be all right?"

"Kate—" Michael started. There was so much to say. "About last night. I don't think it was a mistake. With us."

"I know. I wanted you," she said. "I couldn't tell you how much."

Michael was relieved. He moved closer to her. Their thighs touched. He put a hand on her belly. "Nice clothes," he said. "Did you go to a thrift store?" He leaned down and kissed her stomach. Her ribs. He moved the damp shirt up. He should have thought to take it off before tying her arm. He pictured her shirt bunched around her upper arms, behind her head. He kissed her stomach. The muscles tensed.

"Help me out, guys," Trevin's voice carried down the block. "There's this guy—I gotta get him out—"

Kate's breathing became shallow. "No," she said, but in a tone that meant *yes*.

"I want you," Michael said. "I don't care if these assholes see it. No blanket. Just us. Skin to skin. I want to be with you. Don't think I don't know what it means." He undid the button of her jeans. He started to feel warm, despite his damp clothes. He straddled her.

"I'm going. To kill you," she said. "Don't make me. I told you. Please. Michael. I'm not fucking around."

"The safe word is *juniper berry*," he said. He put a hand under her shirt, and leaned down to kiss her.

She turned her face away. "I'm not playing. Your games. I swear. Please. Don't do this," she said in a voice thick with emotion. "It's hard enough. As it is. Oh, God." Her hips moved against his.

He kissed her neck. Her nipple was so hard in his fingers. He wanted to see how it would feel in his mouth. He did. She took in a breath. He kissed her ear, and her cheek. Finally, she let him kiss her mouth. She opened her lips. Their tongues met. He tasted her. He wanted her more than he'd wanted anyone. There was something magical between them. It was meant to be. She put her tongue inside his ear. It made him twitch. He touched her hair, holding her head to him.

"Something's happening," she said. Her voice next to his ear was awfully deep.

"Kate?" He knew what was happening; he didn't want to stop it.

His ear stung. He put a hand to it. He saw blood. "Kate?" he asked. She was chewing. That didn't matter. He touched her cheek. Love was all about the moment. He untied one of her wrists. Freed, her fingers pulled at his shirt. He used the rope to tie his other wrist to hers. That way, if anyone found them, they'd know what had happened. That he'd gone willingly. Then he leaned to kiss Kate, readying himself.

chapter seventeen

ten years later

Kate no longer asked one of the other bartenders at Patient Zero to walk her back to her car at the end of the night. Half of the customers still called it Cato's; the employees hadn't gotten around to making a new sign. Most of the storefronts on Piedmont Avenue were back to being occupied by retailers, though the really boutiquey stores selling things like handmade organic fair-wage baby clothes were gone. Evolutionary dead ends.

She dried a glass with a towel, setting it in the rack. Business was slow tonight. She watched the television, which showed Piedmont High School's production of *The Tempest*. Prospero was eighteen at best, but had the *gravitas* of someone who remembered everything. "Full fathom five," Kate mouthed along with Ariel.

Derek sat down at the bar. Kate poured him a shot. Employees weren't supposed to drink on the job, but everyone did it. "You're up after Audrey," he said. "She's got another two songs after this." His cheek had a long shiny scar, and he was missing an eyebrow. Kate had never gotten the nerve to ask him how it had happened. She could guess well enough. Still, some people were into that. Evidence of the new order.

"There's almost no one here," she said. "Won't be much in tips."

Audrey was dancing to "Rodeo" by Juvenile. In the colored spotlights, you hardly saw how gray her skin was.

"Like the new shirt." He drank from his cup.

"It'd look great on your floor, right?" That was one of his lines. He flirted out of habit, as she did. The shirt had been an impulse buy from a street vendor, a baby tee on which was printed *No Bugchasers* in pink letters. It rode up, showing off the Ouroboros tattoo around her hips that had cost several weeks' take. The pain and exhilaration from being tattooed had been the closest she'd come to an orgasm with someone else in years.

"Any floor, baby. Try me."

"That drunk still hanging around outside?" Kate asked, mostly to change the subject. She didn't have to tell him that it was bad for business.

"I can't do anything about it. I've told him to go away. He's one of them. It's a little tactless, hanging around in front of this place. PTSD, sure, fine, but we've all been through worse than he has. I wish the council would do something about them."

"Most homeless people are mentally ill," Kate said. "There just isn't funding. Prop Eight failed. It's the damn three-quarters majority requirement."

"New government, same old problems. People would rather have the power on, and the water running, never mind getting some of these potholes fixed. That's what the Reparation was *supposed* to be about. Not just jobs. Not just safety. I drove into the city the other day—"

"'When you ride alone, you ride with Hitler,'" Kate quoted. She'd gotten it from a novel about kids whose parents were making the bomb during WWII. Gas coupons and rationing. The public libraries were gone, but Patient Zero had a take-one-leave-one bookshelf.

"I picked up some people from the casual carpool. But listen to this, at the tollbooth they made us all sign a waiver. Sheet full of names, on both sides. Bridge has finally been declared unsound, but what's the option? Walk through the BART tunnel? No, thank you."

"You could drive down to the 92. It's a newer bridge."

"Yeah, but it's out of the way. Another hour or two, depending on traffic. I don't have the gas credit for that. Everything takes longer, these days. You're old enough to remember how it was."

The song finished. Drake's "Best I Ever Had" started. Audrey flipped upside down on the pole. Her hair hung down like a mop. She wore it long to cover her scars. Kate watched her. Audrey had a beautiful body. She'd gotten ripped, ab muscles visible. Sometimes they'd trade backrubs after their respective sets. The pole took it out of you. But she never touched Audrey at home. In the beginning, they'd both been afraid to live alone. They split the bills, and they didn't talk much except for work. It was like being married, except that neither of them was seeing anyone else.

"I'll watch the store if you want to get ready," Derek said. "This'll be your last set before the power goes out."

Kate poured herself a shot. "All right, I guess. Only for you." She drained it, trying to psych herself up. She went into what used to be a storage closet. She took off her shirt and bra. She pinched her nipples erect, then put clamps on them, grimacing. A clamp had fallen off once, during her act. She changed into white panties. Then she put on a black leather hood with holes for her eyes, nose, and mouth. She used the hood not because her face was scarred but because it wasn't.

Patient Zero was a fetish bar. The fetish was survivors like her, but there was overlap with the BDSM community. She and Audrey were lucky that they'd each been locked up. Most zombies had been shot on sight by the time research groups at UCSF and Stanford had come up with antiretrovirals that worked. Audrey's song ended. The applause faded. Derek called out, not bothering to use the mic: "Next up, put your hands together for our very talented *Kyrie Eleison!*"

Kate made her way to the stage. She stood, looking at the

mirrored ceiling, and waited for the song to start. She'd picked "Easy Come, Easy Go" by the bluegrass Jugtown Pirates as her first piece. They still played the bar circuit, mostly in San Francisco. The stand-up bass player reminded her of Michael; he made the same goofy faces. She'd chosen the song for the chorus: "Life keeps moving along." And because people thought it was funny. When the crowd was particularly frisky, she'd swap it out for their song "My Baby Left and Became a Stripper." She climbed up the pole, swirling around. She made eye contact with the audience. It was mostly middle-aged guys who smelled of beer and work sweat. She touched herself. It was a job. "Bonnie and Clyde" by Haystak was next.

A slender guy came in and sat down. Kate felt the blood leave her head. It couldn't be. It was. Walter. Or his father. No, it was him. She felt weak. So he hadn't died.

She kept dancing. He wouldn't recognize her, the hood covering her face. "Comfortable" by Lil Wayne came on. She did a belly roll, making the snake's tail twitch. She refused to be self-conscious. When the song was over, she collected her money from the floor and bolted from the stage.

She sat in the closet for a while after changing back into her clothes. She counted the cash. Almost fifty, in Bear Republic dollars plus a few wrinkled US dollars. End-of-the-night take. The United States was a joke; bankrupted from the Siege. New England had incorporated. Southern California was now the Orange Republic; Northern California and Oregon the Bear Republic. States printed their own money, but everyone still took US currency. She put the bills in her pocket, then checked her reflection in a mirror that had been manufactured decades ago to fit in a high schooler's locker. Her skin was pale and gray in the light from the single incandescent bulb. They'd shaved her head in the hospital, years ago, and she'd decided she liked it that way. It was a kind of penance. Too little, too late, but it was something. She put on lipstick and smiled at herself.

The light went out. It must be midnight already. She came out of the closet. Derek was lighting candles. Audrey had gotten her guitar and was sitting on a stool on the stage in the semidark, playing Tracy Chapman songs. A few of the customers had stayed to look up her skirt and sing along; others drifted to the bar.

Walter sat by himself, head propped on his hands, examining his bottle of beer. He wore a Stanford sweatshirt with the anti-zombie logo. Kate went behind the bar. She grabbed another bottle of beer from the melted ice in the cooler, and set it in front of him. He looked up.

"Fancy meeting you in a place like this," she said.

He blinked a few times. "Kate?" he said, tasting the word as if for the first time. "I didn't know. Oh, God. I'm so sorry." His face did some complicated things. "How *are* you?"

His voice sounded like she remembered. That was hard.

"Surviving," she said. "Glad to see you are, too. I'm one of the lucky ones. I was in the hospital for a while. Then moved into a tiny apartment by the lake with my friend Audrey. I lost touch with a lot of people. Went off the grid, basically."

"Happens, especially when phones and the Internet are on-again, off-again. I lost all of my email to a server crash." Was he trying to explain why he hadn't tried to contact her, or was he saying that he understood why she hadn't contacted him? She rather liked the idea that all of their correspondence was gone.

"So you're working here?" he asked.

"It's all right. Not a lot of jobs for people like me."

"If I'd known, maybe I could have brought a whip." He smiled as if he already regretted the joke.

"I've got it under control, thank you very much. Antiretrovirals. The whip sound doesn't work once the drugs are in your system. You see the size of those speakers? I'm not sensitive to sound any more, for sure. Glad to see I didn't give it to you, though."

He took a sip. He'd aged. It was in his face, and his posture. "I've been looking for you, believe it or not. For years. I needed to see you, Katie. I asked around at Mills, after they opened again, but no one knew anything. I needed to know that you were OK."

"Yeah." She shook her head. "Yeah, I just told you that I was in school to impress you."

He looked away. "I guess I deserved that."

"I actually do write, now," she added, softening her voice. "Not for publication, though." She thought of a quick poem. *The world does not end / How precious your guilt / How poisonous your love.*

"Kate, give me a hand?" Derek called from the other end of the bar. Now that the dancing was over, the drinking had picked up.

"Sorry. 'Scuse me." Kate touched Walter's hand, out of habit. His skin was soft, in an age where most people worked outdoors. He flinched, just a little, but she noticed. Probably he'd never been touched by a zombie before. People always expected her skin to be cold.

"Wait—when are you off shift? I'd love to buy you a burger or something." In the old days, they'd eaten steak. He must have come down, from whatever he did then to whatever he did now. The panic during the Siege had killed off the remaining banks. His 401(k) was surely lost. Retirement was a joke.

"I'm vegetarian, these days. I'll never eat flesh again." She smiled, trying to look malevolent. If she scared him away, she wouldn't have to talk to him. "Be right there," she called to Derek.

"Touché." Walter wasn't sure whether to laugh. That meant she made him nervous. Good. "Pizza?" he asked. "There's a place down the block that serves late."

She considered.

"Please?"

"Excuse me," she said. She moved to the other end of the bar and mixed a Manhattan for a white-haired man who always tipped. She threw in an extra cherry.

"That guy bothering you?" Derek asked.

"No. Just someone I used to know. We went out a few times." She saw no reason to conceal it.

"Really?"

"Before."

"I was going to say. You never date."

"It's not the zombie thing. I just had a bad experience once."

"With *this* guy?" Derek's face darkened.

"Oh, no. Another guy. It's all conflated in my brain, though. I don't like to talk about it. I'm not embarrassed; it just tends to weird people out. Violence might turn people on, here, but trauma turns them off. There *is* a difference."

"Well, you looked haunted, cutie. Just tell me if you want me to get rid of him."

"Thanks." She bumped her hip against his, checking first to see that he wasn't holding anything that would spill. He smiled. She slung bottles of beer, made here in Oakland, and mixed a few cocktails. When business calmed down, she leaned against the back counter. It was good to have work. Derek stood next to her.

"Stick with your own kind," he said under his breath. "I don't have to tell you why. The vitalists don't understand what it's like. They'll parade you around to show how PC they are, dating a zombie, but they get over it fast. It's all a fantasy. And they're lousy in bed. Afraid to touch you."

"Believe me. It's not like that. I'm not dating *anyone*. This guy, he wants to get the guilt monkey off his back. He ran out on me during the Siege."

"Everyone did shit they regret. *Especially* us."

She nodded. *Honesty / until it hurts / No safe word.* "I ate my friend. I don't talk about it."

"So did I!" Derek said. "I ate my *girlfriend*. How sick was that? I mean, I took it home to her. It was my fault. I think of her every day." He poured a shot for each of them from the well. The alcohol burned on the back of her throat.

"Yeah. I mean, I don't remember all of it," she added. "I tied myself up and told my friend to go away. But he didn't. Then I woke up in a hospital. I saw pictures. What was left. They couldn't even take a dental impression. His face was gone. He'd tied himself to me." She'd never told this to anyone, outside of the hospital shrink. *The kiss of death / a shotgun / smears the lipstick.*

"And we remind them of it, so the only jobs we can get are working for tips in a fetish bar. I guess there's always farming, but we're not safe outside of urban areas. We're barely safe *in* them."

Kate put her arm in Derek's. He at least understood. On Tuesdays, he danced and she emceed. He squeezed her arm against his side, then let go.

"You don't owe him anything, darling."

"No," she said. "I suppose not."

After last call, Walter was still there. He'd had a few beers, but he wasn't drunk in her professional opinion. She busied herself cleaning, wiping down the bar and then the pole. She carried a cooler of melted ice to one of the two single-stall bathrooms, dumping it into the graywater reservoir that was hooked up to the toilet. The bathroom walls were riddled with graffiti. She found a Sharpie. She wrote: *Water washes blood / You can't tell me / it's OK.*

She used the toilet, flushed, then washed her hands in the sink. There was a knock, and she went to the door, in case it was a customer.

"Leave the mopping up to me," Derek said. "You're not making it any easier by putting it off. If you're going to go talk to him. Which I'm still not sure you should."

"I owe him this much," she said, realizing she'd made a decision. "I owe myself this much. Wish me luck. And thanks."

"Luck," Derek said. "I'll give Audrey a ride home."

"You're the best." She retrieved a sweatshirt from the closet and went to collect Walter.

"Thanks for waiting. Shall we?" she said.

Walter stood. He seemed shorter than he used to be. She followed him. The street was quiet. The guy who'd been hanging around outside had gone to wherever they went. Since the BART train had ceased, homeless people had claimed the tunnel. It was always dark down there, or so she'd heard, and there were often fires. Drunks smoking in their cardboard beds. Kate had signed a petition to clear out the tunnel and close it down.

"Thanks for seeing me," Walter said. "It means a lot."

"No worries."

"It's not exactly like old times. I never did take you to the Claremont. I owe you that, I suppose." He reached for her hand.

She squeezed it to be polite, then dropped it, ignoring his last comment. "Well, nothing is. So what are you doing these days?"

"Lawyers always have work. Contracting for the government, mostly. The office is gone. Squatters moved in, last I heard. I got one of those efficiencies downtown, and I work from there. I miss the way things used to be."

"Everyone does. I never thought I'd pine for retail work. That's what I did, back when. I never told you about it. There's a lot I didn't tell you."

He nodded. "Customer service is good for the soul."

"Have you ever done it?" She thought, after she'd said it, that she could have made a joke about him not having a soul, and was glad she hadn't.

"I do it all the time. Unless you're talking about retail customer service. I was a trolley-cart kid. My first job. They'd just invented them."

"Seriously. They'd just invented *kids*?"

"Sort of. I was a prototype. But I *did* work retail."

It was easy to slip back into the joking. They could segue from there to anything. She stopped. They walked down Piedmont Avenue. She let him lead.

Walter cleared his throat. "So you're living with someone named Audrey these days, you said?"

"She's all right. We used to work together, and we work together now. Chick singing on stage? Between us we make enough for rent and utilities. She still misses cable and Netflix, but I don't mind so much. We watch old movies and news on the indie stations when the power's on, or read borrowed books."

A homeless guy stood in their path, muttering. He wore a hat and several jackets, despite the warmth of the evening.

"Let's cross here." She put a hand on Walter's arm and steered him towards the street. She kept talking. "Doesn't matter that Hollywood's dead, or New York publishing. There's already enough culture to last anyone's lifetime. I saw *Casablanca* the other day for the first time. I can understand why a generation of women were in love with Bogey."

The homeless guy's eyes widened. She forced herself to look away. It was dark. Maybe he hadn't seen her skin. She always hated this, the yelling that would follow. Sometimes they'd walk after her, like Mary's little lamb, picking up other crazies as they went. She often wore hoods, sunglasses, makeup, anything that would cover her skin.

"Kate?" the homeless guy said. "Is that you?"

She stopped in the middle of the street, stunned. She had to see who it was. "Sorry, I don't normally get recognized by street people," she said to Walter. She took a breath, and turned around.

She had to look at him for a moment before it clicked into place. Their old boss from Trader Joe's, the one Michael always referred to as Fearless Leader. "Shit," she said, groping for his name. "Darren? How are you?" It was a dumb question, but she didn't know what else to say.

"You're one of them," he said. His face darkened. "It's your fault. All of this happened." He swayed. "Because of you."

She hissed at him, making her best zombie face. He backed into a wall. From the smell, he'd wet himself. She walked away.

"For God's sake, Kate, why'd you do that?" Walter caught up with her.

"Can't reason with those people. Thought he'd be different, maybe. Knew him from back in the day."

"How did you know he didn't have a gun? You could get yourself killed like that."

She gave him credit for not saying, "You could have killed both of us."

"I don't. I just like to see the way they react." She was only half-joking.

"It's dangerous. What if they attack the next, er, one, after you've yanked their chain?"

He held the door for her. They went into the pizza place.

"We're zombies. Just say it. What would you have me do, shrink like a violet? Pretend I'm not what I am? I didn't choose to be like this. But I'm out and proud, like Popeye said."

He smiled then. "It was 'I yam what I yam.'"

"Just seeing if you knew that."

"You're young for Popeye references."

"I watched the cartoons."

"Cartoons? I read the comics."

They sat on plastic chairs at a table next to the wall, among the single-slice crowd. There were candles on the tables, classing the place up, but the kitchen on the other side of the counter was lit with camping lanterns. She felt sober.

"You're right, though," she said. "I half expect to get killed one of these days. Once, not long after I got out of the hospital, I was jumped by a group of them. They dropped me off at the emergency room, after, the nurse said. Rolled me out on the sidewalk like a batch of bad dough. Which meant that someone with a car had been involved. It wasn't just the street crazies. I didn't scar much."

"Oh, wow. I'm sorry to hear that." Walter reached for her hand, on the table, and she moved her hands into her lap. She couldn't believe that she'd been attracted to him. It had been so long ago; it was as if it had never happened.

"People were scared," she said. "They still are. And sometimes it's in my interest to have that particular person moving away from me. You just have to have control of the moment." She picked up the wrinkled paper menu that was wedged behind an empty napkin dispenser. The dispenser was clearly there for this function alone; paper was precious. The menu was handwritten on half a sheet, and listed toppings and prices.

"I hadn't heard anything about ratpacking coming back," he said, after a moment.

She didn't bother to pretend that she knew what he was talking about. "Is that an East Bay motorcycle gang reference? The Rats?"

"No, it was this series of random attacks in the early nineties.

Four or five guys would get out of their car, beat someone within an inch of their life, and drive away. It wasn't gang-related. They didn't know the victim. It was just utterly random."

"Hate crimes is hate crimes." She passed him the menu. They talked about what to get. A girl with legs up to her ears came to the table and took their order. A whole pie. Mushrooms and black olives. Water to drink. They both watched her walk away, her ass high and round in her shorts.

"Hey, I'm sorry about that day," he said. "I should have taken you with me."

"Everyone feels that way," she said. "I haven't talked with anyone who doesn't regret something." He *had* offered to take her with him. He just hadn't wanted her to come; that much had been obvious.

He shook his head. She feared he might cry. This would not be the place, or the time. Not that there ever really was a right place and time. She reached for his hand, not because he would have wanted her to, but because she wanted to. His grip was strong. He turned his face to the wall. She looked at their hands together. Pink and gray. As long as she took her pills, she was safe, never mind that most people had already gotten the vaccine; the Bear Republic sponsored treatment and prevention. Her skin, though, was stuck like this. She moved her hand into her lap.

He passed both hands over his face, collecting himself. "So I went home, that day," he said. "And I barricaded myself in. I tried to call my wife. Over and over."

She let him talk, knowing where this was going. "She didn't make it, did she? I'm sorry."

He shook his head. "I suspected it at first, and then I knew it after the third day. After the power was gone, and I was drinking from the hot water heater. When it went straight to voicemail, when I called. But that's another conversation, not something I intended to burden you with. It was a long time ago, and it's not why I'm here. I felt terrible leaving you. You were—" he looked to the wall. "Very special. Someone I cared a lot about."

Kate nodded. "I cared about you, too," she said. "It took me a while to understand that. I mean, that was the game we were playing, that we didn't care. I was doing what I did with you because I wasn't going to get hurt."

"Oh," he said.

"It was a long time ago. I was a kid. But I've thought about you."

There was a moment of silence between them.

"Do you see your folks often?" he asked. "How'd they fare? They OK?"

He hadn't asked about her family before. "They're holding up. Mom's on the community garden council, and queen of the school board. Dad's an alderman at their church. He designs and builds solar cars with his old bowling team. I call them from the bar about once a week to check in. They know what I do for a living, and they're OK with it. My brother's in construction, but he prefers demolition. He came out, and the 'rents met his boyfriend during the Siege. Then he broke up with the boyfriend. The next one was a nut, everyone agrees, but there were some interesting guys in there, and those are just the ones I know about. Every relationship you're in will fail until one doesn't. So I've heard."

Walter half-smiled. "That's a cutthroat way of putting it. I guess it depends on how you define failure."

"But anyway, yeah. It wasn't as bad back home. Though I haven't seen them since planes flew, and I don't know when I'll see them next. I could take the Hound, but the waiting list for a ticket is so long, and I can't really afford to be away from work. Plus you have to be willing to drive the bus; I heard it's gone co-op. And I don't know how I'd get the gas credit to drive Focahontas, my old Focus. She needs a new radiator. I only use her for work, and only then because it's too far to walk safely this late at night."

"I'm sure you can work something out. Maybe I can help you. I'm glad they're all safe, at least." He paused, considering his words. "So what happened to you and that kid, that day? Did you find your friend? What was his name, Mike?"

"His name was Michael."

Walter nodded at the past tense. "I'm sorry."

"We met up at Alcatraz. That kid, Trevin, came with us. I hear from him occasionally. He's in nursing school."

"Kate," Walter said. "Was it—I mean, what happened to you?"

"You really want to know?"

"Please."

So Kate told him. The whole thing. She started from the beginning. It had been so long, she was afraid she'd lose the details, but the images never went away. They only got a little easier, as time passed. She allowed herself to say everything that she remembered. About Jamie and Cameron. Michael. How she'd felt. How she'd lied.

The pizza was served on a hubcap, with two paper plates and two napkins, and two paper cups of water. She distributed the plates and napkins, and took a slice. She talked about Paul, and the boat. Arriving at the Rock. She told him about Rob. How she still dreamed about it. The trauma of rape, wrapped inside the trauma of her own expected death, and the trauma of nearly killing someone. She took another slice, leaving the crust on her plate. "And I tied myself down, and Michael showed up, and we were locked in together. I tried to get him out. After that, I don't remember anything. But I saw pictures."

"Oh, kitten," Walter said. He wasn't eating. "It's my fault, for not taking you with me."

"No." She'd considered this. "I have lots of regrets. You're not one of them." She realized that this could be interpreted to mean that dating him was not something she regretted. She supposed that was a fair interpretation.

"Pizza's good," she said. "Some days, the only hot meal I get is toast." She knew that by talking around money, he might think she was asking for help. She didn't care. She wasn't trying to fool around with implications and subtext. It was too much work. She was saying what occurred to her to say. "So Charles Dickens walks into a bar, orders a martini," she said to fill the silence. "'Olive, or twist?' the barkeep says."

Walter laughed, though it wasn't funny enough for a laugh. "Sorry, I'm just recovering. I'm serious, I've been looking for you. Wandering around the local bars and streets like a lost thing. I never suspected you'd be a—well." He couldn't say *zombie*. "Was that you dancing?"

"Yeah," she said.

"I—Christ, child. Why hide your face like that?"

"It's a shtick. Customers eat it up. Everyone's gotta sell something. While I'm still young enough, that's what I have." He should know.

"And later? Won't you go to school, get your own nursing degree, or that MFA? Something practical?"

She laughed. "MFAs are hardly practical. Only if I wanted to teach. And who's going to hire me? Who will listen to me? Who, these days, is even going to *want* a liberal arts degree? It's as useless as an MBA. Think of all those Harvard grads digging graves and planting golf courses with crops."

"But don't you think about it? Where you're going?" He meant, *don't you want to grow up? Get out of the bar?*

"I don't know how long I'm going to live," she said. "There are no long-term studies. Which is not to say that I don't think about it. But I try not to think about it too much." *The past / is a series / of bad decisions.*

He was quiet for a minute. He'd taken a few bites, but was still working on his first slice. He used to polish off his plates: entrees and sides, salads and desserts, coffee and brandy. "Shit. I miss you. I need to see you again."

She took a third slice to have something to do with her hands. "Who are you kidding?" she asked.

He looked away. Her stomach turned. "You think you can just pick this up where you left off?" she asked, unable to meet his eyes. "Because this train has gone. Sorry."

"Not the sex, that's not what I mean. It's you. The zombie thing doesn't bother me."

The bill arrived. She let Walter take it to the counter and pay. Kate stood, wiped her mouth with a napkin, and bussed the table, throwing away their half-eaten slices.

"Thanks," she said when he came back. She was standing, holding the remaining pizza sandwiched between their plates.

"Let me walk you to your car?" he said. It was too late to do anything else.

She acquiesced. This late, the street was at its quietest. Even the crazies had settled down for the night.

"Can I get your phone number?" he asked. "Or your email address?"

She didn't have a lot of friends. It seemed like a waste to throw one away. She probably shouldn't have told Walter the whole story. He was the only person alive who knew it. Yet she didn't regret telling him.

"Sorry," she said. "You just remind me too much of it all." *Departing / is sweet / only when tomorrow is like today.*

"Oh."

They walked in silence for a while.

"Do you mind if I stop in and see you?" he asked.

It was good that he was asking. He might do it anyway, whatever she said. "I rather do mind, actually. I don't like to think of you seeing me like that."

"OK." It wasn't, by his tone of voice.

She stepped into the street and unlocked her car door. "This is it," she said.

"So this is it." He followed her to the door. He took a piece of paper from his pocket, and wrote something onto it. "If you change your mind. My address, and my phone number. If there was something I could do, I owe it to you. Get you the gas credit you need to go home, and the car repairs. I mean it. It would be the least I can do." He pressed the paper into her hand.

She got into her car. She didn't offer to give Walter a ride back to his. "You wouldn't believe the day I had," she said. She patted the console between the seats. Some of Michael's cremated remains were there, in a Nalgene bottle. She had another one in the apartment, and a film canister's worth in the dressing closet at work. She drove the few miles home, and went inside. She brought the piece of paper with her.

"Hiya," Audrey said. She was lying on the couch, reading a paperback by candlelight.

"Hi." Kate set the pizza onto the coffee table. "If you're hungry."

"How'd it go?" Audrey asked. She took a piece of the pizza.

"All right. I talked a lot. He wants to see me again. Gave me his phone number."

"And?"

Kate considered the cramped writing. "He offered to get me the gas credit to drive home. And he wants to be my friend."

"Better take a few burly dudes, if you go," Audrey said. "You could probably find some on the ride board. I don't want you to come home lynched."

"Good point. I guess I could do that." She found a pen. *Want you / to want me / after the moment is over* she wrote on the back of the paper with Walter's information. She made her decision. She held the paper above the candle, turning it to watch it burn.

"Guess that's a no, then," Audrey said. "You're ruthless." There was approval in her voice. "Don't want to go home?"

"I do, just not on his credit. He means well. I think. I just can't be around him. You know I dated him, before?" Kate sat on the couch.

"I get it. I don't talk to anyone that I knew back then, either. Aside from the awkward oh-you're-still-alive-too-isn't-that-peachy conversation. It's easier to lose touch." Audrey's breath was fragrant with liquor. She held up her Harlequin in the candlelight. "You know something, though? I miss sex. The way it used to be. Romance. Stability."

"Those are all different things."

"I mean, I haven't been kissed in years, except for Derek, and he's a total player. They're all afraid of me. Every guy I meet. They think it's hot, at a distance; they'll totally walk through the mall holding hands, as if anyone wants to do that once they've gotten out of high school. But they don't know what to do when you get them alone. I'd just about murder someone to be held. Which is what they're afraid of, I guess."

"I didn't know you were dating anyone. *Noli me tangere*, that's how I feel about it."

"*Mole whey tangerine?* Hardly would call it dating, anyway."

Kate leaned against Audrey. "Latin. It means *don't touch me.*" She fingered Audrey's hair. It was damp, and smelled of the coconut shampoo from the co-op. The good kind.

"What are you doing?" Audrey asked.

"Nothing." Kate found Audrey's shoulders. She rubbed them. The girl was made of knots. Audrey let out a breath and put a hand on Kate's knee. It was very late; dawn would come soon. Until then, they were alone. Safe. Darkness abetted privacy.

"I was with a girl, once," Kate said. "You know. Before."

"At that party, right?"

Kate thought about what she was doing. Once you'd started touching someone, things changed. Audrey's fingers tightened on her knee. Kate thought about what it would be like to kiss her. To be kissed. She wondered why they hadn't done this before. Years had passed, and Audrey had been there. Audrey would be there.

"Her name was Jamie. She was good," Kate said. *Stick to your own kind*, Derek had said.

"Like, how?" Audrey turned around.

"Like this."

"I think zombies have more fun. For sure. I mean, can you imagine just randomly being able to eat flesh? I mean, how fun? ... Like, don't you ever think about that, like when you're giving a blowjob? Don't you think about just biting down?"

–Jenna Jameson
on *Up Close with Carrie Keagan* at NGTV.com

afterword

The Zombie Walks are real; check out www.zombiewalk.com for one near you. So's the Zeppelin: a company called Airship Ventures operates a passenger blimp around the Bay Area for tours. *Passage of Darkness: The Ethnobiology of the Haitian Zombie* by Wade Davis describes documented cases of Haitian zombies, and talks about how zombies are controlled by whips — it's worth a read (and my copy *did* come inscribed to Kelly). "Cupid's Disease" is an article by Oliver Sacks in *The Man Who Mistook His Wife For A Hat: And Other Clinical Tales*, discussing a 90-year-old woman who had self-diagnosed her sudden flirtatiousness as a result of long-dormant syphilis; she didn't want to be cured.

Other than that, I made everything (and everyone) up. There's no such thing as zombies.

—Amelia Beamer

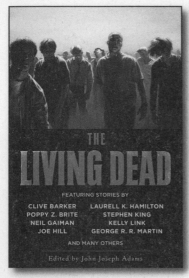
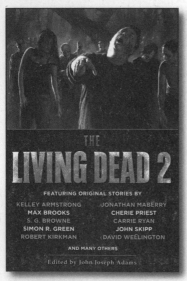

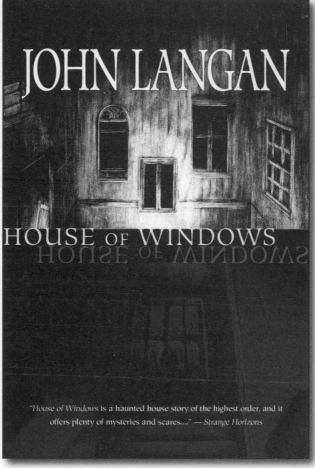

"*House of Windows* is a haunted house story of the highest order, and it offers plenty of mysteries and scares...." — *Strange Horizons*

When a young writer finds himself cornered by a beautiful widow in the waning hours of a late-night cocktail party, he seeks at first to escape, to return to his wife and infant son. But the tale she weaves, of her missing husband, a renowned English professor, and her lost stepson, a soldier killed on a battlefield on the other side of the world, and of phantasmal visions, a family curse, and a house... the Belvedere House, a striking mansion whose features suggest a face hidden just out of view, draws him in, capturing him.

What follows is a deeply psychological ghost story of memory and malediction, loss and remorse. From John Langan (*Mr. Gaunt and Other Uneasy Encounters*) comes *House of Windows*, a chilling novel in the tradition of Peter Straub, Joe Hill, and Laird Barron.

about amelia

Amelia Beamer works as an editor and reviewer for *Locus: The Magazine of the Science Fiction and Fantasy Field*. She has won several literary awards and has published fiction and poetry in *Lady Churchill's Rosebud Wristlet*, *Interfictions 2*, *Red Cedar Review*, a tie-in story to *The Loving Dead* in *The Living Dead 2* (Night Shade Books, September 2010), and other venues.

As an independent scholar she has published papers in *Foundation: The International Review of Science Fiction* and the *Journal of the Fantastic in the Arts*. She has a B.A. in English Literature with high honors from Michigan State University, and attended Clarion East in 2004. She lives in Oakland, CA. *The Loving Dead* is her first novel. Visit her at ameliabeamer.com.